"I wonder if women have always used cooking as an escape route." Drew chuckled.

"I'm not using cooking as an escape route," Christy said levelly. "If I don't stir the chili, it'll burn."

Drew watched her through the kitchen doorway and could tell by her movements that she wasn't nearly as calm as she was pretending to be.

Swinging around to face him, she asked, "Ready to eat?"

"Now?" he protested. Food was the last thing on his mind.

"I thought you were starving," Christy reminded him.

Instantly she realized she'd used a bad choice of words. Drew's kiss had shown her they were both starving . . . for the kind of passion they'd shared a long time ago. But she'd learned, the hard way, not to trust that passion. She didn't dare risk letting herself go with Drew again. . . .

Dear Reader,

If you're looking for an extra-special reading experience—something rich and memorable, something deeply emotional, something totally romantic—your search is over! For in your hands you hold one of Silhouette's extremely **Special Editions**.

Dedicated to the proposition that *not* all romances are created equal, Silhouette **Special Edition** aims to deliver the best and the brightest in women's fiction—six books each month by such stellar authors as Nora Roberts, Lynda Trent, Tracy Sinclair and Ginna Gray, along with some dazzling new writers destined to become tomorrow's romance stars.

Pick and choose among titles if you must—we hope you'll soon equate all Silhouette **Special Editions** with consistently gratifying romance reading.

And don't forget the two Silhouette *Classics* at your bookseller's each month—reissues of the most beloved Silhouette **Special Editions** and Silhouette *Intimate Moments* of yesteryear.

Today's bestsellers, tomorrow's *Classics*—that's Silhouette **Special Edition**. We hope you'll stay with us in the months to come, because month after month, we intend to become more special than ever.

From all the authors and editors of Silhouette **Special Edition**,
Warmest wishes,

Leslie Kazanjian
Senior Editor

MAGGI CHARLES
A Different Drummer

Silhouette Special Edition

Published by Silhouette Books New York

America's Publisher of Contemporary Romance

To Steve...
for many reasons

SILHOUETTE BOOKS
300 East 42nd St., New York, N.Y. 10017

ISBN: 0-373-09459-0

First Silhouette Books printing June 1988

All the characters in this book are fictitious. Any resemblance to actual persons, living or dead, is purely coincidental.

® are Trademarks used under license and are registered in the United States Patent and Trademark Office and in other countries.

Printed in the U.S.A.

Books by Maggi Charles

Silhouette Romance

Magic Crescendo #134

Silhouette Intimate Moments

Love's Other Language #90

Silhouette Special Edition

Love's Golden Shadow #23
Love's Tender Trial #45
The Mirror Image #158
That Special Sunday #258
Autumn Reckoning #269
Focus on Love #305
Yesterday's Tomorrow #336
Shadow on the Sun #362
The Star Seeker #381
Army Daughter #429
A Different Drummer #459

MAGGI CHARLES

is a confirmed traveler who readily admits that "people and places fascinate me." A prolific author, who is also known to her romance fans as Meg Hudson, Ms. Charles states that if she didn't become a writer she would have been a musician, having studied piano and harp. A native New Yorker, she is the mother of two sons and currently resides in Cape Cod, Massachusetts, with her husband.

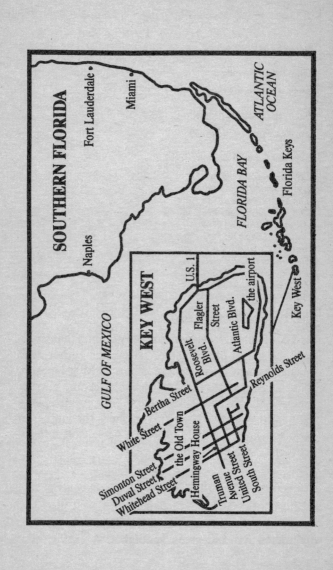

If a man does not keep pace with his companions, perhaps it is because he hears a different drummer. Let him step to the music which he hears, however measured or far away.

Henry David Thoreau

Chapter One

The last place in the world he would have expected to find her was in a bar off Duval Street. Not merely *in* a bar but *behind* a bar!

When the private detective he'd hired to track her down had reported that she was in Key West working at a place called Fancy's, he'd been certain they were mistaken. Perhaps they'd confused her with a look-alike or another young woman with the same name. Still, it was the best lead he'd had, which was why he'd personally trekked down from Westport, even though doing so had seriously upset his schedule.

He needed to see for himself. To be sure.

Well, he was seeing. It had taken a moment for his eyes to adjust from the brilliant sunlight to this shadowed interior. The bar was decorated like a thatched hut and lighted with muted red and green spotlights. A cheap, psuedo-

Polynesian ambiance, he thought distastefully. Yet there was no mistaking her.

It was definitely Christy.

His eyes narrowed. She'd carried out the tropical motif in her working garb. She was wearing a tannish grass skirt topped by a short bright red camisole. Multicolored paper leis garlanded her slim neck. Worst of all, between the skirt and the camisole there was a revealing band of milk-white flesh.

Stiffening, he yearned to cross the room in a few strides and forcefully yank her outside. Instead he bided his time. He moved from the entrance to a vantage point against the wall where he could fade into the dark shadows. The effect was like being at the rear of a theater, focusing on the action on the lighted stage.

She was busy. Very busy. And . . . she appeared to be loving every minute of it. He saw her quick smile. Heard her laugh. Thought about how long it was since she'd smiled or laughed for *him*. And was startled by the sudden surge of jealousy that bolted through him with the force of an adrenaline shot.

His self-deprecating smile was wry. To think he'd seriously believed he'd long since gotten over her.

Slowly, and more than a little reluctantly, he narrowed the gap between wall and bar and slid onto a just-vacated stool. Now that the moment of encounter was at hand he wasn't looking forward to initiating it.

She was so busy pleasing her clients that he had a chance to observe her for a few more seconds before she became aware of his presence. To his added surprise, he discovered that looking at her actually hurt. He'd forgotten how lovely she was. No . . . the fact was he'd forced himself not to remember. Now it was almost as if he were seeing her for the first time.

She was five-four, but the way she carried herself made her seem taller. Her ashy, naturally blond hair fell past her shoulders but was swept up off her neck and pulled into a ponytail of sorts by a large red plastic clip. She had a beautiful complexion—with pearly skin and cheeks slightly flushed with a rosy pink. Evidently she'd been staying out of the sun in Key West or was deliberately trying not to tan.

He knew from experience how expressive her eyes were and how unusual their color was. Like spring violets set perfectly in an oval face complimented by a straight nose and a sensuous warm mouth. Looking at that mouth, he winced. It was too easy to remember how her lips had tasted, how they'd once passionately meshed with his. Those were memories it was imperative to keep buried.

She mixed a frothy strawberry daiquiri and placed it on the bar in front of the man sitting next to him. She still hadn't looked directly at him. He imagined she sensed she had a new customer and was taking care of her other patrons first. So before she noticed him, he seized the initiative and spoke her name.

"Hello, Christy," he said.

Her eyes flew upward, widening in shock when she saw him. He saw her throat work, saw her fight for control. He had to admit that she'd always been gutsy. She was gutsy now as she won her small battle and said, in a near-normal voice, "Hello, Drew."

Drew Delahunt would have sworn that he'd worked her out of his system. But in that revealing instant, he knew how wrong he'd been—and resented it. He'd been observing her for only a few minutes, she'd spoken just two words to him. Yet suddenly the healing of a year—the year that had inched by since she'd left him—was torn to shreds.

His expressive mouth tightened into a study in bitterness as he remembered the agony of that winter evening when he'd found the note she'd left behind. It had happened the week before Valentine's Day. So, through the days that followed, the hearts and flowers in every shop window he passed had telegraphed silent messages to him, underlining his misery.

He remembered how he'd retreated to a lair of calculated solitude. Then, gradually, the healing process had taken over. The scars, raw at first, had healed and hardened. Finally the time had come when he'd taken up the reins of his life, once more in control. Or so he'd thought!

Now the pain was surfacing all over again.

"May I get you something?" she asked politely.

She was offering him a drink as if he were merely a customer who'd happened in off the street. He gritted his teeth, forcing himself to remember his innate good manners. "Thank you, no," he told her. "I need to talk to you."

Briefly she faltered. She glanced around to see if anyone needed a drink, then said softly, "I work until midnight, Drew."

Midnight!

He had visions of her walking the streets of Key West alone late at night, heading back from this bar to wherever she was living. The pictures that raced through his mind were appalling. It was a miracle that someone hadn't dragged her into an alley and robbed her, or stabbed her or worse....

Drew flinched as his imagination ran riot. Then he sternly reminded himself that whatever she did wasn't any of his business anymore.

"Midnight?" he echoed disapprovingly.

She nodded. "I work late on Saturdays."

"Very well," he conceded, inadvertently giving the impression that he was making a gracious gesture. "I'll meet you outside at midnight."

She frowned slightly. "I'm not sure I can do that, Drew. I mean, I have an engagement when I finish here."

An *engagement*, for God's sake!

Drew fought back fury and automatically slipped on the protective mask he'd learned long ago to keep at hand for instant camouflage. It was a cloak of cold mock indifference that had—as he knew only too well—so often put Christy off.

"I flew down here especially to talk to you, Christy," he informed her. "If you have a date after work, I'll have to ask you to break it."

"It doesn't seem to me we have anything to talk about," she said, obviously angry.

"I disagree," he stated coldly. "We have something extremely important to talk about." He paused deliberately, then said, "I want a divorce, Christy."

Five minutes later, Christina DiMartino watched Drew exit the bar and quick tears covered her eyes with a thin film. The man who climbed onto the stool Drew had just vacated asked solicitously, "Something wrong, sweetheart?"

He was a captain of one of the shrimp boats berthed at the big marina only a few blocks away and a regular at Fancy's.

Christy shook her head. "Just got something in my eye, Luigi," she fibbed.

"Like hell you did," he contradicted, his dark face twisting into a scowl. He was a big burly man, old enough to be her father. As a matter of fact, he treated Christy like a daughter. It seemed to please him that she was, like himself, of Italian descent, although he teased her about her family coming from Milan, in the north, while his roots were Sicilian.

"You just tell me what that guy did and I'll even the score!" he said threateningly.

Christy managed the facsimile of a laugh. "No one did anything," she placated him. "Honest."

"Honest?"

"Yes."

"Well then, beautiful, I'll have a Dos Equis."

She poured Luigi's bottle of beer into a frosty mug, then turned to her next customer. Fancy's always hummed on Saturday nights, especially at this time of year. February was a peak season month when tourists vastly outnumbered the Key West residents. Fancy's catered primarily to the locals, but that only made it all the more alluring to the tourists. They came by the droves in bright colored Bermuda shorts, knee socks, knit short-sleeved shirts emblazoned with reptile insignias, and ridiculous straw hats. After four months in Key West, Christy preferred the locals.

Time passed quickly on a busy Saturday night, and Christy was almost able to thrust Drew Delahunt to the back of her mind. Still, he lodged in her thoughts like a thorn that kept pricking and hurting. But there was nothing new about that, she thought sadly.

When midnight arrived, Cal Fancy emerged to take over the bar until closing time. Usually Christy was so tired and her feet hurt enough that she was glad to take off. Tonight, though, she lingered, washing glasses that she didn't need to wash and wiping down the bar not once but twice.

At last Cal asked, "What's with you? Got a Miss Clean complex? Skedaddle, will you?" He gave her a fatherly pat on the fanny to emphasize his point.

Christy was tempted to say she'd rather stay and help till closing time but knew her request would get a quick negative response. Cal worried about her going home late by herself and she appreciated his concern. She lived on the south side of town off Whitehead Street, not far from the lovely old house enshrined as Ernest Hemingway's Key West home. However, most of her solitary ten-minute walk was along Duval Street, the town's main thoroughfare. Duval

Street was always brightly lit, with plenty of people strolling around.

She went into a back room and changed from her work outfit to a slim, pale yellow sheath. Then she switched her straw slippers to comfortable leather flats. She cast a brief glance in the mirror. She needed lipstick, but decided not to bother—she had no intention of fixing herself up for Drew.

He was waiting for her just outside the door. Despite herself, Christy momentarily lost her breath when she saw him. She hadn't forgotten how handsome he was. Rather she'd carefully submerged that fact—along with many others—after the cold winter day she'd walked out of the Delahunt's Westport, Connecticut estate.

She was determined to keep her feelings on an even keel, yet she couldn't help noticing that Drew looked weary. She couldn't help but see the fine lines etched around his eyes, lines that hadn't been there a year ago, and the grooves of tension, also new, edging the sides of his mouth.

Regardless, he was still the handsomest man she'd ever seen. The mere sight of his thick black hair made her want to cry. Despite her resolve to be strong, she remembered the feeling of running her fingers through those wonderful strands far too vividly. His eyebrows, equally dark, arched perfectly over eyes that were not only steel in color but could be steel in coldness...or, at other moments, as meltingly tender as a summer dawn. She'd often thought his profile could have easily graced a Greek coin. He was tall—the top of her head barely reached his shoulder—and looked quite unlike a man who spent most of his time sitting at a desk dealing in the icebound world of business and high finance. He was broad-shouldered, lean-waisted, well muscled in all the right places...as she had every reason to know.

"I was beginning to wonder if you'd already left," he said, with no trace of a smile. "Is there somewhere we can talk?"

"Another bar, maybe," Christy suggested. "Captain Tony's or Sloppy Joe's."

"They'd both be mobbed, wouldn't they? And noisy?"

She shrugged. "I suppose so."

"We need a little privacy, Christy. Not to mention quiet."

"Well, there's a Chinese restaurant not too far from here that stays open late."

"All right."

They walked in silence while cold currents vibrated between them, and Christy shivered despite the warmth of the night. If Drew was aware of her involuntary movement, he gave no indication of it. He'd never been more stony, she thought unhappily, and wondered how she could possibly cope with that.

There were a number of late night people lingering in the Chinese restaurant. Drew asked the waiter for a booth in the rear, as far away from everyone else as possible. Red paper lanterns hung from the ceilings, casting a dim light. The aroma of incense wafted through the air and Oriental music—strange to Western ears—was playing in the background.

"Would you like a drink?" Drew asked politely.

"Just tea, please."

To her surprise, he ordered a Scotch for himself, giving her a clue that he wasn't as much in control as he seemed.

The waiter brought the whiskey and a pot of oolong tea. "Would you like something to eat?" Drew asked her.

At that moment, Christy couldn't have cared less about eating. But she said, shrugging slightly, "Oh, maybe a couple of appetizers."

Drew ordered egg rolls and shrimp, then sipped his drink as if it were much needed medicine. "How long have you been down here?" he finally asked.

"In Key West? A little over four months."

"Where did you go when you left Westport?"

"Is this going to be an inquisition, Drew?"

"No, but I'd like to fill in the gaps. It's taken a while to catch up with you."

Puzzled, she asked, "What's that supposed to mean?"

"It means I hired a firm of detectives to find you."

Christy leaned back and surveyed him through narrowed eyes. "So *that's* how you knew I was in Key West!"

Drew nodded. "Actually, they picked up your trace in Miami—after considerable effort, I might add."

"I wasn't trying to hide, Drew."

"For someone who wasn't trying to hide, you did a pretty good job of it." He set down his glass. "I realize," he said coolly, "that the name of the game was staying away from me. You proved to be very resourceful, Christy. Still, it was misdirected resourcefulness and a complete waste of energy on your part. You simply could have approached me, you know. There was no need to do what you did."

"Wasn't there?" she asked levelly.

To her amazement, she saw him flush slightly and his tone became unusually defensive, "No, there wasn't."

Christy sighed. "I think you know that's not true."

"I disagree," he replied, still strangely defensive.

He met her eyes, and Christy saw in those gray depths something else that surprised her. Hurt. It flashed briefly but it was there. Only to disappear before he added, "Couldn't you have *told* me instead of walking out of my life and leaving a scimpy note?"

"Let's just say I lacked what it would have taken to do that, okay?" Christy said softly.

Drew shook his head. "When I came back that evening after the Bennisons' cocktail party and found you gone, I couldn't believe it. Your note sounded like...well, like some sort of childish invention. I thought by midnight you'd be back. When you weren't, it gradually dawned on me that you'd simply walked out of my house as if it were a transient way station in your life."

"Not *your* house," Christy corrected, still speaking softly. "Your mother's house."

"Ah." His eyes, cold as cold steel, zeroed in on her. "So that was the problem."

"I'd say that was only part of the problem, Drew," she said, maintaining her cool. "We had other problems that had nothing to do with your mother."

"You're telling me!" he retorted bitterly. "Believe me, I had plenty of time to mull things over after you left. Days and weeks during which I reflected on what had gone wrong."

"And I'm sure you reached some very definite conclusions," Christy prompted. "After all, you're used to thinking things through logically. Then you arrive at a verdict that no one can possibly refute."

Drew grimaced. "Forever snide, aren't you?"

"It's the truth, Drew. I act impulsively, you react logically. I'd say that's been pretty much the story of our life together, wouldn't you?"

He exhaled impatiently. "I didn't come here to discuss our personality conflicts," he told her. "It's too late in the day for that."

Before she could respond, Drew signaled the waiter to bring him another drink. Christy held her breath. In a minute or two he would bring up that word again. Divorce. She cringed from the sound of it. But what had she expected? That, one day Drew would loom up on the horizon riding a white horse, and would carry her off to some enchanted oasis in the desert where they could live happily ever after?

No, she was facing truth now, instead of fantasy. She knew Drew was deadly serious, or he would never have condescended to make this trip to Key West himself. He would have had someone else perform the chore for him.

She was prepared to fight him. Even though Drew had all the advantages on his side—wealth, power, an influential family name, family support—while she had nothing. She'd had nothing when Drew married her and took her to Westport. And...she'd taken nothing with her when she'd left. The few possessions that she'd truly considered *hers* fit easily into a suitcase. The beautiful clothes, the jewels, the wedding gifts that had been showered on them, she'd left behind. Along with trunks full of painful memories.

Drew concentrated on his second drink. Then he addressed her. "You made your point when you walked out, Christy," he said. "You couldn't have been more abundantly clear, as I came to realize once the initial shock was over."

She wanted to ask him how long it had taken to get over the "initial shock." An hour? A day? A week? Could she dare hope that he'd suffered for an entire month?

"Later, I realized that there had been signposts of which, unfortunately, I was unaware. If I'd been more...observant, perhaps things might have been different.

When she didn't respond to that, Drew toyed with his glass and stared at the swirling amber liquid. "In your note, you wrote that our basic problem was that we never belonged together in the first place. I'll admit I had to work my way through that. It certainly wasn't something I could immediately accept. But the more I reflected on it, the more I realized you were right. So, I accept your diagnosis that we never belonged together in the first place. And with that in mind, I think we should also accept the fact that the moment's come when we should both have our freedom."

Drew saw Christy's throat work convulsively, saw her eyes widen in shock. In the restaurant's dim reddish light their unusual color was intensified.

She asked, in a curiously toneless voice, "Have you met someone else?"

He supposed he should have had the sense to realize she'd make that assumption. The crazy thing was he hadn't been able to bear the thought of being with anyone but her. Without meeting her eyes, he said, "No, there isn't anyone else." And knew at once that he'd waited too long to say it and that she didn't believe him. He went on with calculated smoothness, "Even if I had met someone else, it wouldn't have any bearing on our problem. What concerns me is the question of dealing with first things first. And the obvious 'first' on both our lists should be the matter of our freedom."

"I see."

"My lawyers could have arranged this for me," Drew pointed out, "but I wanted to tell you myself. That is, I wanted to discuss it with you myself."

Christy suddenly felt numb. Numb, and so terribly fearful that she didn't dare look at him.

"Obviously," Drew stated, "divorce is the logical solution for us. It's only recently, of course, that I discovered you were living in Florida. Knowing that, I had my attorneys check out the laws involving our situation. As it happens, the requirements are more liberal in Florida than they are in Connecticut. In both states divorces are granted on grounds of incompatibility, with no time period necessary between the interlocutory and the final decree. In Connecticut, however, the principals must have been living apart for eighteen months, which would mean that we'd have six more months to go to meet the legal requirement. In Florida there is no such proviso. The petitioner merely has to have been a resident of the state for six months."

Drew managed a stiff smile. "It would seem expedient for you to file here," he said. "I can assure you that my attorneys will do everything in their power to make the path easy for you. Needless to say, I'll take care of the financial details involved."

"How very generous of you," Christy said dryly.

"Do I detect that familiar snide note in your voice?" he asked, frowning.

"I suppose you do," she conceded. "I mean, you make the whole thing sound so damned easy."

"It doesn't have to be difficult."

"Doesn't it?"

"No." The stiff smile returned. "We're both consenting adults, after all," Drew pointed out. "I think at this point we both understand what we want."

Christy shook her head. "You don't have any idea what I want," she said dully. So saying, she reached for a golden butterfly shrimp as if the conversation were closed.

Drew sat back and waited for her to expand on her accusation. He needed her to spell out what it was she wanted that he didn't have any idea of. When she continued to eat her shrimp without saying another word, he felt certain that it could only be one thing.

"I'm prepared to give you whatever you ask for where money is concerned," he informed her bluntly, "and I don't mean merely in connection with the divorce. What I'm saying is, I'm prepared to settle a generous sum of money upon you."

Christy met his inquiring gaze. "In return for my promise that I won't contest a divorce if you go ahead and file for one in Connecticut?"

"Well," he admitted uncomfortably, "I suppose it could be put that way."

She finished her shrimp and very deliberately took a sip of tea. "You think," she said then, "that what I want from you is money?"

"What else am I supposed to think?"

The sadness in her lovely eyes came as yet another surprise to Drew, and he knew she was being honest when she told him, "I don't know, Drew. But if you'd done any

thinking at all, you might have figured out that if all I
wanted from you were money, I wouldn't have left.''

"I don't quite follow that."

"I had money when I was living with you," she informed him. "And clothes and jewels and a gorgeous home
and a gorgeous car and a yacht docked right in our back-
yard. I also had a handsome husband. Sounds like a scenario any girl in her right mind would settle for, doesn't it?"
she queried reasonably.

"Come off it, Christy!" Drew shot back. "Obviously
there's more to it than that. Just what, exactly, is your
point?"

"I said I had a handsome husband," Christy said steadily.
"Past tense, Drew. Because almost from the moment we got
married, he was just that...nothing more. *You* were just that
and nothing more. You took me to your mother's house as
if I were another package you'd bought at Bloomingdale's.
Then you installed me there. Oh, you were considerate and
appreciative and polite and even passionate—in the beginning. But people can develop a passion for the things they
buy at Bloomingdale's, can't they?"

She saw, by the tight line of his jaw, that she'd made him
angry. She wished desperately that he would lash out at her.
Instead, in his usual way, he became colder.

"I begin to see," he said, "that it was folly on my part to
make this trip. One of my attorneys could have handled it
better. So... from now on, this matter between us will be in
the hands of the law firm."

"'*This matter between us?*'"

"The divorce," Drew said. Despite the coldness of his
voice, he appeared distraught as he rapidly polished off his
second drink.

Christy drew a long, even breath. Then, quietly, she said,
"I won't file for a divorce, Drew."

He nodded, his mouth again tightening. "I suppose I should have expected as much," he observed dispassionately. "In that case, I'll instruct my attorneys to file in Connecticut as soon as the time requirement for our separation has been fulfilled. Possibly there may be steps they can take to expedite matters."

He was reaching in his coat pocket for his trim leather billfold and extracted a credit card.

He was acting as if they were concluding a business meeting, and Christy's resentment brimmed. Still, she was determined not to lose her temper.

She matched his coldness as she said, "I don't really care where or when you file for divorce, Drew. Wherever or whenever that happens, I'll contest it."

Drew sat back and surveyed her coldly. She imagined she could see his brain working with mathematical precision. As if to verify that, he said, "Okay. We'll scrap Plan A if you insist and institute Plan B in its place."

"What's that supposed to mean?"

"Personally I'd think you'd welcome, with even more than the proverbial open arms, the thought of a divorce with a settlement in your favor," Drew said dispassionately. "However, it's a long time since I've pretended I could understand you. Thus, since you're opposed to the divorce, I'm prepared to offer you an alternative. I'm willing to take you back to Westport with me and to have you assume your place as my wife—on a six-month trial basis."

"What?" Christy demanded, her indignation surging.

"You heard me. If you can fit in this time, Christy, perhaps we can salvage our marriage after all. To an extent, that is. Meaning, I have no illusions about us. I'd even suggest our marriage be in name only, except I want children. In *that* sense, I can pledge that I'd bother you with my presence only for as long as it takes for you to become pregnant. I'd arrange for you to have ample funds of your own. In essence we'd both be free. Naturally, I'd expect you to remember your position as my wife and to gauge your activities accordingly.''

"How decent of you," Christy murmured.

Drew shot her a suspicious glance. "There really isn't any need to be so consistently snide."

"How about you?" she challenged. "Is there any need for you to be so . . . so self-righteous, so pompous?"

"You're the one who left *me*, remember?"

"Then why would you want me back?" she snapped defensively.

Drew didn't answer her immediately. He sat silent and still. A dramatic pause? Christy wondered. Or was he actually having trouble formulating his reply?

Finally he said, "In part, I'm thinking of appearance. My mother, my associates—"

"But certainly not of me!"

"You're wrong about that, Christy."

"Of course I'm wrong."

Drew sighed. Carefully he said, "After six months if we still found our situation irreparable, I'd be prepared to offer you a generous settlement."

"In return for what?"

"In return for a divorce of course."

"I see," Christy muttered. But she didn't see. She wished desperately that she had the ability to read his thoughts. Even Drew Delahunt couldn't be this crass. Drew had been many other things, she admitted, but he'd never been crass.

She gathered up her faltering courage. "Look, Drew, there's no way I could go back to Westport and act out a charade for you for even six days let alone six months."

He nodded as if he'd expected her to say that. "Then," he said, "divorce it is."

Christy shook her head. "No," she said through gritted teeth. "Divorce it isn't!"

"What are you saying, Christy?"

"I've already told you. I'll contest a divorce. I mean that. I don't have your resources, true. But I'll still do whatever I have to to preserve our marriage."

Chapter Two

The waiter picked up the credit card and quickly moved off toward the cash register. Drew stared at Christy, speechless. Finally he demanded hoarsely, "Why, Christy? Why are you doing this?"

"I'm not going to give up my marriage just because...just because you ask me to," she retorted, faltering slightly.

"Christy, for God's sake! If you wanted to 'preserve' our marriage, as you so quaintly put it, why did you walk out on me?"

"Because we needed space," she answered resolutely. "Definite physical, geographical space. And time away from each other. At least I did. I was suffocating, Drew. I felt that at any minute I'd never be able to catch my breath again. Never be able to be *me* again. I was losing myself in your identity. Or maybe your family's identity. We'd already lost everything we had between us in the beginning. Once upon a time, Drew, we had so much...."

She turned those powerful eyes on him again and he winced. She was right. They'd had a great, great deal in the beginning. But by the time she'd left him, they'd lost it or misplaced it. And he'd been such a blind fool he hadn't even realized how bad things had become.

Why did memories have to hurt so damned much?

Drew shook his head as if that might put the past back where it belonged. "What is it you really want, Christy?" he asked, his voice strained.

"I just told you."

Impatience surfaced. "Don't be ridiculous!" he snapped. "It's not possible."

"To put our marriage back together?"

"Yes."

"Are you so sure?"

Drew exhaled deeply, composing himself. "For a long time after you left I would have given almost anything to try. Then, as I already told you, I took the contents of your note to heart."

"I wish I'd never written that note," Christy murmured.

The waiter returned with Drew's credit card and receipt. He took both, and placed them carefully in his billfold. Watching him, Christy couldn't repress the comment, "You're so *programmed*."

He looked up, his eyebrows furrowing. Still holding the billfold, he tapped it and said, "I suppose you're referring to the fact that I attempt to keep things in order."

She smiled gently, a dangerously disarming smile. "I still can't balance my checkbook," she confessed. "Even now when there isn't that much to balance!" She bit her lip, realizing how that must have sounded. "What I meant was..."

"It doesn't matter," Drew cut in. Still frowning, he added, "Look, Christy, we can't stay here all night, and this has to be settled. I have to fly back to New York tomorrow morning."

"Business, I'll bet."

He glared at her. "Yes, damn it! Business."

The ready admission gave Christy a sinking feeling. She supposed she'd subconsciously been hoping that *this* was more important than business. That, however briefly, the affairs of Delahunt, Marcy and Bainbridge would take second place in Drew's life.

She told herself bitterly she should have known better. She told herself she was a fool . . . wanting to salvage a marriage that had already beaten itself to shreds on the rocks, where it had floundered for so long. She asked herself why any woman would be such an idiot as to persist, when the man she was attempting to bring back into her life was glancing at his wristwatch as if he had an immediate appointment with a destiny that didn't include her.

And she knew the answer.

She still loved him.

Before the impact of that knowledge could wash over Christy, Drew abruptly stood up, startling her. "Let's get out of here," he urged.

Outside the night was moist and warm and tropical. A golden crescent moon hung lopsided in a sable sky. Stars glittered like tempting diamonds ready to be snatched. Evidently Drew made the connection. He said, "I presume you sold your jewelery?"

It was Christy's turn to wince. "You took if for granted that I would, didn't you?"

They were walking under a streetlight, bathed in its amber glow. Drew said reasonably, "Well, yes. It would have been a logical step. After all you had to have something to live on. I don't know how much money you had left in your personal checking account, but I doubt it was enough to take you very far."

Christy felt an odd sense of triumph in telling him, "My jewelry is in the safe-deposit box, Drew. Remember, you insisted I have my own safe-deposit box? I still have the key, which I've been meaning to send back to you. Now that you're here, I'll give it to you."

"Damn it, Christy!"

They stared at each other through the warm shadowy night before she said calmly, "Look, I'd never sell the jewelry, simply because it belongs to you."

"I gave it to *you*, for God's sake!"

"No, you gave it to the person you wanted me to be. Since I never really became that person it still belongs to you."

"That's the craziest reasoning I've ever heard!"

"Well, it happens to be my reasoning. As for my personal checking account—that money is yours, as well. There's a fair sum, actually. I never spent much of the allowance you gave me, Drew, except to get you a present once in a while...."

Her voice trailed off as she remembered trying to find things for his birthday and at Christmas. Gifts that would seem significant when compared to the elaborate, expensive family presents he would find under the big tree, or on the birthday table. The crazy little things she'd picked for him when they were first married were no longer appropriate, she'd realized dismally. So there was nothing left. He was a man who had everything. Drew Cabot Delahunt III. Born with a platinum spoon in his mouth. Scion of one of New England's wealthiest families.

If she'd known who he was when she met him, Christy would have turned on her heels and run a thousand miles the other way!

They met in the summer in the little seaside town of Ogunquit, Maine. After four years at Brown, Drew had gone on to Harvard Business School. Then, armed with another bright new degree, he'd headed north to Ogunquit where a wealthy friend of the family loaned him a house on picturesque Perkins Cove. After a summer's respite, he would be returning to New York and assuming his place in the family business.

Christy *had* learned that much about him. What she hadn't learned was that the "family business" involved one of the world's major financial conglomerates.

In Ogunquit she'd been waitressing at a small pierside restaurant famous for its clam chowder. She and Drew had merely quipped together the first couple of times he'd come in. Then one day he'd asked her to have dinner with him at a lobster place over in nearby York. After that first date they'd spent every possible minute together.

She'd let him think she was a college girl waitressing summers. Actually that was stretching the truth only slightly. She *was* a college girl in a sense. She was taking night courses in literature and psychology at a community college near her home in Springfield, Massachusetts. During the day she worked at one job or another—working had always been a necessary way of life for her. The night courses were aimed at learning things that might open up new worlds so that some day she would be able to graduate from the kind of jobs she'd always had to something that bore the label "career." She was just nineteen when she met Drew, and she had great visions about what she would do with her life.

Then, in late August they'd eloped. It hadn't been until much later that Christy realized what a crazy thing it was to do. She still hadn't connected Drew Delahunt with *the* Delahunts of Park Avenue, Westport and Palm Beach. And she still hadn't met Drew's mother, Millicent Payne Delahunt, who took one aristocratic look at her new daughter-in-law and reduced her to dust. Only to act so unbearably *nice* as she tried to reconstruct her.

"We can't just stand here, Christy. Don't you have a place where you live, where we can talk?"

He was assuming she had a room somewhere. Actually, she had an apartment in an old "conch" house on White-head Street. It wasn't exactly spacious, but she loved its pastel walls and quaint high-ceilinged charm. There was plenty of room for a "conference" with Drew, but she wasn't ready to take him home. Not yet. Maybe not ever, she thought hopelessly.

She hedged, "It's too late to take you back to the house, Drew."

"Damn!" he muttered. "All right, then. I have a rental car parked in a public lot back in that direction." He pointed.

"Mallory Square?"

"Yes, that sounds right. I suppose we can get it and drive around until we settle this."

"Where are you staying?"

He named one of the glossy motor inns that lined Roosevelt Boulevard at the eastern end of Key West, a modern tourist area that most locals—including herself, now that she'd been here a while—considered a separate part of town, if not a separate town altogether.

"Let's get your car," she said.

They started walking along Duval Street. Again they were silent. Now and then they passed a bar where the sound of throbbing music vibrated outside, making Christy all the more aware of their own lack of joy. Now and then they heard laughter, making the absence of laughter between them seem all the more acute. And when they saw a couple disappear into a shadowed doorway to embrace, their apartness was all the more pronounced.

They located Drew's rental car and drove through a gate where he paid the parking charges to a silver-haired attendant sitting on a high stool in a glass booth. The man had a miniature TV for company.

"What a job," Drew commented dryly, after pulling ahead. At the edge of the street he asked, "Where shall we go?"

"I don't know," Christy admitted. "I haven't driven at all since I've been here. I usually walk around the Old Town, though sometimes I ride my bike. Bicycles are a way of life in Key West."

Drew drove out onto the street and Christy leaned back, not caring where he went. Just getting used to being with him, just trying to accept that they were together again—though on very shaky soil, she realized—was enough.

Before long he came to a marina where shrimp boats, in for the night, loomed out of the darkness like giant white nautical ghosts. Drew pulled up by the edge of a dock and parked. Then he sat back and expelled a long frustrated sigh.

"I've been trying to make sense of what you're asking, Christy," he said. "About attempting to put our marriage together again, that is. I must admit I'm not getting anywhere. Twelve months is a long time. Too long, perhaps."

"Aren't you even willing to try?" she asked, the smallness of her voice distressing her.

"How?" he asked, as if someone had brought an investment problem to him that required his expert advice, and he wasn't about to make a statement until he'd reached a conclusion. "How would one begin?"

"By trying," she said simply.

"How would one try?"

"I . . . I've thought about that."

"Have you considered coming back to Westport?"

"No, Drew. As I said, I can't do that."

"What, then?"

"Well, it seems to me that a first step for us would be to back up and find ourselves again." She listened to her words and felt as awkward as she sounded.

Drew's laugh was bitter. "Find ourselves again, Christy? This isn't a game of hide and seek."

"Please, Drew. We won't get anywhere if you start making fun of what I say."

There was a touching dignity to the way she spoke, something that reached him. He looked across at her face mostly in the shadows and said, "I'm sorry. I'll try my best to listen. I'm really more receptive than you think."

"You mean, you're changing your mind?"

He shook his head slowly. "Personally I'm convinced we've come to the end of the road. Unfortunately I don't think you can save something that's spent itself out, but I am willing to listen to whatever you have in mind."

A hint of the tenderness she'd once known flickered in Drew's eyes. "This," she began carefully, "is digressing, but you asked me where I went after I left Westport. Well, I went to Ogunquit."

He stared at her. "In February?"

"Yes, in February."

"Was there anything open?" he asked, astonished.

"People *do* live there in the winter, Drew," she informed him. "It isn't just a summer resort. There weren't as many things open as there are in July, but, yes, there were places open. I was able to find a room and get a job."

"You got a *job*?"

"That's what I said."

"Why?"

"I think I mentioned I left your money behind," Christy said patiently. "I took eighty dollars that was on your dresser. As I said, I'd like to give it to you before you leave Key West, along with the key to the safety-deposit box."

"As you like," Drew said with feigned indifference. But actually, he was anything but indifferent. Once again, Christy had surprised him. He knew she was gutsy, but he'd never thought of her as possessing pure *grit*. To leave home and husband and go off into the world with eighty dollars in her pocket and no plans formulated, nothing worked out, no one to turn to. He couldn't envision it.

"What kind of a job did you get?" he asked curiously.

Christy smiled, remembering. "Well," she said, "first I got work as a chambermaid at the inn where I was staying. They're open all year, and the girl they had was getting married and moving to Portland."

"You worked as a chambermaid, Christy? I don't understand you. *Cleaning* for pay, when you could have sold the damned jewelry, taken a trip around the world and given yourself a chance to think about what you really wanted to do?"

"Honest work is honest work, Drew," she countered. "That's something you've never had to face up to."

He gritted his teeth at that but said nothing. And out of the blue a crazy idea filtered through Christy's mind, but she temporarily set it aside. "I only stayed in Ogunquit three weeks," she went on. "By then I was working another job in a little superette."

He glared at her, and Christy quickly continued. "Anyway, I decided to work my way south. I thought it would be easier to get jobs in some of the southern resort areas, so I headed to Myrtle Beach, South Carolina."

"What ever made you think of Myrtle Beach?"

"I saw an ad in the travel section of the Sunday paper. Anyway, I stayed in Myrtle Beach for three months." She smiled at the memory. "I got a pretty good job as a swimming instructor at a spa there."

"I taught you to swim," Drew growled.

"Yes, you did. Thank you."

"I don't suppose you also managed to get a job as a sailing instructor? I taught you to sail, too," he recalled.

"Actually that came a bit later. After Myrtle Beach, I headed to Jekyll Island, Georgia."

"I don't believe this."

"I can assure you it's all true. I bought an old Volkswagen for four hundred dollars, drove to Jekyll Island and got a job as both a swimming and sailing instructor at a resort there. By then it was the middle of summer. Business seemed surprisingly good to me, but they said it wasn't as brisk as it might have been. I stayed two months, though, and then I wondered where to go next."

"Do tell," Drew marveled.

"I thought about going back north but decided against it."

"I can't imagine why," he observed dryly.

Christy ignored that and said, "I decided it would be wiser to head farther south, so I drove to Miami. Miami Beach actually."

"I see."

"It was easy to find jobs there. Then one day I saw an ad for a bartending course."

"I'm beginning to think I'm dreaming this," Drew mumbled.

"Believe me, it was all very real. Anyway, I took the course and passed. I have my bartender's certificate. Then someone said Key West would be a great place for me to get a job bartending, and here I am."

"Working in that tacky joint I found you in," he finished.

"Fancy's is not a 'tacky joint,'" Christy objected. "In fact, Cal Fancy is one of the nicest men I've ever known."

"I wonder at your taste, Christy."

"There's no need to be nasty, Drew," she said, again exhibiting that touching dignity.

"I'm sorry," he said, and he was. Sorry about more things than he could count on fingers and toes. "How long do you plan to stay in Key West?" he asked cautiously.

"I don't know. Through the rest of the winter certainly. Then I might head for California or possibly Alaska unless..."

"Unless what?"

"Unless it works out for us," Christy said softly, her voice so low that Drew could barely hear her.

A heavy sadness came over him. He tried to work his way through its murkiness but only felt he was sinking deeper. He admired what Christy had done. Admired her gutsiness, her resourcefulness, her fierce independence. Yet what she'd just told him had only widened the gap between them, rather than the reverse.

He could imagine what his friends and business associates—to say nothing of his relatives—would say if they discovered that his wife, his *wife*, had been chambermaiding and waiting on tables and tending bars all the way down the eastern seaboard. And that she intended to travel toward the golden sunset, then swing north for a close look at the aurora borealis!

No one he knew would believe the story. No one he knew could *possibly* believe it. The people he knew had never had to wonder about where their next dollar—or thousand dollars—was coming from. And that was especially true for himself.

Until now he'd been the one who'd been hurt. Christy had walked out on him—Christy had done the wounding. It had never occurred to him that she, too, must have suffered deeply during these past twelve months.

He smiled gently, trying to take the sting out of what he was about to say. "It's no use, Christy. Just accept that, will you? At least we never got to the point of hating each other . . . though we still could, unless we deal with our differences like two sensible adults."

"I could never hate you," she said unsteadily.

Drew suppressed the emotion that stirred within him. "Nor I you, Christy. I was bitter, however." He paused, remembering just *how* bitter. And frustrated, hurt and possessed of an agony he'd never known before—the helpless agony of losing someone.

"Anyway," he went on slowly, "that passed with time. Now, I can honestly say that all I want is what's best for both of us."

"Which is?"

"Which is for you not to balk at this divorce. Despite what you've been through, I'm urging you to put a little of your considerable pride aside and remember you *are* my wife."

"That's exactly what I've been remembering, Drew."

He tried again. "What I mean is, under the law you're entitled to certain benefits because we've been married."

"What benefits are *you* entitled to?" she countered.

"Christy, that's not the point. Stop being so difficult, will you, and listen to me? My lawyers will work out what's fair. Exactly what's fair—no more and no less—for your having given up six years of your life. Six years that should have been among the best for you."

"They weren't all bad."

He bypassed that and continued. "I'll stay out of the arrangements my lawyers make, except . . . I'll ask them to engage a reputable law firm here in Florida to represent you. So, there's no need for either of us to become personally involved in the divorce after tonight."

"Or with each other?"

He forced himself not to look at her, though his heart was aching. "Or with each other," he agreed huskily.

In the thunderous silence that followed, Christy stared out at the white shadows of the shrimp boats, lost in a private reverie. Her mind whirled through the past—the fantasy summer with Drew in Ogunquit, their romantic elopement, the years of tension in Westport, her ultimate flight to freedom. It was like watching a movie, a sad movie with a predictable ending. Except that she wasn't ready for the final scene.

A full minute passed before she said, her voice quiet yet firm, "I still can't accept that, Drew."

Drew leaned closer, certain that he'd misunderstood her. "What did you say?" he asked.

"I can't accept that," Christy repeated. "Maybe you'll hate me after you've heard what I'm going to tell you, but I've spent a lot of time thinking this out, Drew. I knew the moment would come when we'd have to meet. I didn't expect it to be in Key West, like this. I thought I would contact you—quite soon, actually—and then we'd meet in a neutral place like . . . well, like Washington, D.C. But it's happened like this, and maybe that's just as well. We've met, and we both know where we stand. You want a divorce. I don't. Especially not without giving our marriage one last try. If you won't go for that . . ."

"Yes?"

Christy's mind was racing. She knew she had to come up with something drastic, something she would never do, although she could never let Drew know that. She remembered how much he hated sensationalism and an idea occurred to her.

"Okay," she stated defiantly. "I'll contact one of those tabloids you see in the supermarkets. You know, the type that's all headlines and scandal stories. I'll give them my story about why I walked out on my millionaire husband and became a bartender."

Drew muttered a series of choice oaths under his breath before Christy added, almost companionably, "Go ahead and swear out loud if it'll make you feel better."

"Thanks, but I'll pass."

"Okay then, what do you think?"

Drew turned and faced her. "Suppose I tell you to go ahead and sell your smutty story? I won't be the only one blackened by it. You know how they'll make you look, don't you?"

"Yes, but I don't much care," Christy retorted.

"Sticks and stones can't hurt you, is that it?"

"Not sticks and stones thrown by total strangers, no." She spoke steadily but her pulse was pounding. What she was saying was true, except this man sitting across from her didn't have to throw sticks and stones to hurt her. With him she felt hopelessly vulnerable.

He shook his head reprovingly and said, "I can't believe you'd really do that. Could you really be that cheap?"

Was it a stick or a stone? Whichever, it hurt. Christy flinched inside but managed to say calmly, "People do strange things to fight for what they believe in, Drew."

"It's remarkable how moral you make that sound!"

"I'm not trying to sound moral."

"All right then," he decided abruptly. "Come back to Westport with me if that's what you want. It'll be a charade, I warn you. But I'll play my part as well as you play yours."

Christy met his steel gaze and considered questioning his hearing. "No, Drew."

Drew actually sighed. "Look," he groaned, "I've had a rotten week. I have a million things on my mind. I shouldn't have left at all, but as I said, I felt it only fair to offer you the options in person. And what do you do? You chase me around in verbal circles that don't make any sense. You want to put our marriage back together, but you don't want to live with me. How am I supposed to rationalize that?''

"That's not what I said," Christy answered patiently.

"Then perhaps something's gone wrong with my hearing."

"Not with your hearing, Drew. Only with your perception of what you hear."

He glared at her suspiciously. "Along with the bartending course did you take another psychology class?" he quipped.

"I wish I had the time," Christy replied levelly. "Anyway, my conclusions are really quite simple. What it amounts to is that after we got married, I moved into your world, body and soul. But you never put so much as your big toe into mine. You never even met my father, Drew. Every plan we ever made to drive to Springfield fell through. Then, when he died, you were in London at an international monetary conference. I went to the funeral alone, in your big Mercedes, all decked out in your clothes and jewelry. I never felt more out of place."

"Go on," Drew said.

"I still have relatives there. An aunt and uncle, some cousins. They'd welcome me anytime. If they thought I needed help they would scrape the barrel for their last cent and give it to me. That's the kind of people they are."

"What are you saying?"

"I'm saying that my grandparents came to this country from Italy. They had it hard, but they made their way. Each generation's done a little better than the generation before. They've worked, worked like hell for what they've got."

The question "And I haven't?" was on the tip of Drew's tongue, but he bit it back. Instead he asked rather acidly, "If you feel that way about them, why didn't you go back to Springfield after you left Westport?"

"I thought about it," Christy admitted. "You've been accusing me of false pride and maybe that's what it was. No one likes to admit failure. Not about something as important as . . . a marriage."

Her voice had cracked. And Drew knew she hadn't turned away from him simply to peer at the shrimp boats. Again emotion welled, prompting him to ask the question that had tormented him for the longest year of his life.

"Christy," he murmured, "what made you leave the way you did?"

There was a moment's pause before she whispered brokenly, "The Bennisons' party."

"The Bennisons' party?"

Drew couldn't have felt more astonished. He'd always imagined that someone must have slighted her in a way he didn't know about. Very possibly his mother, he thought grimly. He'd even approached Millicent and put several probing questions to her. But if Millicent had said or done anything to cause Christy to flee, she was surely unaware of it. She'd appeared more shocked by Christy's desertion than he had.

He said, scratching his memory, "What about the Bennisons' party? As I recall, you didn't want to go. You said you had a headache."

"And you knew I didn't?"

"I suspected you didn't, yes. Was that the last straw? Because I went to the party without you?"

"That, and the fact that it was my birthday."

"What?" he asked, his voice hollow.

"February eighth. My birthday. My twenty-fifth birthday to be precise. The completion of my first quarter century, and there was no one around to celebrate it with me. You went off to New York on the seven-whatever-it-was that morning, just as you always did. You came home early for you—around five, I think—and you were in a tremendous hurry to change your shirt and tie for the party. When you realized I wasn't dressed and ready to go, you were annoyed, to say the least. And when I told you I just plain wasn't going, you walked out . . . on my birthday.''

Drew stared across at her, appalled and speechless.

''I can't begin to describe how I felt after the front door slammed behind you, after you roared off down the driveway. I'd been soaking up tension and resentment like a huge sponge for some time. All of sudden I reached the saturation point and everything spilled over. I was more hurt than you could know, Drew. Luckily for me, I was also incredibly angry. What it boiled down to was sink or swim. That night what I wanted more than anything else in the world was to teach you a lesson. I wanted to wound your pride, the one area where I knew I could get you.''

''Well,'' Drew said wryly, ''I'd say you succeeded.''

''Did I?'' Christy queried uncertainly. ''I'm not so sure.'' She hesitated, then said, ''There was one thing I took from you. A bottle of champagne. I got a bottle of champagne from the wine cellar without any of your servants seeing me, and I took it up to our bedroom and popped the cork. It was cool but not chilled and it fizzed wonderfully. I watched the bubbles, then I eventually drank the entire bottle. After that I packed my suitcase and left. You did get the car back, didn't you? I said in the note that I'd leave it in the parking lot at the bus station.''

''It was your car,'' Drew protested weakly. ''Not that it makes a damned bit of difference, though thank God you didn't crash or have the police pull you over,'' he added roughly.

''I was too angry to feel intoxicated.''

Drew closed his eyes and shook his head. ''You fail to understand, Christy, that I considered all of my belongings yours, too. At the same time I wanted you to own your own things, have your own money, have some control over your life."

"I had no control over my life, Drew."

He'd been sitting bolt upright, but now he slumped back against the upholstery. "Why in God's name didn't my secretary remind me it was your birthday?" he demanded rhetorically, his nerves unraveling. Then he realized what he'd said.

"That rather says it all, doesn't it?" Christy mused.

Chapter Three

It was a warm night but Christy shivered.

"You're not cold, are you?" Drew asked swiftly.

"With the temperature hovering around seventy? Hardly? I . . . I'm just tired, that's all. This was my early day."

He frowned. "I thought it was your late day."

"At Fancy's, yes. But on Saturdays and Mondays I do the breakfast shift in a restaurant over on Front Street. Most afternoons I work at McKenzie Studios. They sell paintings, prints, crafts. . . ."

"You have three different jobs, Christy?" Drew asked disbelievingly.

"Yes, but they're all part-time."

"Do you really need to work that much to get by?"

Christy smiled ruefully. "Living in Key West isn't cheap, Drew," she told him. "Especially now that we're into peak season."

"Three jobs . . . peak season," Drew mumbled.

Christy brushed that off. "The problem is," she said, "I'm not functioning too clearly at the moment."

"You mean you're nearing exhaustion and you desperately need sleep?" Drew interpreted.

"Yes, I guess that's what I mean. I need a clear head to say what I want to say to you, Drew. I don't want to muddle it up."

She sounded so appealing it took considerable self-control on Drew's part not to reach over and draw her into his arms. He wanted to comfort her, console her, take care of her—all the things he should have wanted long before now. As it was, he sensed that consolation was the last thing Christy wanted from him tonight.

He'd booked a morning flight out of Key West International Airport. Now he decided to change it to a later hour. As long as he was back in New York the first thing Monday morning ready to negotiate a large gold purchase, things would work out.

"I'll drive you home," he said abruptly. "Why don't we meet in the morning? If you already have a lawyer here you trust, you might want him to be present."

"Consulting lawyers has been a low priority for me, Drew," Christy told him wearily. "And you don't need to drive me home."

"What do you expect me to do? Let you walk home alone at this hour of the night?"

A few seconds passed before Christy said softly, "No." Still, she didn't want him to know where she lived. If the private investigators he'd hired had traced her as far as Key West but hadn't uncovered her local address, then that was worth keeping secret a little while longer.

She said, "If you'll let me out near the Hemingway house, that will be fine."

"Why not in front of your own house?"

"The Hemingway house will be fine," she repeated.

"Are you living with someone, Christy?"

The question came like a shot out of the dark, and Christy blurted out the first answer that came to her mind. "Don't you think living with you was enough?" she demanded. "Believe me, I've had absolutely no desire to move in with anyone else."

Drew was silent. Finally, he said, "I suppose I had that coming. However, if you don't have a roommate, why the secrecy about where you live?"

Christy faced him defiantly. "Just for once, Drew, will you do something I ask without making a federal case of it?"

"Okay," he muttered.

She directed him back to Duval Street. Even at this late hour there were people strolling, an occasional bicyclist and activity in the bars. Drew drove along slowly, taking everything in. He'd reached the corner of Olivia Street when Christy said, "This is good."

He stopped the car by the curb, then asked coldly, "Where and when do you want me to meet you in the morning?"

"Well, there's a little café a couple of doors down from Fancy's. They serve *beignets* and good French coffee. Why don't we meet there at eight o'clock?"

"Sure you don't want to sleep later than that? It is Sunday, you know."

Christy shook her head as she slipped out of the car. "I can never sleep late even when I get the chance," she said, peeking back inside. "I'm too used to getting up early."

"Oh. Well then, I'll see you in the morning."

"Okay, Drew. Good night."

She lived two blocks past the entrance to the Hemingway house on Whitehead Street, but she took the precaution of continuing down Duval, wondering if Drew would follow her.

He didn't. He drove off in a way that clearly conveyed his impatience with her. She watched his taillights disappear around the corner, then she reversed direction and headed home. The short walk seemed eternal, and by the time she reached her front door, Christy was shaking.

It was nearly two in the morning and the lights in Ben and Terry Descartes's first floor apartment were out, but still she edged by their door on tiptoe. She didn't want to be involved in anyone else's problems tonight, and lately Ben and Terry were having more than their share.

She climbed the narrow staircase, let herself into her apartment and sagged against the closed door. It took a few minutes to muster enough energy to take a cool shower, put on a shorty nightgown and crawl into bed.

By seven, though, Christy was wide awake. Maybe it was the climate, so entirely the opposite of Connecticut in February. Her apartment wasn't air-conditioned, and she found it difficult to sleep when the nights were so warm.

Despite having much less sleep than most people needed, she usually awoke rested and ready to face her day. This Sunday was different. As she stretched and looked down from her open French window at the charming garden behind her house, it felt as if all her energy had been left in her dreams.

This was her day off. She dressed in pink shorts and a matching pink shirt and slipped on flat white sandals. She headed down the shady side of the street as she walked to the café. She'd never been much of a sun worshipper because she was so fair, and the sun could be pretty intense in Key West, even in the morning.

Drew was already at the café when Christy arrived. He was sitting at a window table sipping coffee. He looked as tired as she felt, and she doubted if he'd slept any better than she had. Still, he was clean shaven and wearing a light blue sport shirt, and as she hungrily traced each line of his beloved profile she knew that never again would she feel about another man as she did about Drew.

Which is both strange and sad, she thought, considering she was barely twenty-six years old.

The thought of her upcoming birthday made her remember her last one. Drew had seemed genuinely shocked at the story she'd told him, but had run true to form by blaming his secretary rather than himself for his forgetfulness.

All of his life Drew had been surrounded by servants and secretaries and assistants to take care of "details" for him. On that cold February evening a year ago, Christy had vented her frustration over having become a "detail" in her husband's well-ordered life. She drank a bottle of his best champagne, then walked out the door.

Just as she remembered this, Drew looked up. Their eyes met and Christy was taken aback by the bleakness she saw. He looked like a man who'd lost something, or someone, very precious to him. Oddly that gave her hope. Maybe there was a chance, even the slightest of chances, that Drew might listen to the zany idea she'd dreamed up and agree to give it a try!

The first glimmer of the idea had come to her in the Chinese restaurant in the wee hours of the morning. Later the idea, gaining dimensions, had returned to haunt her sleep. Now she knew that her future could well hinge on a plan totally foreign to Drew's nature.

He stood as she neared the table, tall, impeccable, his manners as perfect as always. Drew, she thought, would be polite to his worst enemy until the swords were actually drawn. Then she honestly didn't know what he'd do. She'd never seen him in a crisis situation.

She ordered coffee and *beignets*, and urged him to try the delicious, sugar-sprinkled French specialty. He rather sourly replied that he wasn't hungry.

"Maybe later," he conceded.

The French roast coffee was laden with chicory, and Christy sweetened it to her taste and felt a revival of strength with her first sip. Gradually her head—which had been more than a little addled since her first glimpse of Drew at Fancy's—began to clear. She started to feel considerably more in command not only of herself but of her present situation.

Unfortunately the café wasn't a good spot in which to plot one's future. It was a typical Sunday morning in Key West. People were sitting around reading papers, others were talking and laughing. The general atmosphere made a person feel glad to be alive and not in the mood for a heavy discussion.

Christy glanced at Drew, whose attention was clearly elsewhere. She wondered where it was and concluded it was probably on business. Something international in impact, she was sure, that involved more money than she could even think about.

On that wavelength, she asked, "What time is your flight?"

Still far away he glanced at his watch. "Damn," he muttered, suddenly coming to. "I forgot to change the reservation . . . which means I should have been at the airport ten minutes ago."

"Maybe if we got a taxi . . ."

He shook his head.

"I could turn in your rental car for you," Christy offered.

"No."

They edged their way out of the café and walked toward Duval street. It was early enough so the tourists weren't out in full force. Morning sunshine sprinkled the white buildings, filtered through the purple and rose bougainvillea that cascaded over walls and fences and splashed the exotic palm trees.

"Well," Drew asked, "where do we go to talk this time?"

"The Hemingway house opens at nine," Christy suggested.

"I'm not in the mood for a literary excursion," Drew said dryly.

"I wasn't thinking of that. There are chairs and benches out in the gardens, which are lush and shady, so they stay pretty cool. It won't be crowded till later, too."

"Fine," he agreed, surprising her.

Again they walked in silence. It seemed to have become a habit, Christy observed. After ten minutes, they reached the lovely old Spanish-mission-style home where Ernest Hemingway had done some of his best writing. Drew paid an admittance fee inside the gate, then he and Christy strolled along a brick walkway that took them around the house to the tropical garden in the rear.

"Hemingway bought this place back in 1931 for practically nothing," Christy said. "It was run down, but little by little he restored it. We really should take the tour, Drew. You can see where he worked...."

"No thanks," Drew cut in.

"I just thought you might find it interesting, that's all."

"I'm sure I would, at another time. Have you been boning up on your literature, too, by any chance?"

"No!" she snapped, swinging around to confront him. "And I wish every time I say anything about anything you wouldn't assume I'm parroting something I've just learned and will soon forget."

Drew stopped at that and looked down at her. It had never occurred to him that Christy might think he was being disparaging when he half-teased her about her passion for learning. "How about those Victorian-looking garden chairs over under that enormous whatever-it-is. Shall we sit there?" he suggested evenly.

The chairs flanked an ornately carved round table upon which a large black and white cat drowsed happily. Overhead a canopy of lush greenery shaded the small oasis. Underfoot there was an equally lush carpet of philodendron.

The fire in Christy's eyes died as she recognized a surprising tenderness in Drew's expression. "Have you been noticing the cats?" she asked. "Hemingway loved cats and took in any strays that came to the door. Many of his cats had six toes, and a lot of their descendants—the cats you see here—have carried on the trait. They're given free rein of the house and grounds and fed like kings. And," she added, before Drew could say anything, "no comments, please. I didn't learn that in a night course on Key West history."

Drew smiled. He'd often smiled at the things she said and did, and Christy hadn't always liked that. Remembering this, she said levelly, "You can be awfully patronizing, you know."

"I've never meant to patronize you, Christy."

"Maybe not, but that smile of yours . . ."

He realized what she was getting at, but wasn't about to tell her that he smiled at her antics only because they brightened his life so much.

Why had he never told her that?

As he sat down in a garden chair that had once belonged to Ernest Hemingway, Drew was thinking that for a literate and vocal person who normally held his own very well, he'd become increasingly unable to communicate with Christy as their marriage had progressed.

At first he couldn't pinpoint why. Then it came to him that the answer was quite simple. He'd taken it for granted that she knew how he felt about her. He'd taken *her* for granted. Almost from the moment they married he'd become deeply involved in the affairs of Delahunt, Marcy and Bainbridge—to the detriment of just about everything else.

Occasionally—not nearly often enough, he realized now—he'd stolen time to be with her. He'd taught her to swim and sail, loving her reactions to every new experience. Yet even then he'd left too much of himself on Wall Street in the vast sixty-second floor chambers that comprised the firm's executive offices. Too much had been thrust on him too quickly. And he'd only been twenty-five years old . . . the same age Christy was now.

Christy's age. *February.* My God, her twenty-sixth birthday was the day after tomorrow!

This time, Drew thought grimly, he wasn't going to forget her birthday—no matter what conclusions the two of them reached this morning.

She'd reached out a slender hand and was petting the huge cat. Watching her brought an unaccustomed lump to Drew's throat. There was something poignantly maternal in her gesture. And that reminded him how she'd always wanted children—and he hadn't.

There'd been so many adjustments to make. Parenthood had seemed to him an added complication, especially in the beginning. Christy was only nineteen. They had plenty of time to have children. And he, in his mid-twenties, had been thrust into a position that should have been occupied by a man almost twice his age.

Fortunately his mother had remained behind the scenes. Drew had many ropes to learn, and Millicent Delahunt made sure he learned them right with no chicanery on the part of anyone who, in the process of teaching him, might also be thinking of slitting his throat businesswise.

In any event being Drew Delahunt III was a major advantage. The firm had been founded by his great-grandfather, the first Drew Delahunt, not long after the turn of the century. International finance had been far less complicated in those days, but complicated enough. The original Drew Delahunt had been an astute and careful man, qualities he had passed along to his descendants—perhaps to too great a degree, Drew now thought ruefully.

The second Drew Delahunt had been reared, as had subsequent generations of the family, in the proverbial lap of luxury. Born shortly before the onset of the First World War, he'd assumed his rightful place as a pillar of New York business and society and had carried both positions well.

Drew suspected that his own father might have been more of a renegade at heart. He'd been born in the midst of the Great Depression, an economic catastrophe that the family and firm had weathered remarkably well. It was a wonder he hadn't been named Drew the Third, but his mother had decreed otherwise. Her maiden name had been Rogers, so that's what she called him. Not Roger, but Rogers. It was a distinction Rogers Delahunt had to cope with throughout his life.

Drew, however, had been named according to Delahunt family tradition, a tradition to which he'd always felt himself hidebound. It had been taken for granted that he would go into the firm. In college he'd had his moments of rebellion, not at all certain that he wanted to be a leading financier. But during his last year at Brown, his father had suddenly died. A massive coronary hit him one morning as he was awakening and within minutes he was dead.

Millicent had taken over. Millicent, briefly vulnerable in her grief, had rallied with the inner strength that had become her trademark. She'd assumed control of her husband's vast empire, virtually guarding her son's inheritance. Once Drew was through at Harvard Business School, she'd stepped back—not down, just back. Fortunately for Drew she'd stayed in the wings, because many times he'd needed her desperately.

At the very beginning of his learning process, with the knowledge that older and wiser advisers were constantly leaning over his shoulder despite Millicent, he was also beginning a marriage. A marriage to a girl literally as different from everything he'd ever known as day was from night.

Christy was day, he thought now. Everything else was night. Her brightness still shined for him as it always had. Watching her stroke the cat, he was wrenched by a terrible ache and knew, more than ever what a damned fool he'd been to come to Key West.

"Have you given our problem any further thought?" he asked, forcing a board-meeting calm into his voice and manner.

Christy nodded, not looking up. The cat stretched its neck, loudly purring its content and Drew felt a sudden pang of envy.

"I'd like to strike a bargain with you, Drew."

"What kind of bargain?" he asked warily.

She looked up and met his gaze, her eyes sapphire in the muted garden light. "I'd like you to give me one month of your life."

Drew was stunned, quietly drowning in her blond beauty. "A month of my life? I'm afraid I don't understand."

Christy smiled wistfully. "No, I don't imagine you do. So, I'll explain. And if you agree to give me a month of your life, it'll be all I ever ask you for. At the end of it, either we'll decide to stay together, or I'll file for divorce here in Florida, as you've asked, without saying a word to anyone."

"I see," Drew murmured, but he didn't see at all. He tried to fathom what she was getting at. "Are you asking me to stay here in Key West for a month?" he asked finally.

"Yes, among other things."

"What other things?"

"Well, I'm also asking you to get a job."

"A job, Christy?" he exploded. "Just exactly what do you think I have now?"

"I'd say you have a position," she answered sedately.

"Oh, come on," he muttered impatiently. "I'm not interested in definitions. I have a job, believe me. It consumes most of my time and all of my energy."

"Your *position* does," she corrected. "Yes, I'm very well aware of that."

Drew expelled a frustrated breath, knowing that he had to reason with her. "Look, I've already missed my plane and I have to make arrangements to get a later flight out of here. Will you kindly get down to basics and make your point?"

"So this meeting will be over?"

Drew, again silent, suddenly realized he had no desire to end this "meeting," as Christy had termed it. He wished they could forget their problems and simply relax together in the beautiful tropical atmosphere that surrounded Ernest Hemingway's home.

Two more cats, one gray, one tortoiseshell, were rubbing Christy's ankle, vying with the first for her attention. She reached down and patted each in turn. Only then did she face Drew again.

"I think a big problem between us is the fact that we come from two such different worlds, Drew. I'm not talking about snob values or that sort of thing. I'm talking about something much more elemental. You see, you moved me into your world—whether or not I adjusted to it is another matter—but you never, as I said before, made any effort at all to enter mine.

"I've thought about that a lot, Drew. Your problem is that you've been incredibly protected."

"What?" he thundered.

"Please, Drew. You don't need to shout. I mean exactly that. You've never known what it's like to have to fend for yourself. You've never known what it's like not to know where your next dollar or your next meal is coming from, or if you'll manage to save up enough rent money to keep a roof over your head."

"Suppose I haven't?" he challenged. "Are you trying to say that poverty is ennobling? I think it was Somerset Maugham who wrote that poverty is not one damned bit ennobling."

Christy grinned. "Have you been taking a literature course at some night school in Manhattan, Drew?"

She was impossible! He wanted to throw up his hands in despair, but not as badly as he wanted to kiss the tantalizing curve of her neck and make urgent, passionate love to her—something they hadn't done for much, much too long.

"Look, I was only teasing," she said quickly. "But I'm very serious about what I just said. You've always lived in your private ivory tower, Drew. A remote sanctuary from what people like me call the 'real world.' I think the only time I felt you were in touch was in Maine. And that was sort of a last fling for you, wasn't it?"

"What do you mean?"

"I didn't realize it at the time, of course. I didn't realize it until quite recently, one day when I was trying to figure out why things happened the way they did. It came to me that in Maine you were experiencing the last of your youth before you were trapped in your family's business. You knew that once you walked through those doors on Wall Street you'd have to fit into the image that had been carved out for you. You knew there'd be no future time or room for levity," she finished.

Drew sat back and regarded her levelly. "That was quite a speech," he admitted sincerely.

"Am I right?"

He knew he should tell her she was wrong. Way off base. But he couldn't because she *was* right. Entirely too right. He nodded slowly. "I suppose so," he said.

He was watching a fourth cat join the felines already sitting at Christy's feet so he didn't see the flash of triumph that crossed her face. But he heard it in her voice as she said, "Well, then, maybe you'll understand why I want what I want from you."

"I wouldn't count on it."

She disregarded that and said, "What I want, Drew, is for you to assume an entirely different role from the one you're used to. For the next month I want you to pretend you're something you're not. I want you to turn in your rental car and give me all the plastic you carry around. You don't have to worry about what you give me. I'll put it all in a safe-deposit box and, at the end of a month, it'll be yours again. In exchange I'll give you back that eighty dollars I took from your dresser a year ago. I want you to know what it feels like to have no job, no home and hardly any money to your name. Believe me, it totally alters a person's perception of the world."

"I suppose as the next step you want me to job hunt as you did, and so on and so on and so on?" he demanded.

"That's right."

Drew sat back and regarded Christy anew. Suddenly he felt old and tired. She seemed so young and refreshingly beautiful in contrast. "You know, of course, that your request is out of the question," he said, the weight of his world pressing down on him.

"No, I don't know that."

"What would you have me tell the many people who count on my doing what I do?" he asked her.

"There must be someone who could take over for a month," she answered.

"Unfortunately, there isn't."

"Suppose you had a heart attack?"

Drew winced as he thought of his father. "Suppose I did?" he asked.

"Someone would have to take over, wouldn't they? Maybe you hate hearing this, Drew, but there's not a single indispensable person in the whole world. Maybe that's something else no one's ever told you, but believe me it's something you learn very early where I come from."

He swallowed hard, digesting what she'd just said, recognizing the truth of her words. "Okay," he said, "suppose I did divest myself of all my worldly goods, then called the firm and said I wouldn't be back for a month? What then, Christy? As you've pointed out, Key West isn't a cheap place to live, especially now. Finding a place to live with only eighty dollars would be a long shot, wouldn't it? Even if I read through today's paper and managed to find work, it would still be a few days before I got paid, right? So what would you suggest I do? Sleep on the beach? Or sneak back in here at night and use one of Hemingway's benches?"

Christy drew a deep breath, then started to skate carefully over some very thin ice. "When people are down to their last few dollars, it's nice to have friends," she told him.

Drew pounced on that. "But I don't have any friends in Key West. You know that, Christy."

She couldn't look at him. She concentrated on the cats assembled around her, now six in number. "You have me," she pointed out softly. "Until you get a job and find a place of your own, you can stay with me."

Chapter Four

A bus load of tourists had descended on the Hemingway house and people were swarming out onto the verandas. Other tourists were discovering the gardens with voluble exclamations of delight that carried through the sultry air.

"Damn," Drew muttered under his breath, feeling his privacy had been invaded. "This would have to happen now."

"Actually, we had more time to ourselves here than I thought we would," Christy admitted reluctantly. "This is one of Key West's top attractions, you know."

"So we're forced to share it, is that what you're saying?"

"Well, perhaps you could buy the place and post No Admittance signs all around the house and grounds," Christy mused dryly.

The implication that she thought him incredibly spoiled was as plain as day, and that infuriated Drew. The one thing he'd never been was *spoiled*, he thought savagely. He started to tell her so, but knew he'd sound defensive if he uttered the words. Anyway, there was no point in merely *telling* Christy he wasn't spoiled. She needed proof.

Maybe, he decided suddenly, that would be exactly what he would give her!

The idea bore through Drew with a force that completely displaced his usual logic. He'd never felt the need to prove himself to anyone, yet here in Key West with Christy...

She sighed. "It really isn't your fault," she said softly.

Still smoldering, he demanded, "What isn't my fault?"

"The way you are. Any more than the way I am is my fault," Christy said, devoting her attention to the menagerie around her. Watching her, Drew wouldn't have believed he could be so envious of a cat!

"Thoreau wrote about that," Christy said thoughtfully. "And yes, before you say anything, I *did* learn that in one of my literature courses."

"What did Thoreau write about?" Drew asked hoarsely, distracted by the way she was stroking the cat's fur. It reminded him of the early days of their marriage when, after lovemaking, Christy would gently run her fingers up and down his back.

Their lovemaking had been incredibly uninhibited—in the beginning. Then, like everything else in their relationship, the intimate moments had become less frequent and more strained. Admittedly Drew had become apprehensive when he learned how much Christy wanted a child and he'd become cautious. At the same time, his position was making demands far beyond what he'd expected. Even with Millicent's help, those first years at the helm had been difficult and his marriage had been wrongly allowed to fend for itself.

"Drew?" Christy asked. "Are you with me?"

"Yes, of course," he told her quickly.

"Well, you asked what Thoreau said . . ."

"Yes, I did."

"Well, he basically said that every person's perception of the world is different—that we all hear different drummers, and we should listen to our own music, despite what others say or do."

"You think I hear a different drummer?"

"Than I do? Yes, you always have."

"I see."

"Do you really?" she asked, her lovely eyes mirroring her anxious tone. When Drew didn't immediately answer her, she added, "Look, I'm really not trying to sound critical."

"Did I say you were?"

"No, but . . ."

"Then don't jump to conclusions, okay?"

The garden was filling up with people at this point, prompting Drew to get abruptly to his feet. His voice, though, was curiously calm as he said, "We'd better get along."

Christy nodded agreement and slowly stood up. She reached out to give several of her feline friends last affectionate pets and, for a moment, Drew thought she was going to collapse. Her face was strained, her mouth tense. She looked small and very tired. And it took all of Drew's self-control to resist taking her in his arms.

"I suppose you're going to book a later flight?" she asked.

For answer he took her arm and steered her back along the brick pathway to the front of the house. Brushing past yet another influx of tourists they finally reached the sidewalk.

"Wait, Drew. I need to catch my breath."

Drew looked down into eyes that had never seemed more enormous, and something in their expression—a quality he couldn't define—actually made him hurt. Their sadness, perhaps?

"Are you okay?" he asked uncertainly.

For a moment Christy seemed far away. Then, visibly getting a grip on herself, she said, "Where did you park your car?"

"Same place as last night."

"That's quite a walk, Drew. I . . . I'm sorry."

"Sorry? Sorry about what?"

"I wouldn't have dragged you off in this direction if I'd thought of the long walk back you'll have."

"I'm capable of walking a fair distance," he informed her. "In fact," he added, a brief smile playing across his face, "I can *run* a fair distance. For your information I ran the New York Marathon last fall."

"You did?"

"Uh-huh."

"That's more than a 'fair' distance, isn't it?"

"I suppose it is, yes. I didn't break any records, but I did keep up an eight-minute pace the whole way."

Christy shook her head. "Well," she said, "you always did keep yourself physically fit. Still, where did you ever find the time to train for a marathon?"

"I made the time," he said soberly. "Now, as to the car . . . will you walk with me, or would you rather I go get it then come back and pick you up?"

"Neither, Drew."

"Neither?" he echoed. "What's that supposed to mean?"

"It means I think we should bring this meeting to a close."

Drew stopped in his tracks and waited for Christy to turn and look at him. When she did, he said, "You expect me to simply fly back to New York and wait for your scandal story to come out, is that it?"

The expression that crossed her face told Drew that no matter what he did or didn't do, Christy would never carry out that particular threat. She couldn't. She was too fine a person. How could he have lived in the same house with her for five years and not realized what a fine person she was?

A raw emotion older than time surged through him and he nearly groaned aloud. He felt like he was experiencing an internal earthquake. "Well, *is* that what you expect me to do?" he demanded, more brusquely than he'd intended.

"I . . . have to think things over," Christy evaded.

"Well I don't," he countered firmly.

She looked at him, confusion assailing her mind and her heart. After all these months on her own, Drew's tangible presence was a shock. It was like being whisked back in time, and yet some of the tension that had built those high brick walls between them was gone. The laid-back ambience of Key West was a contributing factor, to be sure. But in the last few minutes, something seemed different about Drew himself.

It was a beautiful blue sky morning, tropical and warm. As they passed an open air café, Drew suggested, almost amiably, "Shall we take a break, Christy?"

"If you want to."

"Would you like to?"

"Sure," she said indifferently.

They spotted a vacant table for two near the sidewalk. Drew held Christy's chair for her, then said, "Excuse me a minute, will you?" So saying, he made his way between the tables to a cigarette machine by the waitress station.

As he took his seat opposite her, Christy couldn't repress her surprise. "I don't remember ever seeing you smoke before," she commented.

"It's a bad habit I've just recently taken up," Drew acknowledged. "Actually I smoked for a couple of years at prep school. In college I stopped. Anyway, I don't give in to it very often."

"You shouldn't give in to it at all."

He smiled wearily as he lit a cigarette, inhaled, then blew out a long stream of smoke. "An occasional cigarette can be very relaxing," he said.

"That was my father's standard excuse."

"I'm not making excuses," Drew stated patiently, then quickly smiled up at the waitress who'd arrived to take their order. "Christy?" he prompted, still smiling.

"Just coffee, please," she managed, avoiding his eyes.

"Coffee and a croissant for me," he ordered politely.

The waitress nodded pleasantly and moved away. After a moment, Drew asked Christy, "Why don't we get the car and then stop by your place so you can pick up a bathing suit? There's a swimming pool at the motel, and a jacuzzi, and a pool bar. A good swim followed by a cold drink would be great, don't you think?"

It was a flip suggestion, quite unlike him. Drew recognized this as soon as he finished speaking, and was surprised at himself for adopting such a casual attitude when there was nothing to be casual about.

Christy frowned. "I don't know, Drew. You're making it sound like you're asking me for a date."

"Would that be all bad?" he asked.

Christy looked across at him in disbelief. What had come over him? The Drew she was married to was too controlled to be impulsive, a fact no one knew better than she did. Years ago, in Maine, he'd been impulsive—and young and carefree and wonderful. But those times seemed like another life, a life so remote she couldn't believe she'd actually experienced it.

Drew was surveying his cigarette with the cool of a serious gambler. Another surprise, as he was anything but that! Especially where she was concerned, he'd always held the winning cards. Until that night she folded her hand and quietly walked away.

Now it was a new game he was dealing. A game he'd dreamed up back in Hemingway's garden, Christy decided. Certainly, a change had come over him. Except he was still acting as if his hand was the only one that counted.

The waitress set their coffees on the little table, then went to get Drew's croissant. At that cue Christy got to her feet. "I think I'll be going," she said.

"Oh?" Drew asked. His casual tone belied the look in his eyes. Not for the first time, Christy met his clear gray gaze and felt as if a rose thorn had pricked her heart. The pain was fleeting and emotional and riveted her to the spot.

"I thought you had the day off," he said.

"I do," she said nodding.

"Then I take it you don't want to come swimming with me?"

"No."

"Well then, how about going for a drive? Up to Islamorada, perhaps. When I was at Brown, a bunch of us came down to the Keys on spring break. There was a place on Islamorada, a restaurant right on the water. It was a beautiful spot—I'll bet it's still there."

Was this Drew talking? As if he were a college student on vacation? As if he actually wanted to relax and play? Christy shook her head uncomprehendingly and sat down carefully before she fell down.

"I take it," he said, his silvery eyes still zeroed in on her, "that a trek to Islamorada also doesn't appeal?" He accepted his croissant, took a bite and shrugged. "Well then," he said, "why don't *you* suggest something?" He held Christy's gaze and smiled, entirely disarming her. "Make it good though, okay?" he suggested. "I'd like to have a little fun on my final fling before I pare myself down to eighty bucks."

Christy heard his words and was staggered. She stared across at Drew, expecting to read in his expression a sign that he was making fun of her. But his handsome face was both honest and serious as he said, "I'm giving you that month you asked for."

Christy waited in Drew's rental car while he checked out of the motel and thought she was hallucinating when he tossed a clothes carrier and matching flight bag into the rear seat before he slid in behind the wheel.

"Can we drop my stuff off at your place?" he asked. "Or should I turn the car in first and go it on foot?"

"We can stop at my place," she agreed weakly.

"You're sure that's allowed?" he inquired.

"Yes," she managed, holding her tongue.

Still, she wanted to kick him. He was acting disarmingly civil, but underneath that polished exterior lurked his usual, high-handed self. Christy yearned to wipe the rather smug smile off his face, but decided to simmer down until she figured out what he was up to. If Drew really intended to give her plan a try... well, things would be different after today, she thought, with a smug smile of her own.

He wouldn't feel the pinch immediately, but reducing the resources of Drew Delahunt III to only eighty dollars cash *would* be an enormous step down. He'd be forced to look at people and life and work—forced to consider his own survival, in fact—in a drastically different light. Assuming, of course, he played the game by her rules.

Strangely enough that was the one thing Christy was certain of. The demands Drew placed on himself precluded any form of dishonesty or cheating. Also, Drew would never start something he didn't intend to finish. Or accept a challenge he didn't intend to succeed at.

"So, Christy, where do you live?"

The question, posed casually, triggered a feeling of panic that literally froze her vocal chords. Christy had a sudden vision of her apartment as she'd left it this morning—a total mess. The bed sheets were lying bunched up in a heap, her clothes were scattered all over the place, the kitchen sink was full of dishes, a stack of newspapers and magazines took up half of her couch. The list went on. A list she'd intended to tackle later in the afternoon. As it was...

Drew Delahunt was the unmessiest person she'd ever known. His thick dark hair was always cut and combed just so, his clothes were always cleaned and pressed, he always looked clean shaven. She'd sometimes thought, when they were living under the same roof, that he must have programmed himself to shave in his sleep. Even upon awakening, he looked great—and would smell ever so slightly of some expensive aphrodisiac cologne.

As for that roof she'd lived under, there was a staff of servants to keep the Westport estate in order, and everything the Delahunts owned was exactly that—in order. From the highly polished furniture to the showroom quality Oriental carpets to the crystal chandeliers, not a speck of dust anywhere.

"Christy?" Drew repeated patiently.

She was silently cursing the fact that her lingerie was literally decorating her apartment and wondered how Drew would react to that.

She turned her attention back to Drew and gave him directions to her house.

Christy knew there was nothing tricky about the route, yet Drew drove along the streets of Key West like he'd been living there for years. He even started humming to himself as if he couldn't have been happier!

As they pulled up in front of the house, Christy's heart sank even further. The place was no gem, though it was an architectural treasure in the "conch" style native to Key

West. The owners were slowly renovating it and had begun by putting on a new tin roof. But the yard was a jungle of huge green leaves and creeping green fingers, the far opposite end of the spectrum from the manicured grounds of Westport.

Christy got out of the car and heard Drew's door thud. "So this is your place? It looks fascinating."

She stared across at him, searching for a nuance of hidden meaning, but Drew was studying the house with what appeared to be genuine interest. "Real Key West, isn't it?" he said.

"Very much so," she agreed quickly. "It's a rather ornate example of a conch house."

"Conk?" Drew echoed, noting Christy's pronunciation. "You mean conch, don't you?"

Christy smiled. "They say conk in Key West, Drew. That's one of the first things you learn when you come here. Saying it right helps separate you from the tourists. Although . . . you hardly look like a native."

"So I've noticed," Drew concurred.

"Anyway, the conchs were the original settlers here."

"I see," he said gravely.

The property was separated from the sidewalk by a faded picket fence. As Christy proceeded Drew through the gate, she said, "In case you're wondering, the outside of the house is meant to be that way. I mean, it may look to you as if the exterior needs painting, but that's sun-bleached wood, a very good example of sun-bleached wood, I've been told. The shutters are shot, obviously. And the porch needs refurbishing."

Drew nodded absently as he studied the interesting structure before him. "When was it built, do you know?" he asked.

"About a hundred years ago," Christy informed him. "Many houses were built in Key West in the eighteen seventies, eighties and nineties. They had to import lumber to build here—mahogany from Honduras, cypress from the upper Keys, pine from the Florida Panhandle...."

Christy, speaking faster every second, suddenly stopped. The enormity of what was about to happen washed over her, and her nerves were vibrating like a barbed wire fence in the wind, with the same pain-prickling results.

I'd like you to give me one month of your life....

Those words were already coming back to haunt her.

What could she have been thinking of? she asked herself, her barbed nerves going crazy inside her. This was *Drew Cabot Delahunt III* she was dealing with. A man totally accustomed to living in his own uniquely rarefied environment, an atmosphere of extreme wealth and privilege. To expect him to "descend" to the level of ordinary, mundane human beings and live like "real people" for a month was so consummately ridiculous that she couldn't imagine how she'd whittled the courage to ever suggest the idea.

Drew, she sensed, was waiting for her to say something. She looked up at him unhappily and would have sworn she saw the faintest hint of amusement flicker in his gray eyes. "Well, shall we go inside?" he asked gravely.

"Yes, of course," she managed nervously, realizing he'd been waiting for an invitation. "You might as well bring your stuff up now," she added rather ungraciously.

He favored her with a cool glance at that, but did as she bade, returning to the car and gathering his bags. Christy stepped up onto the low porch, then watched Drew for a moment, frozen in thought, before she fumbled in her handbag for the front door key. She was about to turn the handle when Drew reached over and calmly beat her to it.

"After you," he suggested smoothly, pushing the door open and standing aside so she could precede him.

Involuntarily she turned and looked up into his eyes for a clue of what he was thinking. She had the weird feeling that he should pick her up and carry her over the threshold as if they were bride and groom! The mere idea flooded her with a surge of unexpected warmth. She felt her cheeks grow hot, knew they must be scarlet and was glad that it was shady in the narrow corridor they were facing.

The Descartes's door was just opposite the stairway that flanked one wall. Ben and Terry were not only her neighbors, they were her best friends in Key West. Still, they had no idea that she'd ever been married—was married, in fact—to a well-known millionaire financier. Nor was she about to tell them now, and she hoped the old wooden floorboards wouldn't creak too loudly as she and Drew stepped inside.

At the foot of the stairs, Christy hesitated. She was tempted to draw Drew back into the sunlight and take him somewhere so they could decide how to explain away his identity and the reason he was staying with her. Cal Fancy would also have to know about Drew, she realized dismally, as would a number of other people she knew locally. If anyone discovered that she had this handsome guest secretly staying with her, she'd never hear the end of it.

"Do you live on this floor, or upstairs?" Drew asked, interrupting her thoughts.

Though his voice was pitched normally, it seemed to Christy that his question thundered along the hall. She wanted to clap her hand over his mouth so he couldn't say anything further. As it was, she gave him a small shove toward the stairs and urged him upward in something of a stage whisper.

Drew, looking slightly puzzled, started up the stairs with Christy following close on his heels to the point of pushing him. At the top he turned, frowning. "What was all that about?" he demanded. Then, to her astonishment, he actually grinned. "Haven't you paid your rent?" he teased.

"Yes, I've paid my rent!" she snapped, squeezing by him on the small landing and pushing open her door. "Please, go on in, will you?" she insisted, not attempting to camouflage the urgency of her tone.

Drew strode through the open door, took two steps into Christy's living room, then abruptly halted, wondering what in God's name he'd gotten himself into. The room was fairly large, with a high ceiling and tall French windows at one end leading onto a deck. It could be a pleasant enough room, Drew imagined reasonably, if it were decorated decently. It was potentially airy, potentially light, except... it was a shambles. He felt as if he'd stumbled into a laundry and a lingerie shop combined.

Christy, he realized, was darting about scooping up flimsy wisps of beige and blue and rose-colored lingerie. Drew chuckled, despite himself. "Spare your energy," he advised. "Just point me in the direction of my room, okay?"

"Sure," she muttered disconsolately. She picked up two or three more items, then dropped the whole pile into a battered old armchair. For a moment she stared at Drew, her eyes huge. Then she looked away and blurted, "You don't have a room."

Drew's eyes narrowed. "Exactly what are you talking about?" he demanded, his lack of sleep the previous night suddenly beginning to catch up with him. "I thought you'd agreed to take me in until I can find a job and amass enough money to get a place of my own."

"I did, I did," Christy assured him, vigorously shaking her silky blond head. "But that doesn't mean I can give you a room."

"What does it mean?" Drew asked skeptically.

"Well, there's only one bedroom," she told him, pointing vaguely over her shoulder, "and that's... um, mine. There's a little closet off the kitchen, though. I'll clean it out and you can have that."

"You expect me to sleep in a closet?"

"No, of course not. That's to keep your things in. As for sleeping..."

Christy had never paid much attention to the studio couch that occupied the wall opposite the French windows, except to make it the dumping ground for her ever increasing collection of magazines, newspapers and paperbacks. Just about every inch was covered by unruly stacks of reading material, several of which had spilled over onto the floor.

In something of a daze, she picked up a pile of newspapers, revealing the couch's garish yellow, pink and fuchsia cover. It needed washing and would have been washed, she assured herself, had she known she'd be having company. "You can sleep here. It's a little lumpy but it's all I have to offer," she said, fighting down a sense of embarrassment.

She waited for his reaction, expecting that after having given her the benefit of his opinion—first silent, then spoken—he would turn on his heel and leave.

"Mmm," he observed thoughtfully. "Would you suggest that I sleep on top of your...library, shall we call it? Or should I risk skin contact with that unusual upholstery? What is that, anyway? A floral design or a nightmare?"

Christy bit her lip and suddenly wanted to cry. She wished she could wail, in fact, and beat her hands and head against the wall. Why was Drew so frustrating to deal with? Why did he have such an infinite capacity to nettle her?

Well, she'd asked for this, she thought fairly. This conch house on Whitehead Street in Key West was the current home—and accurately reflected the present life-style—of Mrs. Drew Delahunt III. If she'd had any sense, she would have said politely, *Yes, Drew, of course I'll be glad to file for a divorce in Florida. You're right, it'll be so much simpler that way.*

As it was, she said stiffly, "I'll clear the couch off, Drew. I'm afraid it won't be quite as comfortable as the bed you're used to, but . . ."

"No problem," he told her.

He flashed a smile at her but when she held his gaze, the smile faded. Christy had seen him look serious thousands of times, yet never more so than he looked right now.

"I accepted your option only after you turned down both of mine," he reminded her. "I may not be perfect, Christy, but I don't go back on my word. Remember that, will you?"

Chapter Five

Christy's eyes mirrored her bewilderment. "Yes, Drew...I know, and I'll remember. But first, there's something I have to ask you."

"What?"

She pushed back a strand of ash-blond hair that had fallen across her forehead and realized her skin felt hot. *She* felt hot. Could emotional turmoil give you a fever?

"Would you like a drink of something?" she asked uncertainly. "I mean, it's kind of hot in here, would you like something cold to drink? Orange juice? Beer? White Zinfandel."

"White Zinfandel?" Drew echoed. "No, I don't think so."

"Well, I think I'll have a glass," Christy decided abruptly. She headed for her kitchen and Drew followed. "Have a seat," she said, gesturing toward a round yellow table set snugly in a corner. "Sure you don't want something to drink?"

Drew shook his head. "What was it you needed to ask me?" he queried, his patience obviously strained.

"Well," she began, pouring her wine, "I may have made a mistake."

His eyebrows rose. "Don't tell me you've decided to back out of the challenge you issued me?"

"Not at all," she said quickly. "I want the month you promised me as much as ever. For your sake more than mine."

Drew's smile was mirthless. "How altruistic of you," he said smoothly.

Christy flinched. That was classic Drew, a behavior which had been surprisingly absent these past few hours. The Drew who'd casually strolled along the streets of Key West, the Drew who'd cast an almost tolerant eye over her apartment had thrown her off guard. That Drew had been so *human.* But now she faced the man with whom she'd lived for five increasingly difficult years, and took refuge in the old cliché that leopards can't change their spots. Rearrange, perhaps, but never change.

Lack of sleep was catching up with Christy, too, and her head was beginning to ache. Sitting down opposite him, she asked wearily, "Why are you doing this, Drew? I need to know why you came down here by yourself instead of just sending someone to represent you?"

He looked faintly annoyed. "I thought we went through that." he said. "I felt I should ask you for a divorce personally."

"Why?"

"Courtesy, I suppose. You *can* understand that, can't you?"

She hated it when he talked down to her! She said tightly, "Yes, Drew, I can understand that. Still, I can't help but think you had another reason for making the trip. A reason that went beyond mere courtesy."

"Mere courtesy, eh?" He sat back and surveyed her, his gray eyes strangely brooding. "Okay," he admitted, "there was another reason. I wanted to see you for myself."

"Why?"

For a long moment he was silent. Finally he said, "To tell you the truth, I'm not sure."

Those words sounded very odd to Christy. She'd never known Drew to be unsure about anything. She sipped her wine, hoping it would relax her. Her temples were starting to throb at this point, and a knot was filling her throat.

"I can't quite buy that, Drew," she managed.

"What can't you buy?"

"That you'd leave your business and fly down here just to see me." *Business* was a misnomer, she thought wryly. *Empire* would be a more accurate description.

Drew observed her wordlessly, his eyes binding her to the spot like bands of cold gray steel. Then, abruptly, he leaned forward and rested his elbows on the table. In a ragged voice unlike anything she'd ever heard, he said, "I'm going to go through this with you one time, Christy. Just once, understand? Then I never want to talk about it again."

Her eyes alone told Drew that she had no idea what he was about to say. Also they were an incredible distraction. He pushed back his chair and moved across to the stove. Briefly he glanced at the floor. Then he looked directly at Christy and rasped, "When I realized that you'd walked out of my life, it hurt, Christy. It hurt like hell!"

"Your pride was wounded, you mean?"

His glare was scathing. "You shredded my pride, if that's any satisfaction to you. I wanted to creep into a corner and pull the walls down around me. In some ways that's exactly what I did. But my pride was only part of it. If I'd had your freedom..."

"My *freedom*?"

"Why the puzzled look? Freedom is exactly what you had. You were able to wander off into oblivion with no responsibility toward anyone but yourself. I, on the other hand, had literally hundreds of people to account to. The people I work closely with, our stockholders, people I deal with all over the world. I couldn't simply walk out on them and suffer alone in silence as I wanted to do. Then, there were friends. My friends. Old family friends. And of course there was my mother. It wasn't long before I knew I would have to think up a very good explanation for your absence."

"To save your face?"

"Call it that if you like. My face, my pride. What the hell difference does it make? The point was, I had to invent a story about you."

She sat up straight. "You what?"

"I told everyone your mother was ill and needed you, so you flew out to California to be with her."

Christy's face paled. "You know my mother's dead, Drew."

"Of course I know that. But I had to latch on to something that would sound valid."

"And you managed to keep up that pretense for a whole year?" she asked incredulously.

"Yes, because from time to time I flew out to visit you. I'd take a few days and go somewhere, covering my tracks very carefully," Drew said. "People thought I'd taken off to be with you. After a couple of months I gradually let it be known that you and I weren't doing too well."

"In other words you were paving the way for the announcement of a divorce."

"Yes."

"Hmm," Christy mused. "I really did upset your plans, didn't I?"

"Do I need to answer that question?" Drew asked tersely.

"I suppose not."

Christy was silent for a while, lost in thought. Then something struck her. "You mentioned that were I willing to go back to Westport with you, you wanted children," she said, sitting up even straighter, feeling as if her arms and legs had turned to stone.

"Yes."

"You never wanted children, Drew."

"That's not true, Christy. I wanted to give us time, that's all. There was so much to deal with." He came back to the table and sat down again, lines of tension grooving his face. "I'm not asking for your sympathy or compassion," he said, "so I won't go into how it was to take over the conglomerate of interests my family's involved in when I was twenty-five years old and newly married. I couldn't expect you to understand."

Christy sprang to her feet and glared at him. "Damn it!" she shouted. "Will you stop putting me down?"

He looked honestly taken aback. "It wasn't my intention to put you down," he said levelly.

"You've always tended to put me down!"

Drew exhaled deeply, then said softly, "If you really think that, I'm . . . sorry."

Christy sank back against her chair and rubbed her temples. "You still haven't told me what I want to know," she said quietly.

"What else is there?"

"Well, my feeling is—and please correct me if I'm wrong—that your facing me in person was a matter of honor with you, as much as it was a courtesy to me."

"I suppose you could call it that."

"Suppose I *had* agreed to go back to Westport with you? For a while, you could have covered tracks so everything would have looked all right, couldn't you?"

"Probably."

"Then," Christy continued, "if our marriage started to fall apart with me right there on the premises and we decided to get a divorce after six months, it would have been okay. No one would ever have had to know that I'd once walked out on you."

"You do have a way of putting things," Drew murmured.

"So you've said before."

"Is there anything else?"

"One other thing, yes. Suppose I got pregnant during those six months, Drew?"

"Suppose you had?"

"What would have happened to the child?"

"What do you mean?"

"It's very simple, really. Let's assume the trial period ended in failure, as I think you'll have to admit it probably would. Then, a baby came along. Under the terms of the divorce, would I have any chance at all of getting the baby? Or is it reasonable to assume the court would decide that being brought up as a Delahunt might be slightly more advantageous to our child?"

"Oh, come on," Drew protested.

"You don't have to answer," she said. "You'd have taken the child, of course. You'd have robbed me of my baby just as you tried to rob me of my very identity—tried to mold me into something I'm not, because what I *am* didn't fit in with your life and your friends."

Drew wanted desperately to protest but didn't. There was a certain truth to what Christy was saying, and it made him sick to recognize it. He'd married her because—as she might have put it—she marched to the step of a different drummer. He'd found her personality enchanting, her free spirit a delight, her beauty so refreshingly natural. He'd envied her uninhibited zest for life, her excitement, her wonder. He'd loved her totally.

After they eloped, things changed. Reality stepped in, along with tremendous responsibility. Drew, anything but free, had tried to crush out of Christy the very things that had appealed to him. Like destroying the petals of a rose one by one, as though the stem might be more beautiful than the blossom.

Yet he'd been unaware of what he was doing. There'd been nothing malicious in his motivation, he'd wanted only the best for her. He'd dressed her in the most fashionable clothes, placed her in a Mercedes and tried to temper her exuberant manner so she didn't always stand out in a room filled with his kind of people.

Christy, of course, had resisted him. Stood up to him. And, finally walked out on him.

Looking at Christy now, so blond and beautiful and free, Drew's heart ached. He'd tried so hard to get over her these past twelve months and at times even thought he'd succeeded. But after only *hours* in her company, he realized he would never get her out of his system. He would never stop loving her, and he was an absolute fool to think otherwise.

"Christy," he said, shattering the silence that had come between them, "if you want out of this month you've asked me for, I'll understand."

Her violet eyes spelled suspicion. "What's that supposed to mean?" she asked carefully.

"It means I can understand that you might have second thoughts about what you've asked me to do. You might not think I can do it." He smiled faintly. "If you think that—if you've wondered if I'll be a problem—I'll go. I won't even make any nasty remarks about the way women change their minds," he promised.

Christy shook her head. "Oh, no, I want the month, Drew," she told him. "It's just ... well, I still don't understand why you agreed to give it to me."

"Because," he said, his tone low and level, "I'd like to show you that I'm not the spoiled, arrogant, selfish, pampered, incompetent individual you seem to think I am."

Fifteen minutes later Drew left her apartment to return his rental car. As he passed the door to the downstairs apartment it opened, revealing a red-haired young woman who looked very tired and very pregnant. She seemed about to speak to him, but then she withdrew and closed the door.

At the car rental office Drew terminated his business, then placed a credit card call to his mother. This, he decided, hearing the phone ringing at the other end of the line, would be the last in-character move for the next thirty days. At the same time, he couldn't simply disappear without telling Millicent what he was doing. Who would run the company, for one thing?

Drew and his mother were very close. He not only loved her he admired her profoundly. Most people knew only the social facade of Millicent Payne Delahunt or the business attitude she'd adopted so well. A facade envied by many, her son was aware. Her inner side, especially her private agonies, were known to very few. Drew had been witness to reactions reserved for no one else. Reactions to tragedy, of which Millicent had endured her share—like when his father had suffered a fatal heart attack at age forty-eight, to cite the most recent trauma of her life.

Millicent and Rogers Delahunt had been deeply in love with each other. The peeping, prying world had looked on their union as the meshing of two very wealthy families. The paparazzi had done their job, the scandal writers had invented their stories of lurid extramarital romance. All for a buck, Drew had thought bitterly so many, many times.

Possessed of a quality called dignity, Millicent and Rogers had never stooped to refute a single untrue tale. Instead they had cultivated the stony indifference that would become something of a Delahunt trademark. What that trademark really did was camouflage an inner loneliness peculiar to old-line wealth. It was only natural that Drew would learn this from his parents. Only natural that he would present that so-called haughty mien to a sometimes hostile world, including the young woman he loved so dearly, Christy DiMartino.

He was the only remaining Delahunt child. As thus, he was scion of the family and sole inheritor. He'd never forgotten that his mother had lost two other children, one in infancy, another at the age of three. The three-year-old, a beautiful little girl named Lucinda, had been kidnapped. Rogers, despite police protests, had met the kidnappers' demands. But after he'd paid the exorbitant cash ransom, his little daughter's body had been found in a culvert beside the Connecticut Turnpike.

That was one of the many tragedies Millicent had endured over the years. There was also the suicide of her father after her mother deserted him, and the trauma of having the brother she adored die in a car crash while driving blind drunk.

Millicent had weathered many storms, her son remembered now, during that supposedly perfect life of hers. And it had been incredibly difficult for her to grasp the reins of the Delahunt conglomerate after her husband's death. Not the least of her problems was withstanding the astonishing avarice of several key individuals who would have done anything in their power, legal or illegal, to sweep her off the throne and keep Drew from ever ascending it.

All these thoughts flashed through Drew's mind in a moment, and his voice was tender as he said, "Hello, Millie."

It was his private name for her, spoken only when there was no one else around.

"Drew," she exclaimed. "Where are you? I pictured you flying up the coast about now."

"I'm still in Key West," he told her. And then he began to tell her about finding Christy in Fancy's bar and about how she'd vetoed his options and offered one of her own.

When he'd finished and hung up, Drew moved away from the phone convinced that no one but Millicent would have understood his decision so knowingly. Added to that was her vow to support his stand, no matter what.

As he started walking back toward Whitehead Street, Drew recalled ruefully that the only time Millicent had ever let him down was during her first encounter with Christy.

He and Christy had eloped. They'd driven up to Massachusetts, gotten their blood tests, applied for a license and later were married by a magistrate on Nantucket Island, off the coast of Cape Cod. It had all been very romantic, like a storybook fantasy... until they'd finally reached Westport.

Christy had been completely unprepared for the estate Drew drove her onto, and the Delahunt property was exactly that—an ivy-covered brick mansion of forty rooms set on eight manicured acres. The place had been home to Drew all his life. He was used to the magnificence, the opulence. Only later, much later, did he begin to appreciate how it must have looked through Christy's eyes.

Millicent had been at a charity tea that afternoon. She got home not long after they arrived, dressed to the teeth, the diamonds and sapphires that Drew laughingly referred to as "the crown jewels" flashing as she crossed the drawing room to be introduced to the awestruck young girl who'd become her daughter-in-law.

She'd been staggered when Drew introduced Christy as his wife.

Drew had recognized Millicent's shock, but he'd seen her shocked before, seen her hide it, seen her instantly transform herself into the gracious and imperturbable hostess that she was. But it hadn't happened like that, that day. Millicent had been shaken and, instinctively, a certain coldness had crept into her manner. Drew knew it for what it was—a form of self-protection. Christy, of course, had not.

It had been a bad beginning.

Later Millicent had tried to make amends. By then, though, Christy's pride had become laced with tough, impenetrable scars. She'd effectively kept her mother-in-law beyond arm's length and was never rude to her but never warm either.

For a while Drew had tried to bring the two women together. Then, he'd been too busy taking over the reins of the firm to think much about the chasm between them or about the other chasm that was growing between him and his young wife.

Somewhere along the line, he thought now, something in his education had been remiss. Millicent, so untried in the world of business until forced to take over after her husband's death, had never really learned how to delegate responsibility. She'd been afraid to let go of the reins, and—probably unconsciously—she'd passed that idea on to her son. For so long he'd fought his battles alone, felt that doing so was necessary in order to remain at the top. Only in the last year had he learned it was possible to loosen his grip and still keep control

It was a lesson that applied even more to his relationship with Christy. A lesson learned too late perhaps. But at least a lesson learned. Now all he had to do was prove it to her.

"Hey, you want to come down and let me in," Drew called up from the garden. "I locked myself out."

Christy, hearing him, stepped onto the deck outside the French windows. "I warned you that would happen if you didn't put the latch on the door," she reprimanded him lightly. "I'll have a duplicate set of keys made for you tomorrow."

"Why don't I do that now?"

"Because one, the hardware store isn't open today, and two, keys cost money," Christy answered. "You don't want to dig into your eighty dollars any more than you have to."

"Good point," Drew agreed. "Anyway, I can repay you as soon as I get a job."

A minute later Christy opened the front door. She'd changed into jeans and a lacy pale green top and had a huge white cotton apron tied around her waist. She looked relaxed and happy—positively terrific. As he followed her up the narrow stairs, he felt surprisingly self-conscious.

If only I could loosen up like that, he thought.

A marvelous aroma was emanating from her kitchen. And a remarkable transformation had been effected during his absence. The newspapers, magazines and paperbacks were neatly stacked in one corner, and there was not so much as a scrap of lingerie on public display.

In the kitchen, the round yellow table had been set for four with straw-colored place mats, red cloth napkins and a single red candle.

Drew raised an eyebrow. "Company?" he asked.

"I'd forgotten all about it, but Terry came up just after you left and brought a bottle of Chianti," Christy said. "She said she saw you. Anyway, I'd invited her and Ben for an early Sunday supper."

"So that's why you're cooking," Drew mused. "Am I invited?"

"Of course you're invited. Who did you think that fourth chair is for?"

"I wouldn't know," he answered innocently. "But whatever you're making smells delicious."

"It's my grandmother's spaghetti sauce," Christy said.

"Well, that smell has made me realize I'm starving. All I've had so far today is coffee and one croissant. Don't you eat lunch, Christy?"

"Sometimes, but I hadn't even thought about it to tell you the truth. Did you?"

"Not until now," Drew admitted. "What time are your friends coming?"

"I told them around six."

"Then we have time to go get a snack somewhere."

Christy shook her hand. "You can't afford going out for snacks," she informed him.

"I haven't yet divested myself of my money," he reminded her. "I still have both plastic and cash. We could have one last fling, you know."

She shook her head. "No way, Drew. You're in my territory now so you've got to play by my rules. Anyway, I can't leave the gas stove on if we go out. So," she capitulated, "I'll make you a cheese and tomato sandwich if you're that hungry. You can have a beer with it, okay?"

"Sounds good," Drew agreed.

As he watched her make the sandwich, he was sure his heart skipped several beats. Just observing her doing anything made him feel warm inside.

"Why don't we sit outside," she suggested as she handed him his plate.

"Good idea."

She led him through the French doors onto the deck, a recent modification to the house, Drew realized, noting the unweathered floorboards and railing.

"This is very nice," he commented appreciatively.

"It was one of the main reasons I took the place," Christy said. "We're facing east, so I get the morning rays out here.

The midday sun is just too much for my skin, but the mornings are perfect. Cool fresh air, birds chirping..."

Drew visualized Christy reading the morning paper and sipping her coffee in this relaxed, unhurried atmosphere and felt a pang of envy. By contrast his mornings were one big rush into the city. Except now...

"Is there anything I can do to help?" he asked.

"For dinner? No, I've got it all under control," she said rather absently.

Back in the kitchen she gave the spaghetti sauce a stir. Beside her, Drew was washing his plate. It was the perfect time, she decided.

"Okay, Mr. Delahunt," she said briskly, "the moment of truth has arrived."

"Moment of truth?" he asked, innocently.

"Turn out your pockets and let me have your wallet."

"Oh, *that* moment of truth," he muttered. Still, he did as she said without protest. He fished out every last penny from his pockets, then went and got his billfold from his jacket.

"That's it?" she asked.

"Isn't that enough?"

"Very funny," she told him, counting bills and shaking her head in disbelief. "Seven hundred and sixty-nine dollars," she said finally. "Plus an extra five thousand in traveler's checks. My God, Drew, do you always carry around this much money?"

"It varies," he evaded.

"I can imagine. Probably upward, if anything."

So saying, she disappeared in the direction of her bedroom to return a moment later with a rather worn looking red purse. "We'll put all of it in this," she announced. "Tomorrow I'll rent a safe-deposit at one of the banks. For tonight... well, let's just hope we don't get robbed."

She was tucking away Drew's credit cards and cash as she spoke. "Aren't you forgetting something?" he asked dryly.

Without looking up, she handed him eighty dollars. "Your springboard," she told him.

"Thank you," he said casually.

"That's *it*, you know," Christy warned.

"Yes, I know. So . . . how much do I owe you for rent?"

She looked up suspiciously but Drew was serious. "I thought I told you that's what friends are for," she informed him patiently. "To help out when things aren't going too well."

"Who said things aren't going too well?"

"Look, Drew. Our script reads that you arrived in Key West with eighty dollars to your name, no job and no place to stay. Then you ran across me, and because we knew each other way back I said you could stay at my place until you latched onto something."

"Right," he agreed.

"Which brings me to something else," Christy said.

"What's that?"

"We have to give you a cover with Terry and Ben," she told him.

Drew was perplexed. "Why do I need a cover?"

"Because they don't know I was ever married—that I *am* married," she corrected hastily and hoped she wouldn't blush. "I . . . I'm not wearing my wedding ring, in case you haven't noticed."

Drew was stunned . . . because he *hadn't* noticed. "I still don't see why I need a cover," he growled.

"Look, if any of my friends heard the name Drew Delahunt III it would be like saying John D. Rockefeller."

"You're exaggerating, Christy," Drew said. "I'm not that well-known outside of Wall Street."

"Maybe your face isn't, but your name is," she contradicted. "Anyway, I'd appreciate it if you'd take another last name while you're here."

"Okay, if you say so," Drew agreed. "How about Cabot, my middle name. Would that be okay?"

Christy shook her head. "It sounds...I don't know, it just sounds, that's all."

"How about Payne, my mother's maiden name?"

"I suppose so," Christy groaned. "It's still..."

"New England?" Drew suggested.

"Oh, all right. You're Drew Payne, a friend of my brother's from Springfield, Massachusetts."

"But you don't have a brother, Christy."

She eyed him levelly. "I did have. My brother Marty died of leukemia when he was eight years old."

"You never told me that."

"It's so far in the past, Drew, I hardly ever think about it. Please, don't take it the wrong way that I didn't tell you."

"All right, I won't."

"Thank you," she said softly, then added, "Anyway, if you brought my mother back to life for your purposes then I guess I can bring Marty back to life for a while."

Drew shook his head. "This is getting awfully complicated."

"Not really," Christy disagreed. "Anyway, you'll get used to it. You just have to remember that you're Drew Payne. You know Marty DiMartino back in Springfield, so when you were coming to Key West you said you'd look me up. You could have known me back in Springfield, too, for that matter, when I was a kid."

"Of course."

Christy thought she detected a twinkle of amusement in Drew's steel eyes. A put-down, perhaps? Somehow she didn't think so.

"Anyway, you got down here to Key West and you needed a place to stay until you get a job, so I said you could sleep on the couch for a few nights. I think that sounds plausible, don't you?"

She was so intent that Drew was hard put to repress a smile. That, he knew, wouldn't go over very well, so he managed to say with suitable gravity, "Yes, I think that sounds very plausible."

"Then that's what we'll go with," Christy decided. "There's only one problem," she added, frowning.

"Which is?"

"You," she said succinctly.

"Me?"

"You are just too...perfect," Christy said, faltering only slightly. "Your clothes shriek expense, for one thing. I don't suppose you brought along a pair of jeans or a T-shirt?"

"Sorry, but that's not exactly the costume of the day on Wall Street," he said.

"This isn't Wall Street, Drew. I'm afraid you'd better splurge some of your eighty dollars on a pair of jeans," Christy decided. "And get something prewashed, okay? Otherwise... well, you know what new jeans look like."

"Absolutely," he agreed, on the verge of laughter.

"As for a shirt," Christy went on, ignoring him, "I've got a sweatshirt from Fancy's that's a mile too big for me. It'll have to do for now."

The shirt in question was lime green with the sleeves cut off and the neck cut ragged. The logo depicted Fancy's Polynesian hut with a girl doing the hula. Drew had never worn anything like it in his life and was about to protest that he couldn't possibly do so now. But Christy silenced him by saying, "You don't have to tell me. I know it isn't you. But go along with it for tonight, will you? You'll fit in much better."

"We're playing by your rules," he said nodding.

That Drew should acquiesce so readily to her suggestions was a total surprise. A surprise Christy didn't have any idea how to handle.

Chapter Six

Terry Descartes was wearing a bright yellow smock over her maternity jeans and had tied her red hair in a ponytail with a length of yellow yarn. She was of slight build and quite frail looking, except for the enormous bulge of her pregnancy. Drew guessed her age at close to thirty, and wondered how soon she was due.

Ben was of medium height, rather stocky and had sandy blond hair. His pale blue eyes were almost obscured by the thick glasses he wore, but he had an infectious smile and a strong, friendly handshake. Initially he was more outgoing than Terry. But Terry caught up with him once she'd had a glass of the Chianti.

"The doctor says a little wine is okay, but for the first five months I didn't drink at all," she confided to Drew. "Now it only takes about two sips to make me giddy, so watch out or I'm apt to talk your ear off."

"Go right ahead," Drew invited amiably.

They were sitting side by side on the lumpy studio couch. Ben had insisted that Christy let him toss the salad. "This is what I do a couple of nights a week at a restaurant down near Mallory Dock," he told Drew over his shoulder. "So I'm an expert."

"Actually," Christy said, "Ben's an artist and a very good one."

"I wish more people had your excellent taste," Ben said, with a chuckle. "The checks I've received for selling a painting have been few and far between."

"Last year it was better," Terry observed.

"A lot of people are saying that," Christy said nodding. "Maybe the tourists had more money to spend last year. I've noticed that the majority here now seem to be operating on rather tight vacation budgets."

"Would that we could operate on a tight *vacation* budget," Ben scoffed. He gave the salad one last toss then exclaimed, "There. Perfecto!"

Christy was emptying the boiling contents of a huge pot of spaghetti into a colander she'd placed in the sink. Steam rose in clouds and, for a moment, Drew anxiously thought she was going to burn herself. But she merely said, "There," as she dumped the spaghetti from the colander back into the empty pot. "That's perfecto, too. *Al dente*, just like spaghetti should be."

As the quartet settled themselves around the yellow wooden table, Ben laughed and said, "Close quarters, eh? We'll have to keep track of our elbows."

"It's called camaraderie," Terry informed him. "And normally I wouldn't be taking up so much room."

Christy struck a match and lit the red candle that centered the intimate setting. Then she rose and switched off the overhead light. "That's better," she said, resuming her seat. "If a place doesn't come with atmosphere, you have to create a little."

Drew saw Terry glance rather anxiously toward Ben. "Can you see all right?" she asked him.

"Sure," he answered cheerfully.

Drew sampled Christy's sauce and thought he'd never tasted anything better. "This is terrific, Christy," he murmured appreciatively. "I never knew you could cook like this."

Terry picked up on his statement. "You mean she was holding out on you back in Springfield?"

"I never knew Drew well enough back in Springfield to cook for him," Christy said quickly. "He was my brother's friend."

"Which doesn't mean I didn't have my eye on her," Drew put in wickedly, suddenly deciding that two could play her game. "If I'd known she could cook pasta like this—"

"You might have made an honest woman of her?" Ben ventured, keeping up the tempo.

"Well, I don't know if I'd have gone that far," Drew drawled. "She was kind of young for my taste...back then, I mean. There *are* a few years between us."

Six, you lug, Christy wanted to say to him. Her face was stormy as she met his eyes, temporarily forgetting about acting cautiously in front of the Descarteses. Then, flabbergasting her all the more, Drew actually winked at her!

He looked terrific in the sweatshirt she'd loaned him and his new pair of jeans. He seemed incredibly relaxed and, to her astonishment, was obviously enjoying himself. She stole glances at him as he bantered easily with Terry and Ben, adroitly sidestepping any questions about life back in Springfield that might have aroused their suspicions. At the same time he made observations about the Key West scene that were impossible not to laugh at. He was a visitor all right!

Christy couldn't believe her eyes as Drew polished off his third plate of spaghetti. She'd never seen him eat like that before. Back in the beautifully appointed dining room of the Westport mansion, Drew had always been discreet in his consumption of the gourmet meals he'd been served routinely. Meals prepared by a bona fide chef, she remembered ruefully—the main reason why she hardly ever set foot in the kitchen.

As she watched, Drew poured claret sauce liberally over his spumoni and polished that off, too. Then, as if he'd done this sort of thing all his life, he helped her clear the table and stacked the dishes neatly in the sink.

"Thanks," Christy managed, thrown off-base by his unexpected actions. She turned to her guests, "How about some coffee? I'd offer cappuccino, but I still haven't figured out how to work the machine my aunt sent me for Christmas."

"I'll make cappuccino, if you like," Drew offered casually, catching her off-guard yet again.

"You?" Christy blurted.

"Sure," he said, grinning. "I'm an expert when it comes to making cappuccino."

The crazy thing was...he was. Ten minutes later, they sat around the table enjoying the frothy brew, and even Christy had to admit it was the best cappuccino she'd ever tasted.

The Descarteses left fairly early, Ben stating that Terry needed her rest. At the door Terry said, "I haven't been doing much in the way of entertaining lately, but maybe you two could come for wine and cheese sometime soon. Okay, Drew?"

"I'd like that," he said, sounding so sincere that Christy felt she was about to choke.

"Good. You'll be in town for a while, won't you?"

"I hope to be here for a month. Maybe longer, if I can latch on to something that pays reasonably well."

"There are jobs in Key West, but they come in kind of an odd assortment and none of them will make you rich," Ben warned.

"As long as I can get by, that's all that matters right now," Drew said evenly.

"I'll second that," Ben agreed.

"Come on, Ben," Christy chided. "Your ship's right over the horizon."

"Loaded with gold?"

"Both fame and fortune," she assured him.

"Then let's hope it looms up soon." Ben reached out and gave her a bear hug. "Thanks for everything, Christy. It was great."

She waited until the Descarteses had trekked down the staircase before closing the door. Then she leaned back against it and surveyed Drew. "I guess I should say thanks again," she told him.

"For what?"

"For going along with everything."

"It was no problem."

Back in the kitchen he collected the cups that had come with the cappuccino machine and started filling the sink with hot water. Next he was squirting dishwashing liquid into the water and digging into the dishes.

"What are you doing?" Christy demanded in shock.

"Cleaning up," he announced. "You put on a terrific dinner, so take a break and relax, okay?"

"Well, there's one little thing, Drew."

"What's that?" he asked over his shoulder.

"Water's kind of precious in Key West, so I use the plastic thing under the sink to wash dishes in and the pot I cooked the spaghetti in to rinse them off."

"It's not too late to rectify the situation," Drew observed calmly. Then, after a moment of silence, he swung around and faced her. "However," he added, "if you keep

boring a hole into my back with those gorgeous eyes of
yours, I'm apt to drop a dish and break it. Are you afraid
that I can't even wash a few dishes satisfactorily?''

"It's just that you've never done anything...like that
before," Christy said.

"Really? For your information, I was an Eagle Scout."

"I might have known," she muttered, then added, "So,
where did you learn to make cappuccino?"

"I had an Italian roommate one year at Brown, *signor-
ina*," Drew reported urbanely. "Or I guess I should say, *si-
gnora*. Anyway, he could never have faced his finals without
endless cups of cappuccino. I could hardly *not* have learned
to make it."

"I see."

"Do you, Christy?"

Drew's back was turned to her as he posed the question.
Christy watched as he vigorously scoured out the spaghetti
pot, and the taut play of muscles in his well-toned arms
made her go weak. She'd never negated Drew's physical at-
tractiveness, but now those arms—showcased by the cut-off
sleeves of the sweatshirt—plus everything else that went with
them appeared downright magnetic.

You'd better be careful, she warned herself.

Another thought followed in the wake of caution. *What
makes you think he'd even want you?*

It was a question she hadn't asked herself before, and the
mere idea of his possible rejection stung to a degree she
wouldn't have believed.

Drew repeated his question. "Do you, Christy?" he asked
roughly. "Do you see? You were so obviously amazed tonight to find I could behave like a normal human being that
I wonder if you see anything!"

"I had no idea how you'd behave," she said honestly.

"Thanks a lot!" He flung the comment over his shoulder, and she had the crazy notion that she'd hurt him.

"Look, Drew..." she began.

"Don't try to explain, Christy. You'll only make it worse."

His tone was increasingly belligerent, puzzling her all the more. "Don't cut me off," she said tightly. "You've always cut me off."

"Put you down. Cut you off. The accusations seem to be coming out of the woodwork."

"It's about time, wouldn't you say?"

To her surprise he said, "Perhaps it is. Got a dish towel?"

She moved forward. "Just leave them, Drew. I'll dry them later."

"While I sleep?"

He turned to face her, amusement flickering in his gray eyes. Christy caught her breath, but before she could say a word, Drew went on, "I'm sleeping right in there, am I not?" he said, nodding toward the living room.

"Yes."

"Then I think we'd better finish this now."

"All right, I'll dry."

It felt so...disconcerting, working side by side with Drew. All of a sudden, Christy felt her apartment closing in on her. It was so *small*. The kitchen looked into the living room, and on the other side of that was her bedroom. The notion that Drew would be sleeping on her studio couch tonight, with only a thin wall separating them, hadn't really bothered her—until now.

"Drew?" she asked uncomfortably.

He rinsed off the last cappuccino cup and shook it before he handed it to her. "Yes?"

"About your sleeping here..."

"Mmm. Yes?"

"There's something I have to make very clear. I mean, maybe there's no need to make it clear, but..."

He frowned slightly, but the amusement still lingered in his eyes. "I'm afraid I'm not following you, Christy," he said.

Drew had always had the capacity to unnerve her, and that was one thing that hadn't changed at all. If anything, it had grown worse! Christy was absolutely sure he knew precisely what she was getting at but was just going to play dumb while she wriggled her way through an explanation.

She took the cup from him and gritted her teeth as he said complacently, "Well, that does it. Any other household chores you'd like me to perform before we call it a night?"

"You don't have to perform any chores, Drew. Consider yourself a guest in this house, will you?"

"A paying guest," he corrected. "So it makes sense that I do things to earn my bed and board until I bring in a paycheck, don't you think?" he asked reasonably. Without waiting for her answer, he cautioned, "Now, what was it you were saying a moment ago?"

"I was about to define the relationship between us," Christy replied stiffly.

Drew reached over and squeezed out a sponge he'd overlooked. Setting it behind the faucet, he asked, "What about the relationship between us?"

"That's just it, there isn't any. I mean, there can't be any. What I mean is..."

At Drew's patient look Christy began again. "This is something I should've brought up earlier, Drew." She paused to take a deep breath, then went on, "What I'm trying to say is...I want us both to behave as if you really *are* an old friend of my brother's who just happened to look me up in Key West because you needed a place to stay."

"Did I fail in putting over that pretense with Ben and Terry?" Drew asked, his tone annoyingly bland.

"No, not really. But that was just a beginning. I mean, now there are just the two of us here."

He raised an eyebrow. "You're not worried about my taking advantage of you, are you? Of course we *are* still legally married...."

"Being legally married doesn't have anything to do with it," Christy retorted. "Marriage isn't just a matter of *legality*."

"It shouldn't be," he agreed. "So then, what's bothering you?"

Inadvertently she glanced toward the studio couch and past it toward her bedroom door, flinching when she heard Drew laugh mirthlessly. That laugh belonged to the man she'd left a year ago, not this delightful person who'd shared dinner with her and her friends this evening.

"Proximity?" he suggested. "Is that what's bothering you, Christy?" Deliberately, his gaze followed the path hers had taken a moment before. "Distances are not always easy to measure," he said. "Just now I'd say the distance between that couch and your bed is several light-years long."

Christy was still smarting from the sting of Drew's remark as she closed her bedroom door behind her and crawled under her covers. She'd insisted that he use the bathroom first because she wanted to soak for a while in a hot tub. But even the fragrant bath she'd indulged in hadn't calmed her down.

She twisted and turned as she tried to get to sleep. She was much too aware of Drew's nearness. The thought of him being on the other side of her bedroom door evoked a tension she wasn't sure she could handle. She felt as if she were burning up, felt that the blood in her heart had been injected with a potent serum distilled from the very essence of desire. It coursed through her veins relentlessly while she clenched her fists against its force.

She'd wanted so desperately to go to Drew. It shocked her how much she wanted to bridge the distance between them. She yearned to slide onto the couch next to him, yearned to embrace him passionately, to press herself close against his body and evoke a response from him. She wished that he would take her to him and make love to her so they could recapture that enchanted sensual bond that had held them both captive during those first wonderful months of their relationship.

After a while she started to cry silent tears because she wanted him so much and was sure she couldn't have him. By the time she drifted off to sleep, the pillow under her head was damp straight through to the ticking.

On Monday morning Christy worked a breakfast shift at a restaurant called Violet's on Front Street. After a lunch break she moved on to her salesperson job at McKenzie Studios, around the corner on Duval Street. After a supper break she usually did a four-hour bartending stint at Fancy's.

She didn't have to be at Violet's until eight o'clock but getting to work entailed walking almost the full north-south width of Key West. The distance was about a mile and Christy liked to take her time covering it so she wouldn't arrive sweating. Usually she skipped breakfast and had a cup of coffee and a muffin when she reached the restaurant.

This Monday morning in Key West was, of course, different from any other. Because when she got up, there was a handsome dark-haired man asleep on her studio couch whom she wasn't at all sure she could cope with. And he would be there morning after morning and night after night, maybe for a whole month!

As she brushed her teeth, she was silently muttering that she'd been insane, absolutely insane, to ever get into this wacky arrangement with Drew.

"Crazy, crazy, crazy," she grumbled under her breath as she exited the bathroom, shaking her head. Still grumbling, she promptly collided with Drew, then had to fight back a new surge of treacherous emotional fire as he grabbed her elbows and stopped her cold.

"What's crazy?" he asked huskily.

She couldn't answer him. She could only stare.

Drew was wearing dark blue silk pajamas with his monogram over the breast pocket. Like all his clothes, they were expensive and they looked remarkably unmussed. The same, though, couldn't be said for the rest of him. His hair was tumbling around in an intriguing disarray that made Christy yearn to rake her fingers through it. And he actually needed a shave!

Hadn't she ever gotten up before he did when they were living together? She frowned, wondering about that. Evidently she never had—or certainly, at some point, she would have glimpsed this side of Drew before he converted himself into the perfect image he routinely presented to the world.

The wild thing was that Drew, needing a shave and with his hair uncombed, looked more blatantly attractive and even sexier than ever. Christy winced from the ache of her heightened awareness of him and tried to free herself from his grasp.

"What's crazy, Christy?" he repeated, restraining her.

He wasn't using even a fraction of his strength, she realized, more impressed than taken aback. "Nothing," she answered hastily. "Let me go, will you? I have to get dressed."

She was wearing a white cotton nightgown that was a bit too sheer for comfort. Drew was eyeing both the garment and the curves it covered, she realized abruptly, and her cheeks began to burn. But he only asked, "You have to go somewhere?"

"To work," she told him irritably.

"Kind of early, isn't it?"

"No, Drew, it isn't. I don't have to be at the restaurant until eight, but it takes me twenty minutes to get there. Walking, that is."

"Why don't you ride your bike?"

"It needs some fixing. Anyway, I like to take my time and walk."

"What about breakfast?"

"I'll have coffee there."

"May I join you? Walk with you, that is?"

"Why?" she asked bluntly.

"Well, for one thing I need to buy a paper so I can check out the classifieds," Drew pointed out.

"You don't need to walk all the way to Front Street to buy a paper."

"I'd like to have coffee with you, if there's no particular objection," he said mildly.

"Oh, all right," she gave in. "But not where I work, okay?"

"Whatever you say, Mrs. Delahunt."

She felt like throttling him but headed for the sanctuary of her bedroom instead. A short time later they were sauntering over to Simonton Street together. Christy led him to a corner coffee shop and deli, and they settled in at a gingham-covered table for two.

When Drew looked around for a waitperson, Christy said, "You serve yourself here." She started to get up, but Drew held up a hand, stopping her.

"What would you like?" he asked. "I'll get it."

"Coffee and a pineapple muffin," she told him, fumbling in her handbag and drawing out a couple of crumpled dollar bills. "Here," she added.

Drew looked slightly amused before he said, "That's okay, Christy. This one's on me. Anyway, a couple of hours from now I should be holding down a job. Exactly what kind of job remains to be seen, but still..."

They kept the conversation casual, centering mainly on Key West's unique ambience. They stayed in the same low key after they left the coffee shop. Then, on Front Street, Christy paused beside a little depot where the Conch Tour Train—a colorful motorized trolley of sorts—left for its tour of the historic island town.

"There's no need in your going all the way with me," she stated.

Her choice of words was provocative at the least, Drew thought wryly. It reminded him—not that he really needed a reminder—that he'd had a hard time getting to sleep last night, knowing she was in bed only a few feet away in the next room.

She was watching him through the dark glasses she'd put on, and she looked so inscrutable he couldn't read her expression. He squinted. The sun was dazzling, and the intense reflection of light on the mostly white or pastel buildings was blinding. Sunglasses were one item Drew had forgotten to bring with him, which meant that some of his money would have to be parted with soon if he wanted to get around town comfortably.

"See you later," Christy said blithely.

The question escaped before he could yank it back. "When will you be home?"

"Oh, I should be back by ten or eleven," Christy informed him airily.

"This morning or tonight?"

"Tonight, of course."

"Christy, that's *hours* from now."

"So?"

"Where are you working?"

"I told you, the restaurant, the art studio and at Fancy's. Why?"

"Do you have to work all three places today?"

"Yes, Drew!" she snapped. "There's the small matter of making a living, you know."

Drew took another tack. "What about dinner?"

"I'm not even thinking about dinner right now, Drew. For you, well, I think there's some macaroni and cheese in the freezer, and a couple of cans of soup in the cupboard."

"Right," he said evenly. He hesitated. He didn't want her to go. Stalling for time, he asked, "Aren't you going to wish me luck?"

"Luck?" she echoed, puzzled.

"In finding a job," he explained.

"Of course. Good luck, Drew."

He saw her mouth quiver ever so slightly. It was the only visible sign of emotion on her part, but it was telltale. With considerable effort Drew resisted the impulse to bend down and kiss her.

Christy turned away. There was a variety store a few doors away and Drew started to go inside, determined to try to refrain from turning to watch her as she continued along Front Street. He lost the battle. She was wearing burgundy slacks and a white blouse and her blond hair was held atop her head by another of those plastic clips. There was a mixture of unconscious sexual allure, pride and defiance in her walk. Watching, he realized abruptly that this was Christina DiMartino he was seeing, not Christy Delahunt. And Christina DiMartino was very much her own person. Bleakly he wondered if he would ever again be able to really reach her.

Inside the variety store Drew found sunglasses—cheap sunglasses, a far cry from the expensive brands he preferred. *Her rules,* he repeated to himself as he selected a pair for five dollars that he hoped wouldn't ruin his eyesight. He added a newspaper and couldn't help but count the money he had left before he stuffed it into his pocket. There was less than forty-five dollars—his jeans had cost twenty-three plus tax—but that seemed a reasonable amount to get by on until he was paid for work.

He chose an outdoor café on the shady side of the street. Sipping iced coffee as he scanned the Want Ads—the drink and tip set him back another dollar fifty—Drew was at first amused but then gradually dismayed by the jobs advertised in the Key West paper.

Shrimp boat workers were wanted, as were floral designers, stock clerks, experienced plumbers, a dive boat captain and a counterperson in a local turtle cannery and seafood market. None of those positions seemed quite in line with his capabilities.

So, Drew mused, assessing his situation, just what were his capabilities? He was a Harvard Business School graduate trained to manage a financial empire. But even if Key West had jobs to offer in areas that could use his education and expertise, he didn't dare apply for any of them because it would mean giving a résumé of past experience.

Presently he wasn't Drew Delahunt III, he reminded himself. Rather, he was Drew Payne, who didn't have much of a résumé to draw upon.

"Go for it!" he told himself aloud, then began circling an occasional ad with the slim gold pen he always carried. With a dozen ads circled, he started out and soon realized he should have also invested in a map. Key West was bigger than he'd thought and not having a car began to seem like a real drawback.

After walking for two hours, during which he checked out several dead ends, Drew began to ask himself why he was doing this. Did he really feel such a need to prove himself to Christy?

Maybe, he conceded. But . . . there was more to it than that. Christy's challenge had awakened something deep inside him, something that he hadn't ever been aware of. He hoped it was the same kind of spirit which, in another century, had led people to take to covered wagons and go west in search of gold. Or, in this century, had sent men to the moon.

His quest, admittedly, was limited and essentially self-centered. Yet it was the same kind of pioneering spirit that was motivating him to prove to Christy—and to himself—that he could make his way in the world without family and fortune to back him.

For the first time in his life, Drew recognized the true feeling of being entirely on one's own. The headiness that came with the recognition was in itself a supercharge, but by the time morning had merged into afternoon, he needed more than a supercharge to keep him going.

He'd learned what it meant to have people look at your hopeful face and say no. Sometimes they said it politely, sometimes regretfully, sometimes rudely. He'd discovered that most of the jobs offered in the paper paid poorly, yet the employers wanted all sorts of qualifications for them, especially experience. Experience, in fact, became the big catchword.

Drew was turned down for a position as a host in an expensive restaurant because he lacked experience. He was interviewed for a job as a laundry person but there again experience was the key word. Next he tried for a job in an exclusive gift shop. The ad had said that a good personality was essential, but though he turned on the full voltage of his charm, his lack of experience with exotic shells—the shop's specialty—killed his chance. The same applied to a clerk's job in a hardware store. He'd thought he'd known a lot about hardware but was quickly proven wrong. He also tried for a breakfast cook position in a café and as a cashier in a motel, both to no avail.

Drew stopped for lunch just long enough to imbibe a root beer float. He was wearing dark slacks and a white shirt, chosen because he'd discovered his sports shirts all had his monogram embroidered on the pocket. Virtually everything he owned was decorated with his monogram, something he'd never realized before, either.

It was impossible to always walk on the shady side of the street, and the tropical sun was hot. By midafternoon the shirt was soaked through. Also, his feet were killing him. His polished leather cordovans certainly weren't suitable for this kind of hiking!

Finally, his spirits sagging, he decided to call it a day and head back to Whitehead Street. With Christy away he could soak in her tub and try to soothe his aching body, as well as the bruises to his ego.

As he was passing a chic boutique on Duval Street, he stopped. Throughout the whole day, he hadn't forgotten that tomorrow was Christy's twenty-sixth birthday, nor that he wanted to get her a special present.

Well, the dress displayed in the window was very special. In fact it was Christy. It was made out of a filmy white material with a deep rose underskirt. The neckline was scooped, the sleeves short, the bodice tight fitting. Drew had never considered himself an expert on women's clothes, but he knew just by looking that this dress would mold Christy's lovely figure perfectly.

Impulsively he stalked into the store. A willing salesgirl brought forth the dress. Drew fingered the material, assessed the style again and swallowed hard as he pictured Christy wearing it.

"I'll take it," he said automatically.

"Cash or charge?" the salesgirl asked.

"Well," Drew began slowly, "how much is it?"

"You're lucky," the salesgirl informed him, smiling brightly. "This dress was priced at two hundred twenty-five, but it's on sale for one-fifty."

"One hundred fifty dollars?" Drew demanded.

She glanced at him warily. "Well, yes."

"Sorry, but I don't have that much cash with me."

He saw that she was evaluating his clothing. Despite the dampness and creases, he knew they still looked expensive. "How about a credit card?" she suggested.

Drew nearly reached in his pocket, then remembered all too vividly that he'd handed over all his credit cards to Christy. "Sorry," he muttered. "No plastic, either."

"I'd be willing to take a personal check."

Drew mumbled uncomfortably, "I don't have a checking account."

"Then the only thing I can suggest is layaway."

"What's that?"

The girl looked at him as if he'd stepped off another planet. "You put down a deposit to hold the dress and pay for it as you can," she told him. "When you've paid the full price, it's yours."

Drew thought about that, then said, "Sorry, but it's for a birthday and the birthday's tomorrow. Couldn't we work out something else?"

"Like what?"

"Well, I could give you a deposit and take the dress now, and then later..."

The salesgirl clutched the dress closely, as if she were afraid he was about to snatch it out of her hands. The gesture made him angry.

"Forget it," he snapped, raking her with a scathing glance that made her instinctively back away from him.

He was still bristling as he started the hot and miserable trek home.

Chapter Seven

Drew stood at the front door and swore volubly. To put the cap on his misery, it was locked! That morning both he and Christy had forgotten about his need for keys. Staring at the blank wooden door, Drew fought the impulse to shatter it with his bare fists.

He swore again. And the door opened. Terry Descartes stood before him, wearing a wrinkled blue housecoat. She looked paler than ever, and exhausted.

"I hope you didn't hear what I was just saying," Drew said guiltily.

She laughed. "You should catch Ben's language when he's locked out!"

"Did I make that much noise?"

"Not really, Drew. It's just that my living room window's right there," she said, nodding to her right. "I was lying down on the couch trying to get some breeze, but there isn't much."

"I woke you up," Drew accused himself. "Terry, I'm sorry."

"Honestly, I wasn't asleep. Anyway, I wanted to speak to you about something."

"Oh?"

Terry glanced back toward the staircase, then lowered her voice to a conspiratorial whisper. "Tomorrow's Christy's birthday," she said.

"Yes, I know," Drew answered, automatically lowering his voice, too.

"Well, Ben and I would like to surprise her, and Christy's a hard person to surprise. I'm going to bake a cake and I was hoping we could arrange a little party. Do you suppose you could take her out to dinner, then make an excuse to come back here early?"

Drew thought about his cash on hand and wondered if there was a restaurant in Key West where two people could have a decent dinner for, say, a total of twenty dollars, that including a bottle of champagne. Impossible, obviously, yet he didn't dare spend much more than that. His job hunting experience today had indicated that it might be longer than he thought before he came up with that first paycheck.

"Christy will probably be working tomorrow night," he hedged.

"Mmm . . . she may be at that," Terry admitted. "Look, she'd be working at Fancy's if she's working at all. And I doubt she'd be working late on a Tuesday. Maybe you could meet her over there and buy her a special drink or something, and then the two of you could head back here."

Drew wondered what the going rate for "special drinks" was at Fancy's. "That sounds fine, Terry," he agreed.

"I'll count on you, then," Terry said.

Unexpectedly she smiled, a smile so lovely it brought a lump to Drew's throat. If only she didn't look so *wan*. If she were his wife, he thought, he'd be worried to death about her. But perhaps Ben already was.

Only after he started up the stairs did it dawn on Drew that he might not be able to get into the apartment either. He didn't remember Christy using a key to open the door thus far, or locking it behind them this morning, but . . .

At the top of the stairs these thoughts were shoved aside by an aroma almost as delicious as the spaghetti sauce had smelled yesterday afternoon. Puzzled, Drew was about to try the door. He stepped back startled when Christy opened it for him.

She'd changed into jeans and an apricot-colored T-shirt, and her hair was still twirled up on top of her head. The big white apron was in place, too, and she was holding a large wooden spoon. She looked fresh and lovely and incredibly desirable. And it was all Drew could do to keep from grabbing her and kissing her as he hadn't kissed her for a long, long time.

"What are you doing home?" he asked abruptly.

A frown quickly replaced Christy's smile. "I thought maybe I'd better do something to keep you from starvation, that's all."

"I wasn't about to starve, Christy."

"Please don't tell me you can cook, Drew."

"I can cook," he said wearily. "Remember, there was a time in my life when I was an Eagle Scout? I'm not saying I can prepare a meal that anyone else would want to eat, but I can whip up passable bacon and eggs and I know how to open a can of corned beef hash or beef stew. I can even do a cheeseburger!"

"How about chili?" Christy challenged.

"So that's what smells so fantastic." He smiled. "I guess you're right," he said. "I guess maybe I'm closer to starvation than I realized."

"It should be ready in half an hour or so," Christy told him.

Drew looked across at her as she stirred the steaming chili, found himself staring at a wisp of blond hair curling around the nape of her neck and wanted, terribly so, to touch that neck with tender fingers. "You didn't have to cook for me, Christy," he said huskily. "It was . . . very nice of you. I appreciate it."

"You look beat," she answered, still stirring the chili. "Any luck?"

"Need you ask?" he rejoined bitterly. "Believe me, when I *have* some luck I'll be shouting it from the rooftops."

"Not a very good day, eh?"

"A rotten day," Drew admitted.

He was thinking more about the dress he'd wanted to buy her than about his failure to get a job. He'd wanted to get it for her birthday present so damned much, and had experienced all kinds of frustrations he'd never felt before when he just plain couldn't come up with the money.

One hundred and fifty dollars, he groaned to himself, and slowly began to realize how large a sum that was when you didn't have it. . . .

Christy went over to the fridge, withdrew a cold bottle of beer and handed it to him. "Take this, go take a cool shower, and you'll feel better," she advised. When he stood there staring down at her, she added, "Believe me, I've walked the same mile."

A gamin grin crossed her lovely face, an expression Drew hadn't seen since their very beginning together. It made her look more enchanting than ever and so incredibly appealing. He winced at the memory. Thinking back, he couldn't imagine having had the luck to marry this woman in the first place, let alone having been foolish enough to let things deteriorate between them to the point where she would finally walk straight out his door.

If only she'd come back to me. Drew heard his own inner voice and groaned silently.

Fortunately Christy had turned her attention to the chili again and so didn't witness his silent battle. Drew muttered thanks for the beer, escaped to the bathroom and let blessed cool water pelt his body and his blistered feet. Once he'd dried off, he slipped into his jeans and sweatshirt again, then had to laugh at himself. It had been a long time, if ever, since he'd worn the same clothes two days in a row. Such were the trappings of a limited wardrobe.

There was no question of donning shoes. Barefoot, he walked gingerly into the living room. Christy was clearing the table of magazines and newspapers and noticed his feet.

"Drew, what have you done to yourself?"

"Just a few blisters," he said casually. "No big deal."

"I should have known better," she reprimanded herself.

"Known better about what?"

"I should have warned you about walking around Key West in those dress shoes of yours. They're not exactly designed for all-day treks on hot sidewalks."

"Tell me about it. But I'm the one who should have known better," he reminded her. "I'm the one who's run a marathon, after all."

"Sit down on the couch." She was leaving the room as she spoke and a moment later, she returned with a bath towel and a can of powder.

Before he could protest, she got to her knees in front of him and instructed, "Lift your feet up."

"Christy, come on," he protested. "You're making me feel like a wimp."

"This isn't funny, Drew. Do what I ask. Please."

She laid the towel down on the rug, carefully positioned his feet in the center, then liberally sprinkled on the powder. Next she was massaging in the powder with hands so deft they felt like feathers touching his skin.

"What is that stuff?" Drew managed.

"Boric acid powder," Christy told him. "You're going to have to be careful, Drew. If those blisters break open you could get a nasty infection. That won't help your job hunting one bit."

"I'll be careful," he murmured huskily, his eyes on her beautiful blond hair, her beautiful head, her beautiful hands and her beautiful body.

She looked up and it was too late for Drew to slip on any of the masks he usually kept close at hand. He was uncharacteristically vulnerable just then and conscious only of wanting Christy in a way he'd never wanted anyone before, not even Christy herself. She stirred him so totally he felt like every atom in his body had been rearranged. His need for her was overwhelming.

Their gazes locked. Christy tried to look away but she couldn't. The tug between them was too powerful to pull against. Like a riptide, it momentarily washed everything away—all the resentment, frustration and despair this man had caused her to feel. For this moment, at least, they were back to square one or very close to it. Two people who were experiencing vibes so strong that nothing else mattered.

Drew reached out and tenderly pulled Christy toward him. He felt her initial stiffening but then her resistance melted. She let him draw her into his arms, let him hold her close against him. And nothing in her life had ever felt quite so wonderful to her as Drew's closeness.

She heard him murmur her name, but that was the last thing she heard before Drew's lips found hers and his plunging kiss rocked her all the way to her toenails. When finally he released her, she gasped, more from being startled than because she was out of breath. If he could do this to her with just a kiss, she was on very dangerous ground!

"I have to go stir the chili," she said shakily, carefully getting to her feet.

Drew chuckled. "I wonder if women have always used cooking as an escape route?"

"I'm not using cooking as an escape route," Christy stated levelly. "If I don't stir the chili, it'll burn."

Drew watched her through the kitchen doorway as she turned off the burner and set the pot lid to one side. He could tell by her movements, her body language, that she was nowhere near as calm as she was pretending to be. Swinging around to face him, she asked, "Ready to eat?"

"*Now*, Christy?" Drew protested. He had other things than eating on his mind. His own body was sending him some highly potent signals.

"I thought you were starving," Christy reminded him, then realized she'd used a bad choice of words. Drew's kiss had shown her that they were both starving... for the kind of passion they'd shared a long time ago. But she'd learned the hard way not to trust that passion. She didn't dare risk letting herself go with Drew again.

Fortunately he didn't pursue the issue. After a moment he asked, "Are you going to have supper with me or are you going to run off again?"

Christy hesitated. She'd stopped by Fancy's to see if Cal really needed her tonight and he'd told her business was pretty slow. He had a couple of waitresses to handle the tables and felt he could take care of the bar by himself if she needed a little time off.

She'd been thinking about taking her birthday off but didn't want to skip two nights shifts on the bar. "Pretty slow" sometimes became busy and profitable, but you had to be there to find out. More than anything, though, she'd been remembering all afternoon how sparse the contents of her larder were and how Drew was certain to come home tired and hungry.

"Yes," she said nodding. "Except..."

"I know. Only if I promise not to make any passes, right?"

He smiled wistfully and Christy's heart flipped over. If he'd looked at her like that a year ago in Westport, she thought wryly, she would never have found the strength to walk out on him. Had Drew changed in the past twelve months? Or was she merely seeing a side of him she'd seldom, if ever, seen before?

"I promise I won't make any passes," he said, to her further surprise. "I'd really like to have you around tonight. So, I pledge I'll keep my hands to myself."

"Scout's honor?" she teased.

His mouth twitched. "Scout's honor," he assured her.

Christy's chili was hot, spicy and delicious. As Drew finished a liberal second helping, he shook his head in wonder. "Why have you kept your culinary skills such a deep secret?" he asked.

"Can you imagine me suggesting I cook dinner in Westport?" she asked scathingly.

"Why not?"

"Because that chef of your mother's would have had a heart attack, that's why."

"Come on, Christy," Drew contradicted lightly. "I think he'd have gotten quite a charge out of having you cook now and then."

"I didn't think so. That's why I don't believe I set foot in your kitchen more than half a dozen times," she stated.

"I never knew you wanted to."

Christy felt like telling him there were many things he'd never known she wanted during her five years in Westport, but she bit back the words. They were sitting at the round yellow table and in the flickering light of the candle that separated them, Drew looked wonderful but very tired. If she said much more about Westport, Christy knew they would soon get to the edge of bickering with each other, and she didn't want that. They'd had enough bickering, enough disagreement, in Westport itself.

She was beginning to see that Drew really had no idea how uncomfortable the Delahunt social scene had made her feel. He'd never known she'd felt like a sore thumb at his mother's cocktail parties and dinners. Even worse were the occasional luncheons given by Millicent Delahunt for her female social peers. It wasn't that her mother-in-law's friends had been unkind to her or that Millicent herself had been unkind—after that first, chilly reception. If anything, they'd all been too kind, obviously going out of their way to include her in a world where she didn't belong.

She knew she lacked that innate self-assurance that comes with having been born into wealth. She lacked the polished manners of Millicent Delahunt and her friends and could never quite affect their way of dressing with consummate, understated elegance. She didn't play bridge, as so many of them did, and when Millicent offered to teach her, she was almost rude in the way she declined. Millicent couldn't have known that her refusal was because she was sure she wouldn't catch on fast enough, not because she didn't want to learn.

As a result she'd developed a massive inferiority complex where just about everything regarding the Delahunt life-style was concerned. She was especially wary of Drew's close business associates, most of whom were old enough to be his father. When one man had actually made a pass at her one evening at a party in another Westport mansion, she reacted as if she'd been stung by a hornet.

Later Drew had made light of the incident, further firing her indignation. "Giles had a tad too much to drink," he'd said easily. "He's done that sort of thing before when he's been feeling good, but he's really harmless, I assure you. He probably won't even remember a thing tomorrow and if he does, he'll be ashamed of himself."

Christy forcibly shut off her thoughts, aware that Drew was watching her closely. He was smiling, a tender sad smile of concern.

"Wasn't there anything you liked about Westport?" he asked gently.

"I loved the times when you and I went sailing alone out on the Sound," she answered.

Drew's eyes flickered and Christy knew she'd struck a responsive chord. He kept his beautiful sloop moored just offshore from the house during the summer months and had taken her sailing every other Sunday. They would pack a picnic lunch and motor out from the dock in the Boston Whaler. Then Drew would set the sails and they would glide around Long Island Sound all day leaving the worries of the world behind. He was an expert sailor and an equally expert teacher. And every minute on the water with him had been pure bliss.

"I think back on those as the good times, too," he said softly.

For a moment they were quiet, both lost in memories. Then Drew stood up and stretched. "I'll wash the dishes," he said and started to hobble toward the sink.

"Not tonight you won't," Christy said swiftly. "I want you to get off your feet. I'm sorry I don't have a television but there are plenty of things you might like to read."

He shook his head. "Not until I finish cleaning up, Christy. That's the least I can do. You worked all day then cooked dinner, so fair is fair."

"I'd say you worked all day, too," she offered.

"Job hunting, you mean?" Drew asked skeptically.

"It's just about the worst kind of work, especially when you don't come up with anything. So..."

"Yes?"

"Why don't we split another beer and you can tell me where you looked for work today."

Drew was too tired to disagree. He settled on the studio couch while Christy refilled their beer glasses, and waited for her to curl up in the worn old, armchair before he started talking. Then he recounted the details of his job search around town and discovered, to his surprise, that most of the story was pretty funny. Often Christy chuckled. A couple of times she laughed out loud.

It was a warm night but a gentle breeze was drifting in through the windows. Sweet-scented tropical flowers infiltrated the air with their perfume. Drew thought he identified jasmine as one. And as he continued to tell Christy about the trials and tribulations of his day, he began to feel more relaxed than he'd felt in ages. Relaxed, content and . . . at peace. With the world, with Christy, with himself.

Terry had called it camaraderie at dinner last night. Drew and Christy had experienced fiery passion in the course of their relationship, the ardor of new love, the excitement of committing themselves to a whirlwind marriage. Subsequently they'd encountered colder, uglier feelings that Drew didn't even want to think about. Now, in a setting he'd never have imagined in his wildest fantasies, he was feeling a wonderful rapport with Christy such as he'd never known before.

He suspected, that night, that she headed to bed earlier than she normally would have because she wanted to free the living room for his use. She gave him the tin of powder and told him to sprinkle his feet again once he got into bed. Then she briefly used the bathroom and disappeared into her bedroom, shutting the door behind her.

Drew wished that door would dissolve. He wished that all the tensions that had grown between Christy and himself would disappear, as well. But, he knew life wasn't that easy, nor would it be in the future. If he wanted her back, he would have to work like hell to get her back!

With those thoughts, Drew settled onto the couch and covered himself with a sheet. Within minutes he was asleep, having determined to wake up before Christy in the morning and surprise her with freshly brewed cappuccino in honor of her birthday.

Despite Drew's best intentions Christy was up and around before he was. He heard her stirring in the kitchen, bolted to his feet, wincing at the contact with the floor.

He found her standing at the sink sipping a glass of orange juice. "Hey," he protested, "didn't you know you were supposed to sleep in late?"

"Why?" she asked, surprised.

"Because it's your birthday, you goose." He advanced toward her and kissed her soundly before she grasped what he was doing. "That's in honor of your being twenty-six today," he grinned. "Now, if you'll turn around I'll complete the job with the appropriate spanking."

"The devil you will!" Christy blurted, her eyes glinting. Her glance fell to his feet. "They still don't look too great," she observed.

"They feel a lot better."

"Well, I'd say job hunting today is out of the question."

He shook his head vigorously. "No, Christy. Today's the day I'm going to find work."

"Then you'd better rent a wheelchair to scoot around on your interviews."

Drew laughed easily. "That might not be such a bad idea," he agreed. "Anyway, it brings me to a question. Is there a public bus system in Key West? I thought I saw a bus yesterday but it was from a distance."

"There is a bus line, yes. Though I have no idea where or when the buses run. I usually walk, just because it's pleasant and the distances I travel aren't that great."

"You said your bike needs fixing up, right?"

"Yes."

"Much?"

"I don't know," Christy confessed. "I think it needs a couple of screws or bolts or something."

"Where is it?"

"Chained to the back porch downstairs."

"Maybe I'll look it over," Drew mused. "Or maybe I'll buy a used bike myself when I've made a little money."

"Well, don't spend money on another bicycle until you've checked out mine," she warned prudently. "In fact it's yours if you can fix it."

He grinned at her cheerfully. "I suppose you're working this morning even though it's your birthday?"

"A couple of hours at Violet's, yes. Though I don't have to be in until nine-thirty. I'm covering for a girl who has a dentist's appointment."

"Then if you'll hang on till I get dressed, I'll walk along with you and we can get a cup of coffee on the way."

"Drew," Christy said firmly, "you're not going anywhere today."

"I beg your pardon, lady," he retorted, injecting both humor and firmness into his words. "I have an appointment with myself to purchase a local paper, scan the want ads and then get on with the search. Anyway, I feel it in my bones that by tonight I'll be employed."

"How are you going to get your shoes on, Drew?"

"I'll manage," he assured her.

Christy shook her head, frowning. "Must you always be so obstinate?"

Drew took a long breath, then asked very seriously, "This *is* for real, isn't it?"

"What do you mean?"

"This isn't a game, Christy. This month I gave you entails my doing my damnedest to get a job so I can prove I'm capable of living in the real world. At least the real world as you define it. If we're serious about this, I'm down to my last thirty-odd dollars. But for your generosity I'd soon be having some serious eating and sleeping problems. So unless you were kidding and I'm actually taking a low budget vacation, I've got to get out there today.''

"I don't agree," Christy said tightly.

Drew shrugged his shoulders. "What can I tell you?" he said simply and started into the living room.

She stared after him, her beautiful eyes stormy. "I knew you were stubborn, Drew. But you're being ridiculous," she accused.

"I disagree," he said easily. "But if you want, I'll add ridiculous to the list of adjectives you've recently attributed to my nature. Let's see, there was spoiled, arrogant, protected...."

"All right, all right!" Christy groaned. She nearly stamped her foot, she was so annoyed at him. "Look, if you insist on trying to find work today, I'll make a deal with you."

"What kind of deal?" Drew asked suspiciously.

"Tell me what size shoe you wear and I'll go get you a pair of sandals. Then at least you'll be able to get around without doing any more damage."

He shook his head and said, "Sorry, but I can't afford a pair of new shoes."

"*Cheap* sandals," Christy persisted. "Not anything even close to the expensive footwear you're used to. Anyway, I'll buy them and you can pay me back out of your first paycheck."

Drew gritted his teeth, realizing that what she said made sense. "Okay," he said grudgingly. "Provided you give me the receipt so I'll know exactly what you paid for them."

"Have no fear," Christy promised loftily.

She left a few minutes later for a shoe outlet store that she was certain opened early. Drew sank back on the couch, glad for the chance to rest his feet again. They hurt like hell. Still, if Christy couldn't find him a pair of sandals, he promised himself he'd struggle into his cordovans and set out, no matter how much she protested.

"Beggars can't be choosers," he muttered under his breath.

For the first time in his life, the truth of that adage—and its implications—forcibly struck home. He'd been without the benefits of his fortune for barely two days, but already Drew was becoming aware of how much he'd taken money for granted. Not that money promised a problem-free life. To think that was a supreme fallacy.

Rich people had problems just as poor people did, Drew mused dryly, different kinds of problems, maybe, but just as intense. And, at least, people without money never have to wonder whether someone likes them just because of their wealth.

Funny...he'd never had any doubt on that score with Christy. When they'd first met, she'd had no idea he was wealthy. Nor would she have cared. Money wasn't their problem. Rather, their troubles started when Christy discovered what his being Drew Delahunt III often entailed.

If Christy DiMartino had ever loved him, Drew thought morosely, there was little doubt that she had loved him for himself alone.

And he'd blown it.

Chapter Eight

Wearing the sandals Christy brought him, Drew was able to head out on his job quest, though the going was slow and the initial results as frustrating as they'd been the day before.

He was turned down by a haberdashery and an Italian grocers, because both jobs required having a car. The haberdashery wanted a "runner" to make trips to Miami, while the grocer wanted a delivery person, though neither ad had made those points clear. He was politely discouraged at a popular fast-food restaurant and missed an opening in another clothing store by ten minutes.

The last blow came when he was turned down by an art gallery. As he walked in there, Drew thought he might have a real chance. But he was quickly rejected by the gallery owner in such a rude fashion that it was a shock. The man seemed to automatically dislike him. Back outside on the bright, sun-spattered street, Drew rationalized that most of the paintings were so terrible he probably couldn't have brought himself to sell them anyway. He brooded resentfully, wishing that the guy could see the paintings hanging in the Westport mansion. Any single one of them was worth more than this man's entire collection, Drew muttered under his breath.

At noon Drew paused for lunch in a small, side street restaurant. He ordered iced tea and the cheapest sandwich on the menu, grilled cheese. He was too discouraged to be hungry, but he had the sense to know he needed some sustenance to keep going.

The sandwich was lukewarm, the cheese rubbery. Disgruntled, Drew again reminded himself that beggars couldn't be choosers. Nevertheless, he was in a sour mood when he resumed his quest for a job. Personal appearance, an area where he modestly gave himself a few points, certainly didn't count much in Christy's "real world," he thought ruefully.

The ad for a car salesman stated that there was an immediate opening but previous experience was a must. Nevertheless, Drew decided out of pure desperation to try for the position. This possibility was the last one on his list.

The dealership was on the northern edge of the Old Town. By the time he finished the trek, Drew's feet hurt so much he could hardly stand to take an added step. He felt hot and sweaty and his clothes were rumpled. He knew he looked anything but sartorially splendid, and a car salesman, he imagined, should be a rather spiffy dresser.

The manager at the agency, however, was middle-aged, paunchy and balding and appeared to be suffering from indigestion. He was poring over a stack of mail when Drew was shown into his office.

Almost immediately, he asked Drew about experience and Drew finally resorted to his first deliberate lie. "It's been a few years but I've worked for two dealerships," he managed levelly. "One in New Haven—I'm from Connecticut originally—the other in the Boston suburban area. Milton, to be exact."

The man, who introduced himself as Bill Peters, seemed willing to accept that. Next he asked, "What brings you to Key West?"

"Cold weather," Drew said with a smile. "Too much snow and ice up there in Yankeeland," he added, having detected a definite Southern accent in Bill Peter's speech. "I decided it was time to shake it and get to a place where there's year-round sun."

"Year-round?" Bill Peters picked up on the adjective Drew had deliberately inserted. "You mean you're not just a young snowbird looking to make a few fast bucks?"

"This isn't my first time in the keys," Drew evaded. At least that was the truth. "I like it here. I wouldn't mind staying and settling down for a while if things go my way."

"Then maybe you're the man we've been looking for," Peters decided, as much of a smile as he probably ever managed to achieve crossing his pudgy face.

Fifteen minutes later Drew left the dealership with a new lift to both his spirits and his steps. His feet hurt as much as ever, but it didn't seem to matter anymore. He'd gotten a job! He'd walked right in off the street and gotten a job! True, he would only be receiving minimum wage as a regular salary—and it was so "minimum" he couldn't believe it—but he would get a whopping commission with each car sale he made.

Jubilant about his change of fortune, Drew splurged. He didn't have enough money to buy "Christy's dress," but he did have enough to get her a birthday present. At a vendor's cart on Duval Street, he selected a pair of coral and pearl earrings, their coloring reminding him of Christy's delicate complexion.

Next he stopped at a liquor store and bought a bottle of champagne. As he paid for the purchase, he remembered Christy once saying that he must have been weaned on Dom Perignon. This champagne was a long way from top quality but it looked to be the best of the available brands, though not one he could ever remember having. Still, it would be festive. It was the thought that counted after all.

That morning Christy had brought him a duplicate set of keys when she'd returned with the sandals. Now it gave Drew a strange but pleasant feeling to let himself into the house with his own key. It made him feel as if he and Christy really were sharing this living space.

Once inside he knocked on the Descartes's door. Terry opened it and he saw a smudge of cake frosting on her cheek. He smiled down at her. "Just wanted to check on the time you want us tonight," he said.

"How late is Christy working at Fancy's?" Terry asked. "I saw her when she headed out this morning and she'd decided to put in a few hours behind the bar."

"Hmm, she didn't tell me," Drew confessed. "Maybe I'll call her after a while and check."

"That would help, Drew. Usually she works until eight or nine except on Saturday, when she works late. Anyway, I've asked a few people over. If you can persuade her to get out of there on the early side, it would be great."

"No problem," Drew agreed. Impulsively he thrust the bottle of champagne into Terry's hands. "How about adding this to the stock for the party?" he suggested.

Terry saw the foil-wrapped cork and her eyes widened. "Champagne, yet!" she enthused. She looked, beaming. "Drew, I have the sneaky suspicion you got a job today."

"That I did," Drew reported proudly. "I'll be selling cars for Bill Peters at Conch Town Motors. If you need a new beauty or an old jalopy, stop by and I'll fix you up."

"I'll keep that in mind," Terry laughed. "Listen, are you sure you don't want to share this champagne just with Christy?"

"Absolutely sure."

"That's really nice, Drew. It'll make things special. People are bringing beer and wine but with champagne we can drink a genuine birthday toast to Christy."

"Terrific," Drew managed, a lump in his throat.

Late afternoon shadows were creeping across the living room floor as he opened the door to the apartment. Drew stood on the threshold and experienced a strange sense of emptiness because Christy wasn't there. Even if Terry hadn't told him she was out working, he would have known the apartment was empty. It was as if the warmth had left the place without her around.

It felt great to take a cool bath, then don his Key West clothes—the jeans and sweatshirt. With his new job he would be able to get some mileage out of the dress clothes he'd brought with him. Still, as soon as he could afford it, he promised to buy himself a T-shirt or two.

As he heated up some chili for his supper, Drew couldn't get Christy out of his mind. She worked too hard, damn it. Part-time jobs, admittedly, but often all three in one day. He marveled at her energy, to say nothing of her enthusiasm for just about everything she did.

Christy was a survivor, he realized, and yet she was so much more. She wasn't a live-for-today type of person, yet when reality necessitated her doing so, she managed with a smile. He wondered how she kept it all straight and remembered that she kept a work calendar for the purpose of organizing her time. He'd seen her scribbling on it this morning before she headed off to Violet's.

Possibly the hours she intended to work at Fancy's were jotted down there, Drew realized. If so, he could let Terry know precisely when to expect them back for the surprise party without making a phone call. Christy had let it be known that she preferred not to be called at her places of work.

He glanced around the living room and kitchen, then remembered she'd taken the calendar back into her bedroom. At the bedroom door, he hesitated. This was the first time he'd set foot in her bedroom and the feeling that he was trespassing became very real. The rest of the apartment was shared territory, but this was Christy's private domain.

There was a double bed, which she'd neglected to make up. Drew was tempted to straighten the bed sheets but could imagine how she might react to such a gesture. There was a rather battered dresser, painted white, a matching white table next to the bed and a single wooden chair, painted green.

Drew's mind whirled back to Westport. Though he and Christy shared a master bedroom, they each had a separate suite of rooms for their personal belongings and privacy. Hers consisted of a study with bookshelves, sofa and TV, a wardrobe room considerably larger than this conch house bedroom he was in now and a skylighted bathroom replete with twin sinks and a Jacuzzi. The contrast couldn't have been greater. Yet, spartan though this was, he could appreciate the fact that Christy felt it was hers and hers alone.

In Westport he'd tried to surround her with luxury—beautiful clothes, beautiful jewels, every beautiful *thing* money could by. He could see now that he'd lavished too much on her too soon. Maybe it was because he'd felt the need to compensate for giving her so little of himself, once he'd assumed his position with Delahunt, Marcy and Bainbridge. Admittedly there hadn't been much of Drew the husband left over when he got home from Wall Street. Most nights even the train ride from Grand Central Station to Connecticut had been stressful. Inevitably he found himself in the company of other executives who wanted only to talk shop.

Drew moved toward Christy's bed and saw the indentation her head had made on her pillows. Impulsively he picked up one and pressed his nose against the case. As he hoped he would, he detected a trace of Christy's scent. Not perfume, exactly, though there was a nuance of something flowery. Mostly it was just . . . her.

Drew's throat thickened and, without thinking, he clutched the pillow tightly. It was hardly the same as clutching Christy herself, but it was comforting nonetheless.

Careful there! he cautioned himself. *You're starting to sail out of control.*

He set the pillow back in place, then glanced around for the calendar. It wasn't visible and after a brief bout with his conscience, Drew decided to probe a little. The top dresser drawer seemed a likely place to look, so he opened the drawer and peered inside, only to feel the lump in his throat grow thicker.

In one corner, apart from a tangled mass of feminine undergarments, he spotted a blue leather folder. It wasn't his intention to snoop but having gone this far he couldn't resist. He opened the folder and his eyes fell upon an enlarged photograph of a younger Christy embracing a much younger version of himself long ago in Ogunquit. The shot had been taken on the very afternoon, Drew remembered vividly, when he and Christy had decided to trek down to Massachusetts and get married.

Under the folder were several postcards depicting their favorite Ogunquit restaurants and scenes. And something else neatly wrapped in a sheet of pink tissue.

Drew carefully unfolded the tissue and found himself staring at Christy's wedding ring, a lovely gold band engraved with a pattern of flowers and leaves. He'd found it in an antique shop in Ogunquit and bought it without hesitation simply because it suited her so perfectly.

Placing the ring over the tip of his little finger, Drew felt tears welling in his eyes. It was the rarest of feelings for him, the rarest emotional display, something he couldn't remember having ever permitted himself. He'd been brought up in a stiff-upper-lip family tradition where men didn't cry. He hadn't cried when his little sister's body had been found, or when his uncle had been killed in the car crash, or when his father had suddenly died of a massive coronary. But now he experienced firsthand what tears were like—hot, stinging and full of the pain in his heart.

It took a moment, a long moment, to rein in his emotions. Then he neatly folded the ring back into its square of tissue and closed the dresser drawer. Sobered, somehow chastened, and feeling like the ultimate intruder, he quietly left Christy's room, went outside on the deck and watched the red-orange sun descend slowly through the palms.

Early in the evening, Drew dialed Fancy's and asked for Christy. A moment later she came to the phone.

"Is something wrong, Drew?" she asked quickly.

"No. I just wondered what time you'll be through, that's all."

"You're calling me up about something like *that*?"

"It *is* your birthday, Christy," he reminded her. "I thought maybe I'd stop by and buy you a drink."

As he spoke Drew remembered that he had exactly ten dollars and twenty-eight cents left. The earrings and the champagne had taken a toll on his resources.

"How are your feet?" Christy queried.

"Not too bad. The sandals worked great and after I got home I soaked in a cool tub for a while. I even used more of the foot powder. How about that?"

"You're getting wise," she teased, then said dubiously, "Still, it's a fairly long walk down to Fancy's."

Drew wanted to tell her that no walk in the world would be too long if she were waiting at the end. On the other hand he'd never been given to making flowery statements and imagined Christy would scoff if he made one now.

"I'll manage," he told her lightly.

"Well, it's seven-twenty, so head over whenever you feel like it. I get off at eight but Cal won't care if I leave a few minutes early. It's really slow and the night crew's already here."

Drew walked into Fancy's at a quarter to eight expecting to see Christy still working. Instead a heavyset man with balding black hair and thick black eyebrows was presiding behind the bar, talking to a couple of patrons.

"What can I get you?" he asked as Drew approached.

"Actually I'm looking for Christy," Drew said.·

"Hey, Christy!" the man bellowed.

"You want me?" she called from the back room.

"Someone here for you," she was told.

A second later Christy appeared in a doorway behind the end of the bar, spotted Drew and advanced toward him slowly. She'd changed out of her working costume into an ivory skirt and peach-toned blouse. It occurred to Drew that the colors were almost exactly those of the earrings he'd bought her. Was that an omen that they were finally arriving on the same wavelength?

Still advancing, Christy accused, "What did you do, run down here?"

Drew smiled. "I can't be that early," he said softly. "I mean . . . you're ready, aren't you?"

Christy supposed he didn't realize it, but his voice sounded intimate and sexy. She cast a swift glance at the bartender. Bonzo Clark had been an actor in earlier days and would certainly recognize nuances of tone when he heard them.

"Sure you don't need me, Bonzo?" she asked quickly.

"Go celebrate your birthday," Bonzo advised, his rough voice filled with affection.

They were at the door when Drew said, "Wouldn't you like to have a drink here before we go?"

"Thanks, but no thanks. Tonight I'd just as soon go some place else. Have you been to Sloppy Joe's yet?"

"As a matter of fact, I haven't."

"Then let's walk over there," Christy decided. "It might not be too bad on a Tuesday night, and they make awfully good frozen strawberry daiquiris."

Sloppy Joe's was humming even though it evidently was a slow night elsewhere, but they were able to get a small table wedged into a corner. It was a cavern of a bar replete with Ernest Hemingway memorabilia.

Once they'd settled in, Drew commented, "Whether or not this place was Papa's favorite watering hole, they should light candles to him every night out of sheer gratitude."

"Very true," Christy agreed.

Frozen strawberry daiquiris were not exactly a favorite drink of Drew's—he preferred a good twelve-year-old Scotch on the rocks—but he went along with Christy's selection. *Her rules,* he reminded himself. Still, as he paid for the frosty drinks, he hoped she wouldn't want a second. If she did, it might prove embarrassing moneywise.

A loud reggae band had launched into a popular island tune, threatening safe decibel levels. Drew pitched his voice lower than the din and said, "Hey, I've got a surprise for you. Two surprises in fact."

"What kind of surprise?" Christy asked, leaning closer.

"Don't sound so suspicious."

"Well, there are good surprises and bad surprises."

"These are good surprises, Christy. Do you really think I'd lay a bad surprise on you on your birthday?"

"I suppose not," she admitted.

Her eyes started sparkling despite herself, as Drew reached into his pocket and came up with a little plastic envelope. Handing it to her, he said almost shyly, "I thought you might like these. The colors reminded me of you."

"Earrings, Drew! They're beautiful."

He watched as Christy removed the pearl studs she was wearing and quickly donned his gift. Her eyes were shining now and Drew thought he'd never seen her look more beautiful.

"How do they look?" she asked breathlessly.

"Super," Drew said. "I was right," he added. "The colors complement you perfectly. They're not bad with that outfit you're wearing, either."

"I love them, Drew. It was so sweet of you."

"They're not much, but given the situation..."

"I'll keep them forever," she assured him.

Forever. Drew felt his throat thicken. What was forever going to mean to the two of them? Would they be together? Or separated, once and for all?

He thought about being separated from Christy forever and was suffused by a deep and penetrating misery that made him visibly flinch.

"What is it?" Christy asked anxiously.

"Nothing," Drew said hastily.

"You looked like something hurt you."

"No," he said, trying to force a smile.

Christy's look was a shade too discerning and he was relieved when she said, "Well, what's the other surprise?"

Drew tried to sound completely nonchalant as he said, "Oh, yeah. I have a job."

Christy sprang to her feet impulsively, came around the table and threw her arms around him. She hugged him so fervently that his psyche unraveled in all directions, like a ball of yarn attacked by a kitten.

"Oh, Drew!" she exclaimed. "I'm really proud of you."

Drew realized that people at nearby tables were smiling appreciatively at Christy's enthusiasm. Normally he would have been put off by such a public display of emotion, but right now all he wanted was for Christy to keep on hugging him.

She resumed her seat, then said, "Tell me about it, Drew. How could you be such a clam and keep it to yourself all this time? *Tell* me about it!"

"Well, I'm going to sell cars for Conch Town Motors," Drew reported.

To his surprise Christy frowned skeptically. "Mmm," she said. "What kind of a salary are they paying you?"

"Minimum wage," he admitted. "However, I'll get a hefty commission for each sale."

"Mmm," she murmured again.

"You don't seem to be exactly carried away by my luck," Drew muttered.

"It's not that, Drew. I think it's great...really, I do. I just hope you don't get disappointed, that's all."

"Why should I get disappointed?"

"Because it isn't easy to sell cars."

He laughed. "You haven't heard my sales pitch, lady. So drink up, okay? This is your birthday, you know."

"So it is," she smiled.

They were nearly finished with their drinks when Drew excused himself, ostensibly to go to the men's room. Actually he sought out a phone and called Terry to report they were getting under way.

"If she wants a second drink, I'll just steer her home first. About twenty minutes or so, I'd guess."

Fortunately Christy didn't want a second daiquiri. "I'm pretty bushed," she confessed. "Maybe I'll have a glass of wine when I get home, though. It might give me a second wind."

Drew smiled to himself as they left Sloppy Joe's, knowing that Terry's little surprise party would almost force Christy into that second wind.

The evening air was soft and cool. After a time Drew reached for Christy's hand and she let him take it. Drew had the crazy feeling that he was out on his first date with her and it felt very good. The years seemed to be rolling off his back and he wondered if she felt the same way. But he wasn't about to ask. He didn't want anything to spoil tonight or this rare mood of empathy between them.

When they reached the house and stepped into the hall, Christy said, "I'd intended to stop by and say hello to Ben and Terry, but I noticed their lights are out. I guess they've turned in."

"Probably," Drew mumbled, not daring to look at her.

At that moment to his relief, the door to the Descarteses' apartment flew open and people spilled out into the hall. A spirit of carnival revelry took over as he and Christy were ushered inside. Their apartment was only slightly larger than Christy's, but Drew quickly decided it must have rubber walls. There were people everywhere, all of whom seemed to know and love Christy Delahunt.

Christy DiMartino, he reminded himself quickly.

He was introduced to Cal Fancy, to a shrimp boat captain named Luigi Amoroso—who fixed him with a curiously suspicious eye—and to a bevy of other Key Westers.

They were an interesting, colorful, friendly group of about twenty people. As he talked with a number of individuals and edged into a few group discussions, as well, Drew increasingly felt that each person there probably had a life history worthy of a book. There were few spaces in the flow of conversation and no dull moments whatsoever.

There was snack food in abundance and plenty of beer and wine. But the feature item was the big birthday cake

Terry had decorated beautifully. It held a place of honor on the card table Ben had set up in a corner of the living room.

Most of the time Christy and Drew were separated. Even so he knew she was glancing toward him at regular intervals. Was she trying to make sure he was enjoying himself? he wondered. Or worried about his ability to hold his own?

Actually Christy was wondering how Drew would react to her friends and how they would react to him. But she soon saw that she needn't have worried. Her friends were obviously having no problem welcoming and accepting Drew. And he seemed to be equally accepting of them.

Inadvertently her thoughts traveled back to Westport. She'd once accused Drew, during a bitter argument they'd had not long before she'd left him, of being cold, unyielding and extremely class-conscious. "You're an unmitigated snob!" she'd stormed. "But let me tell you right now, most of the people I knew before we were married—hardworking, less than wealthy people, that is—wouldn't give you standing room."

Well, here in Key West that certainly wasn't the case. These hardworking, less than wealthy friends of hers were giving Drew standing room, and then some. Fortunately they weren't an inquisitive bunch, so it wasn't necessary for Drew to elaborate on his phony background. The fact that he was a friend of Christy's was enough.

Drew was drinking inexpensive red wine and truly enjoying himself. He was even enjoying the warm glow the wine was giving him, and was amused when Christy came over and handed him a paper napkin on which she'd put several crackers and some chunks of cheese.

"I think you'd better eat something," she instructed.

"Why?" Drew asked innocently.

"Because you were weaving a little when you went to get that wineglass refilled a minute ago. I've never seen you weave, Drew," she added in a whisper.

"My wounded feet," he quipped.

"They were all right a little while ago, Mr. Payne," she teased. "But maybe you should be sitting down," she added seriously. "Why push it?"

"I'm not," he grinned.

Christy smiled back. "You look like you're actually having a good time. I kind of thought you might feel like a fish out of water."

"Is that so?" Drew drawled. "Sorry to disappoint you."

"You're not disappointing me, Drew. It's just...well, it's a surprise to see you enjoying yourself so much."

"The all work and no play kid, is that it?"

Christy tried to think of the right thing to say and couldn't. Caution was warning her not to be too hasty in coming to a conclusion about anything involving Drew. Except that just looking at him stirred her senses to such a pitch she had the sudden impulse to grab his hand and lure him out of here to a place where they could be alone. Her apartment? Her bedroom? Her bed?

She forced herself to concentrate on the immediate moment. "Drew," she said hesitantly, "don't...misunderstand me."

He met her eyes levelly. "I'm trying not to, Christy."

She felt herself flushing. Because she saw something in those gray eyes that made her think Drew was mind reading and that he maybe even wished, like she did, that they could escape together.

Again she forced herself to concentrate on the moment and the fact that Drew—this Key West Drew—seemed to be so full of surprises. She wouldn't have believed that, in a gathering like this, Drew Delahunt would have done anything other than to retreat into his most aristocratic of shells.

"Hmm," she murmured to herself.

Just then Ben Descartes called out, "Silence, everybody." His voice surmounted the din and, incredibly, the room grew still.

"Thanks to Drew," Ben announced, "we have some bubbly with which to drink a toast to Christy."

Christy darted a swift reproachful glance at the handsome man standing close behind her. "You held out," she accused in a muttered whisper.

"I did not," he muttered back at a pitch meant for her ears only. "I bought that bottle out of my original eighty dollars. I swear it."

His gray eyes were intent, his face serious, and it surprised Christy to realize how important to him her confidence was. "Okay," she mumbled. "I believe you."

The champagne was served in small paper cups and Cal Fancy proposed the toast. "To Christy," he beamed, "our friend who's even more effervescent than this champagne. She lights up our lives and brightens our sunsets."

"Here, here!" everyone agreed, clapping.

Somebody called out, "Speech!"

"Are you kidding?" Christy shot back. "I'm too choked up to say much more than thank-you."

Drew darted a quick glance at her. Sure enough her eyes were brimming with tears. But these tears, he knew, weren't like the tears he'd sometimes caused her to shed. These were tears of happiness.

The candles were lit on the cake and the moment came for Christy to make a wish. As she stood by the card table, Drew felt something tighten inside and realized he was holding his breath. He felt sure, somehow, that the wish she was about to make involved him. And he was almost afraid to look, for fear she wouldn't manage to blow out all the candles.

"Whew," he exclaimed when she just barely succeeded.

There were laughs and cheers, then a cake knife was thrust into Christy's hands. But before she made that first careful cut, she looked over and met Drew's eyes.

He tried to read the message she was sending him, afraid of reading it wrong. The last thing he wanted was to clutch at false hopes, but, God, Christy was looking at him like she loved him!

Chapter Nine

Drew didn't know whether it was the time of year, the rather out of the way location of the dealership, Bill Peters's negative personality or a combination of all three factors, but business at Conch Town Motors was decidedly slow.

On the bright side he was given a car to use for transportation to and from work. Peters had grumbled that it would look kind of funny to have a car salesman who didn't have a car.

But that was the *only* perk of the job. The car didn't even come with a full tank of gas and Drew certainly didn't have any extra cash for that. Even taking Christy for a drive up to Islamorada would just have to wait—not that she had that much spare time for a day trip anyway.

Nor did he. His schedule was the standard nine to five, but Peters wanted him to pull extra hours working both Thursday and Friday evenings. That left only the weekends for daytime excursions. Or Sundays to be precise, Drew thought, remembering that Saturday was Christy's longest and fullest workday.

Friday was payday, and though Drew realized he'd only been working two days and one evening when he got his first paycheck, he was, nonetheless, shocked at how meager it was. According to his calculations, he'd worked nineteen hours for Peters and he had less then fifty dollars to show for it.

Spending that grand sum would present no problem whatsoever. Drew wanted to take Christy to a good restaurant for dinner, but that was out of the question until he had money to blow. First came taking care of the basics—like sharing the cost of food with her. She was definitely spending more on groceries than she normally did. Nor did it help that he'd had such a ravenous appetite of late.

Drew worked until nine o'clock on Friday night, then drove home tired and hungry. Finding a parking place was a problem—the onslaught of weekend tourists was incredible—and the last thing Drew wanted was to park illegally and risk getting a ticket. Finally after driving around for fifteen minutes, he found a spot several blocks from the house.

As he walked back to Whitehead Street, he was thinking about the conversation he'd had with Bill Peters just before leaving the office.

"You know," Bill had suggested none too tactfully, "it might help if you toned down your appearance a little. There's nothing wrong with a shirt and tie, but haven't you got any ordinary clothes?"

"What kind of ordinary clothes?" Drew had asked perplexed.

"You know, shirts without initials on them. What about those initials, anyway? They aren't even yours."

"Hand-me-downs from a rich cousin," Drew mumbled.

"Guess he must have given you his ties, too. They look like they cost a hundred bucks apiece. Maybe up north people go for that. But down here, well, it's a little out of place. I mean, you always look like you're going to a board meeting or something."

Coming from Bill, that seemed a rather astute observation. But even if he was right, there wasn't much Drew could do about it. He simply didn't own any "ordinary" clothes of the type Bill Peters was referring to. He'd come to Key West wearing a business suit and had carried an extra suit with him. He had a couple of dress shirts, and a few monogrammed sports shirts. That was it.

It was funny in a way. In Westport there was always a freshly pressed suit—a number of suits actually—hanging in his closet ready for use. There were drawers full of clean shirts, a rack full of perfectly creased slacks. He saw now that clothes and their upkeep were another of the many everyday things he'd always taken for granted.

His spirits rose automatically as he let himself into the old conch house, then padded up the stairs. At least he had enough money to take Christy out for beer and pizza, he thought whimsically.

He was ready to make that suggestion to her but was greeted by an empty apartment. Christy had left a note on the kitchen counter saying that Cal got busy and called to ask her to work for a couple of hours.

Drew digested the contents of Christy's note and his appetite faded. He supposed he was acting like a spoiled brat, but he wanted her here. He wanted to talk with her about his first disappointing paycheck. Wanted her to commiserate with him. Wanted to hear her say that things were bound to get better as he gained more experience in the difficult job of selling cars.

He thought about going over to Fancy's and having a drink but knew Christy wouldn't relish his appearance. The morning after her birthday, she'd plainly stated that she didn't like "socializing" during her working hours. "When you're working, you're there to do a job," she said bluntly. "It's not fair to an employer to have his employees chatting with their friends instead of taking care of business."

Drew thought that she took such things too seriously, but he refrained from telling her so. She could easily have pointed out that he'd never had much experience in dealing with hired help per se, which was true. Usually his contact with rank and file employees was filtered through his private secretary, Dorothea Breck. Ms. Breck had worked for Rogers Delahunt for a number of years, and was a master at shielding her former boss's son from virtually everything that went on beyond the doors of the executive suite. As it was, employee complaints went through so many channels before they got to his echelon they practically didn't exist. Drew knew this but saw it now in a different light.

He'd done very little elbow rubbing with the majority of the people who worked for him. He made appearances at Christmas parties and retirement banquets. He endorsed the sending of bouquets to company women or wives who had babies and sympathy flowers to the families who suffered a loss. But there'd been nothing really personal in any of that. It was formality, not much more.

Now, lonely and feeling an out-of-character need for companionship, Drew wandered downstairs and knocked on the Descarteses' door. Terry opened it after a minute, but instead of asking him in, she stepped out into the hall, closing the door behind her.

"What's up?" she whispered, forcing a smile.

Drew noted, once again, the shadows of fatigue that underlined Terry's eloquent dark eyes and wished he hadn't disturbed her. "I'm sorry," he apologized. "I didn't mean to wake you up."

"No, no...it's Ben who's asleep," Terry explained. "He was supposed to work at the salad bar tonight, but he had to leave and come home. One of his headaches..."

"What kind of headaches?" Drew asked carefully.

"Serious ones," Terry admitted heavily. "Unfortunately they seem to be getting worse. More frequent, too. I guess it's part of the whole problem."

"What problem?"

"His eyes," Terry said. "I thought maybe Christy might have mentioned it to you."

"No, she hasn't. Look, Terry..."

"Yes?"

"Do you suppose you could come up and have a beer with me? Or juice or milk?" Drew amended quickly, remembering her pregnancy. "You could leave a note for Ben."

"Ben's probably out for the night, Drew. He took some pretty strong medication for the pain and was just falling asleep when you knocked. Anyway, he'd probably guess I was upstairs if he woke up and didn't find me nearby."

Having Terry for company wasn't like having Christy around, but it helped. Drew ushered her into the old armchair, then got their drinks. Seated on the couch, his long legs stretched out in front of him, he asked, "Would you mind telling me about Ben's eye problem? I remember when we had dinner last Sunday, you asked Ben if he could see all right. I thought maybe he just had poor eyesight, what with the glasses he was wearing. It's more than that, isn't it?"

Terry said slowly, "I don't want to burden you with our troubles, Drew."

"Friends are for listening," he said easily. "And I'd like to consider myself a friend of yours and Ben's."

Terry smiled. "Certainly we consider you a friend, Drew. And we're so happy for Christy...that you're here, I mean. Christy's always full of vim and vigor, but I've personally thought that some of it's a front she puts on. I've caught her unexpectedly a few times when she's been lonely and moody."

"Christy, lonely and moody?" Drew quipped, hoping he'd masked his instinctive reaction to hearing that.

"Oh yes," Terry said soberly. "I've sat up here with her many times. By herself, she's not as upbeat as she seems in a group. I've even had the feeling that she was ... well, sort of grieving."

"Grieving?" Drew echoed hoarsely.

"Uh-huh," Terry said nodding.

"How so, do you think?"

"Well, my guess is that Christy's encountered some serious bumps in her life's path and things still aren't smooth for her, no matter how she makes it seem. I admire her tremendously, Drew. She has so much fire and courage. But I'm really glad she has you here with her, if only for a little while.

"Oh," Terry added, before he could say anything, "I know she thinks of you as kind of another brother. But maybe that's all the more reason why having you here seems to be such a shot in the arm for her."

"I'm glad to hear that," Drew murmured unsteadily and took a hasty swallow of beer.

"Christy's not a complainer," Terry went on. "Sometimes, when it's been obvious that she's down, I've tried to get her to tell me what the problem is. She always changes the subject, though. Always keeps her secrets locked up. I think she's really been hurt. Badly hurt and almost certainly by a man. So be good to her, Drew, will you?"

Drew stared at the tired young woman sitting across from him, shaken by what she'd revealed. He said very slowly, "I'll be good to her, Terry. You can bank on it."

"You're not tied up with anyone up north, are you?"

The question came out inadvertently, and Terry immediately flushed. "Strike that," she implored. "It's none of my business."

Drew chuckled. "You asked," he teased. "for the record, no, I'm not tied up with anyone up north."

Terry returned his laugh. "I guess I'm a romantic at heart," she confessed, "though you wouldn't know it to look at me now! Ben used to call me the hearts and flowers girl. The other night at the birthday party..."

"Yes?"

"Well, with you and Christy...there was sort of a spark between you. Again it's none of my business. But believe me, Christy needs someone like you in her life."

If there had been a trapdoor at his feet, Drew was sure that his astonishment alone would have sprung it and he would have tumbled into a hole ten times deeper than the one Alice in Wonderland fell into.

Choosing his words like he was stepping through a mine field, he said, "The man who winds up with Christy in his life will be luckier, Terry, than I can ever hope to be. Now," he continued, "tell me about Ben. Unless you'd rather not, of course."

"I need to talk about Ben," Terry admitted frankly. "I keep it all bottled up. The only person I ever say anything to is Christy, but lately she's been working so much..."

"I know," Drew agreed. "So talk, will you?"

Terry sighed deeply. "I'm worried about Ben's eyes, Drew," she said steadily. "Very worried about them. Ben's had a vision problem that started when he got an infection in his eyes, oh maybe two and a half years ago. Ever since he's had more and more trouble focusing, his depth perception's been off, he's had headaches. He won't tell me what he knows or, for that matter, what he doesn't know. It's not his favorite subject as you might imagine."

Drew nodded. "What do *you* know?" he asked.

"Well, as I said, he got an infection in his eyes. We were living in Sarasota, up on the Gulf Coast about fifty miles south of Tampa. It might have been from swimming in the gulf during red tide...."

"What's red tide?" Drew interjected.

"It's an algae that kills fish and can cause severe allergic reactions and flulike symptoms in people," Terry said matter-of-factly. "Trouble is, you don't always know if you're swimming in it."

"Nice," Drew commented dryly.

"Yes, well, whether or not that's what caused Ben's infection, the doctor couldn't say. There are any number of ways to contract an eye infection. And it can happen to anyone at any age."

"But Ben's eyesight was fine before that?"

"Fine, with glasses," Terry agreed.

For a moment Drew sat thinking. Then he asked abruptly, "How did you and Ben meet?"

Terry smiled at the memory. "It was on Sea Island in Georgia, almost five years ago," she said. "Ben was an art student, I was in business college. We both had summer jobs at a big old hotel on the shore. We fell in love and had a wonderfully romantic time together. When September rolled around, we decided we wanted to get married more than we wanted to finish school. Neither of our families was very supportive, which is understandable, I suppose, but unfortunate. I mean, it's something you never really get over, having your parents turn their backs on you."

When Drew was silent, Terry went on, "Anyway, that's when we moved to Sarasota. We got jobs and Ben continued with his painting. Have you seen any of his paintings yet?"

"No, I haven't," Drew told her. "I noticed the other night that there were quite a few paintings in your apartment, but

I didn't take a close look to tell you the truth. What with the party and everything..."

"Well, Ben is good," Terry said solemnly. "Very good. Anyway, he wanted time for painting, so he took a variety of part-time jobs, like Christy does. Meantime I was working as a secretary in a real estate office. We had it pretty good until his eyes started bothering him."

"Who has he consulted?" Drew queried.

"At first he wouldn't consult anyone," Terry admitted. "Finally, he went to a walk-in medical clinic. The doctor prescribed some drops and wanted Ben to see an ophthalmologist for a more thorough examination. But we didn't have any medical insurance and Ben didn't want to run up a lot of bills. I might add that he didn't say anything to me about that at the time, or I would have insisted.

"In the meantime, I got pregnant and had a miscarriage. My third miscarriage actually." Terry paused and flashed a rueful smile at Drew. "Sounds pretty grim, doesn't it? Want me to stop?"

"No, I want you to go on. But first I'm going to get another beer. Want some more milk?"

"No thanks, I'm fine."

A minute later Drew resumed his seat on the couch and Terry continued, "After that Ben got restless. Sarasota is a pretty city, but finally we decided we had to move. Key West sounded like a good town for an artist to live in, so we headed down in this big old Pontiac we owned. That was late last spring, just before it starts getting real hot."

Terry paused and shook her head. "Would you believe I never learned how to drive? Crazy, I guess, but I never did. Then, when Ben went to get his license renewed this past fall, he couldn't pass the vision test. Probably it was just as well. We didn't really need the car, and gas money was a luxury we were better off spending on food and rent. Then I got pregnant again, and I've been very, very careful. I guess I'm one of those women who doesn't carry babies easily, but I want to have this one so much, Drew." Terry's eyes suddenly filled with tears. "So much," she whispered.

"How much longer do you have?"

"About a month."

Drew nodded. Then he asked, "What have the doctors here said about Ben?"

"Ben hasn't been to a doctor since we moved to Key West," Terry admitted heavily. "I know that's ridiculous, but I can't get him near one. He can be a very stubborn man, Drew. If I so much as bring it up, he reminds me we're going to need every cent we can put together for the baby. And that's true of course. Ben insists that his eyes and the headaches are no worse and says he'll get medical attention once the baby and I are thriving. I haven't been able to work at all these past few months...."

Terry stopped in mid-thought and stared across at Drew. "I can't believe I'm telling you all this," she confessed.

"Terry, we all need to get things off our chest now and then," Drew said quickly.

It suddenly occurred to him that he'd never gotten things off *his* chest when he'd needed to. He didn't have anyone with whom he could let it all out. He was closest to Millicent, but Millicent had set the example of weathering storms stoically, a course which Drew had followed. He'd always felt guilty about burdening his mother—or anyone else—with his problems. Supposedly he was so fortunate compared to most people. Yet, damn it, he was still human.

Right in the beginning, Drew thought ruefully, he should have confided in Christy. He should have shared the events of his day, especially his problems, with his wife instead of acting as if those things weren't any of her concern.

Why hadn't he? He could only think that it was because Christy had seemed so young and free-spirited. A golden-haired beauty whom he'd wanted to ply with jewels and satins and furs. A bride whom he'd wanted to shield from the harsh realities of the world.

A world she grew up in, he told himself bitterly.

All he'd ever really given her were toys and she'd deserved so much more. How could he have been blind to the fact that she was a woman, not a child?

Terry said softly, "I can listen as well as talk, Drew. Somehow I get the feeling you have a lot on your mind that you're holding in, too."

He smiled wryly. "I suppose I do," he said. "And maybe one of these days, I'll talk. Tonight I don't think I could find the right words."

Terry nodded. "I know what you're saying."

Drew met her eyes and said sincerely, "I admire you, Terry. With what you're going through, I marvel at how you always appear so damned cheerful!"

"It's a matter of conditioning," Terry replied.

So saying, she got to her feet. "I'd better get back downstairs, Drew, just in case Ben does stir." At the door, she added philosophically, "You know, Ben keeps telling me to stop worrying. He says we've always muddled through and we'll make it through again."

"Ben's right," Drew told her.

For the next hour Drew couldn't get the Descarteses off his mind. It struck him, not for the first time, that the distribution of wealth was an incredibly complex phenomenon. A fact of life totally beyond anyone's control. Still, it bothered him to know that with one stroke of a pen he could write a check that would go a long way toward solving Ben and Terry's problems.

He'd signed many checks for many charities over the years, but his actual involvement with their causes was like his relationship with the majority of people who worked for him: impersonal. With the Descarteses, it was different.

They were by no means a charity case—Drew could imagine Ben's justifiable anger at the mere suggestion—but their problems were tangible, right next door.

He stretched out on the couch, pondering this and fate and so much more. And within minutes he was asleep.

When Christy got home shortly after midnight, she found Drew lying on his side, one arm dangling to the floor. As she gazed down at him, a variety of very strong emotions went to war inside her. His hair was tousled, his long lashes brushed his cheeks and, like so many people appear when they're asleep, he looked younger—and considerably more vulnerable.

Maybe it was the wrinkled shirt, the rumpled slacks or simply his bare feet wedged under a cushion. Whatever, Christy's love for Drew brimmed over. She wanted to drop to her knees next to the couch and clasp him. She wanted to gently caress him and express the tenderness she felt for him in her heart.

Tenderness, she realized, was a new ingredient in her feelings for Drew. They'd experienced passion and joy, anger and frustration, but the vibes of caring and affection that were rocking her now were altogether different from anything she'd felt in the past. Different and, she suspected, far more significant.

Passion was by no means missing. Christy knew that it would only take a small gesture on Drew's part to fully arouse her passion. She'd already come so close to the edge with him that she had no illusions about what would happen if he were to wake up right now and gaze deeply into her eyes.

She quietly slipped into her bedroom and got a light blanket from the closet. Then she tiptoed back to the couch and covered Drew. For another long moment she stared down at him. Then she switched off the lights and went to bed.

* * *

Christy accepted the twenty-five dollars from Drew to cover his room and board. When he argued hotly that it wasn't nearly enough, that he wanted to give her his entire paycheck, she reminded him that he'd need money for all sorts of things he was forgetting.

"Like lunches," she said practically. "Unless you'd prefer to brown-bag it."

"It may come to that," Drew muttered. "I've been buying the cheapest sandwiches I can find—like chicken salad at the convenience store—but I still go through a couple of bucks every day."

It was Saturday morning, and Drew had just finished pressing a pair of slacks on an ironing board set up in the living room. Christy sipped her orange juice while he used the bathroom to change. When he emerged a few minutes later wearing a monogrammed sports shirt and with his hair neatly combed, her eyes widened.

"I thought you were trying to get away from that polished image," she remarked.

"This is my last clean shirt," Drew said mirthlessly. "You're going to have to point me in the direction of the nearest laundromat pretty soon, I'm afraid."

Christy couldn't help it. She dissolved into laughter. "That," she chuckled, "I'll have to see to believe."

Drew couldn't decide whether to fire off a retort or join in her laughter. Finally he said, "Well, if you've had your comedy fix for the day, I think I'll head out. Can I drop you at Violet's? You're late, aren't you?"

"I'm taking the morning off," Christy told him. "Violet has more waitresses than she needs and none of us are making what we should in tips. Actually I'm thinking of quitting."

Drew was groaning as he drove to Conch Town Motors. Bill Peters had offered him extra hours, and he was hardly in a position to refuse, which made it all the more infuriating to think that Christy was taking time off. He wanted so much—too much—to be with her. Maybe it was as well, he conceded, that he had to go to work. It was getting harder and harder to keep their "apartness" routine when he was around Christy. She stirred him too much. Sometimes he thought he would go crazy from the constant repression of the feelings that surged endlessly every time he looked at her. During the night he wanted her so much it took all the fortitude he could muster not to break down that barrier of a bedroom door.

Late that morning Drew almost made his first sale. Then, at the last minute, the potential customer said with a smile that he wanted to do a little more looking around but would be back later. He didn't return.

"You'll run into a lot of Be-Backs," Peters commented dryly.

Christy was working her late shift at Fancy's that night so Drew again returned to an empty apartment. It was getting to be a habit, he thought grimly. And for the first time he really began to appreciate how difficult it was for many couples to adjust their working schedules so they would have a few significant hours together.

He ate a quick and lonely supper, then picked out a book from Christy's collection and settled into the armchair. It was a good book, but after half an hour Drew gave up. He was too restless to concentrate.

He didn't want to intrude on the Descarteses, so after a time he slipped out of the house and walked over to Duval Street. Passing the dress shop, he noticed that the dress he'd wanted to buy for Christy was no longer in the window. He wondered if it had been sold or maybe put back into stock. Perhaps if he struck pay dirt with a car sale, he would come back and check.

He continued down Duval Street, which was jammed with traffic and buzzing with all sorts of people. It was a fascinating, lively scene, and Drew allowed himself to be swept up in the crowd. He didn't deliberately program his footsteps to follow the route to Fancy's, but in due course he found himself standing around the corner from the bar.

After five minutes of deliberating Drew decided that it was after all a free country. He had as much right to have a drink in Fancy's as anyone else did. Too bad Christy didn't see it that way, he thought, when she affixed him with a cold stare.

He slid onto the only vacant stool at the bar, then watched as she took and filled three other orders before his. Finally she asked brusquely, "What can I get you?"

"I'd like to have a beer," Drew said politely.

"What kind?"

"Anything. Whatever's on draft."

Christy glanced at him suspiciously, but a moment later she set a frosted mug in front of him. The beer suds were foaming over the top, and he gulped hastily. When the customer next to him left, she stopped in front of Drew. "Why are you here, Drew? I thought I told you that I couldn't socialize."

"I'm not asking you to," he rejoined coolly.

At that she hastily moved down the bar to wait on another customer. Thereafter she scrupulously avoided Drew as he lingered over his beer or deliberately engaged other patrons in conversation whenever there was a slack period. She even let him go ten minutes with an empty glass before she reluctantly refilled it.

At first Drew tried not to let her attitude get to him. But gradually resentment began to build up. Luckily several people who'd been at her birthday party drifted in. They greeted him affably, invited him over to their table and immediately included him in their conversation, which was a lot more than Christy had attempted to do.

Drew deliberately turned on his charm with two young women whom he'd met at the party. To his satisfaction he got some positive responses. It was admittedly a childish attempt to make Christy jealous, and he soon saw it wasn't working. Christy couldn't have acted more indifferent.

That got to Drew, and he made up his mind to do something about it. He had every intention to hang around until she got off at midnight—it was already almost eleven—then walk home with her. He would suggest they stop for a pizza or maybe some Chinese food again, just like they were out on a date. But when they got back to the house, he didn't know what would happen.

The birthday party people left to go dancing, and Drew took another stool at the bar. He gazed at Christy in the her pseudo-Polynesian costume, working the bar in this smoky, dimly lit watering hole, and he loved her so much it hurt.

He was still watching her when he became conscious of someone sliding onto the stool next to him. Glancing sideways, he met the hostile dark eyes of the shrimp boat captain who'd been at the Descarteses.

Almost instantly Christy hurried over. "Well, hello there, Luigi," she chirped. "I was afraid you weren't going to make it tonight."

"Wouldn't be Saturday if I didn't get in to see you, sweetheart," he murmured.

"You know Drew, don't you?"

"Yeah," Luigi acknowledged.

Christy frowned slightly as she sneaked a glance at Drew. He looked like a thundercloud. Something was going on, she realized, but she hadn't the slightest idea what.

Several customers arrived about then, and she became very busy. It wasn't until Cal Fancy emerged from the back room to help out, and the rush subsided, that she managed to get back to where Drew and Luigi were sitting.

To her horror she heard Drew snarl, "Look, it's none of your business."

"So, I'm *making* it my business," Luigi growled. "Christy means a lot to me and you're no good for her. You probably didn't notice, but that first time you came in here I was right behind you when you left. I saw how you'd shaken her up. You're nothing but trouble. So lay off her, understand?"

"What I understand is that this is something we should settle outside," Drew suggested ominously.

Christy couldn't believe her ears. Was this Drew Cabot Delahunt III, challenging a Key West shrimp boat captain to a street brawl?

"Stop!" she commanded, her voice low. She leaned over the bar and grabbed Drew's arm, but he shook her off.

"Stay out of this, Christy," he advised.

"I'm not staying out of anything," she hissed. She turned to Luigi and stated, "You've gotten all the wrong messages about Drew. He and I go back a long way, and what's happened between us isn't anyone else's business. I know you mean well, so I'll tell you this much. Drew and I may not know exactly where we stand with each other, but he's not trouble for me, so don't think that he is."

It was quite a speech, and for a few seconds no one said a word. Finally Luigi exhaled heavily. "I guess maybe I read the wrong signals," he admitted. He turned to Drew and thrust out a large, work-worn hand. "No hard feelings, okay?" he suggested.

"No hard feelings," Drew agreed and shook his hand.

Luigi grinned sheepishly. "You know," he said, "I'm old enough to be Christy's father. Maybe that's why she means a lot to me."

"I can understand that," Drew said solemnly. And added while Christy held her breath, "She means a lot to me, too."

Chapter Ten

Luigi Amoroso finished his Dos Equis and left. Drew said to Christy, "Isn't it about time for you to leave, too?"

Christy hesitated. She still couldn't get over that scene between Drew and Luigi, still couldn't believe that Drew would have gotten into a fight over her. Even after her pulse stopped racing, she felt as if her entire world had been turned upside down. Most of the things Drew had been doing lately were either completely out of character—or else she didn't know him nearly as well as she'd thought.

The way he'd gotten along with her friends the other night in the Descarteses' apartment had really surprised her. Everyone had genuinely liked Drew—except Luigi, she realized now. Then, when a group from the party had turned up at Fancy's tonight and found Drew sitting at the bar, they'd greeted him like an old friend. Christy had even overheard his rather flirtatious repartee with two of the girls, something she could have done without!

Recalling that, she felt an odd emotional twist deep inside. Was it resentment over his having fun on his own? Honesty compelled her to diagnose her feeling as something much more elemental—jealousy.

She'd even felt a little bit jealous of Terry this morning, where Drew was concerned. And that of course was ridiculous. But after Drew had headed off to Conch Town Motors she'd wandered downstairs for a cup of coffee with Terry. It was the first real chance they'd had to be alone since Drew's arrival on the scene, and Terry couldn't say enough nice things about him.

"He asked me up for a drink last night when he found out you were working," she told Christy. "I think he missed your company, and he was too tired to go out."

She went on to confess that she'd unloaded the whole story of Ben's eye problem on Drew, as well as the apprehensions she had about their financial situation and her pregnancy. Drew had been pretty wonderful, she said, in the way he'd listened to her.

"He told me he admired me for the cheerful front I try hard to keep up," she added. "That really gave my spirits a lift."

"Well, Drew's a nice guy," Christy murmured thickly. And though she appreciated what Drew had done for Terry, she began to wish that she had that kind of rapport with him herself. Did he ever really give *her* points for anything?

Don't be so childish and trivial, she admonished herself, and listened attentively when Terry said, "Yes, Drew is a *very* nice guy. And . . . extremely empathetic. I think maybe it's because he's got a few problems of his own. At least that's what I suspect."

Christy felt like her heart had skipped a beat. "What makes you say that?" she asked cautiously.

"Oh, I don't know. Intuition, I guess. I mean, you've got to wonder why a good-looking guy like Drew all of a sudden shows up in Key West with no money, no job, no plans. You don't know why, do you?"

"No, I don't," Christy said softly.

Terry smiled. "Well, I told him anytime he needs a sympathetic ear, mine's available."

Christy didn't know what to say to that.

Now, looking across at Drew through the red-light haze inside Fancy's, she felt a new wave of confusion wash over her. She began to wonder what she'd truly been out to prove when she'd challenged him to give her a month of his time. Had she been so sure he'd fall flat on his face if forced to make his way in her "real world?" Had she *wanted* him to fail, just to prove to herself that the idol she'd worshipped so ardently in the early phases of their marriage really had feet of clay?

"It's ten past midnight, Christy," Drew said impatiently, cutting in on her conjectures. "I'd like to take you home."

"Home." The word stirred something in Christy, made her think of the old cliché about home being where the heart is. If that were true, then she should have been happy in Westport. And yet it hadn't worked out that way.

She met his eyes and said uncomfortably, "Don't take this the wrong way, Drew, but, I promised that group of people down at the end of the bar that I'd go out with them after I got out of here."

Briefly his temper flared. He nearly asked her what had provoked her to do something like that when they needed so desperately to be together. Instead he slipped on a mask and stared at her dispassionately.

Christy immediately noted the mask and just as quickly knew there was something different about it. Strangely it wasn't a "Delahunt mask." Rather she felt it was one she could reach behind. She did so and was startled to discover that a wave of intense disappointment was emanating from this man who appeared to be so cool and indifferent.

She said quickly, "Drew, you're invited to come along of course. We were thinking of going to a pizza place just around the corner."

"No, I don't think so."

"Why not?"

Drew stared at her for a moment before a wide grin suddenly transformed his face into something wonderful to behold. "Why not, indeed?" he agreed.

Five minutes later seated at a big round table lighted by a fake Tiffany lamp, Drew was introduced to a beer truck driver who knew "everybody in Key West," a piano player who'd sprained his wrist, a girl who ran a bicycle shop and the owner of a store called "Unique Batik."

Again, Drew was readily accepted and easily contributed his share to the witty, eclectic conversation. Christy knew he was tired from another long day on his feet, but he completely held his own until the group finally broke up at nearly two in the morning.

As they walked through the warm, sweet scented night, Christy could feel an intangible *something* rising between the two of them. It suffused her; she was certain it suffused Drew too. Passion? Yes, this atmosphere between them contained its full share of potential passion. But there were other ingredients, too. An intensified awareness of each other. An understanding that brought with it a different kind of closeness.

She preceded him into the old conch house and slowly made her way up the staircase. Her pulse was throbbing against her throat. She felt like a bird, long-caged, who somehow knew it was about to be released, and desire fluttered like newly freed wings.

She stood aside to let Drew open the door to the apartment. Then, inside the darkened living room, she turned to face his shadow. He took her into his arms so quickly that Christy instinctively pulled back. But then his lips found hers, and the wave of wanting him that swept over her erased her will to resist him. It was as if all the frustrations of the past year were released at once. All the troubles were for the moment forgotten. Christy yearned to be one with him, yearned to flow with his tide, wanted desperately to feel his love.

Drew felt her body melt against his and embraced her even more tightly. Then, his legs slightly astride, he cupped her face in his hands and kissed her mouth with unbridled passion. At the same time he moved his hands down, pressing his palms seductively against the contours of her body. Expertly he aroused her flame to fire.

A sliver of moonlight slanted through the French doors and crept across the floor. Christy slowly opened her eyes during a long slow kiss and saw Drew's face in the platinum light. His eyes were closed like the eyes of a man in a trance, while his hands continued to move, molding her as if he were a sculptor and she the statue he longed to create.

Then, with exquisite care Drew slowly began to undress her. He slowly slipped off her skirt, then her blouse, then finally her satiny panties and lacy bra. She tried to stand still as he divested her of one garment after another, but the flames twisting inside her were too intense. Long before he'd caressed her very secret center, she was writhing and on fire.

As the moonlight faded then came back again Drew smiled. Staring into Christy's violet eyes, he whispered, "Now... you undress me."

She was so emotionally charged her fingers fumbled and she tugged at his shirt and belt buckle ineffectually.

"Here," he offered huskily. "I'll help."

They stood together in the swath of pale moonlight and slowly succumbed to desire's dance. Entwining and twisting, joining and then separating, touching and feeling, they played upon each other until the music they were silently orchestrating threatened to surge out of control.

Only then did Drew gather Christy in his arms and carry her into her bedroom. There the moonlight was more intense. It bathed her bed in its radiance, bathed them as they came together. And as prelude became fugue, their bodies and souls were joined as they'd never been joined before. Even in those early days of uninhibited passion, their love-making had never achieved the total dimension they were finally achieving now. In the bedroom of a conch house in Key West.

Many minutes passed without a word spoken. And when Christy finally did start to speak, Drew placed a firm finger on her lips.

"Please," he whispered, his tone deep. "Not a word. At least not tonight—is that all right, Christy?"

The moon had vanished behind a cloud, and Christy saw only a dark shape where she knew Drew's face was. After a moment of silence she said uncertainly, "All right."

She lay silent, wondering about this step they'd just taken, worried about it. What had just passed between them brought an entirely new dimension into their relationship. How could they go back to where they'd been before tonight?

Drew, as if sensing her quandary, pulled her toward him, encircled her within the protection of his arms. Finally she curled up against his beloved body, feeling drowsy. And, for a while, she dozed. But then Drew began caressing her slowly, sensuously, provoking desire yet again. Only after they'd reached love's thunderous finale for a second time, did they collapse in each other's arms and fall asleep.

Christy got up early the next morning, washed and dressed as quietly as possible and slipped out of the apartment. She needed a little time, a little space before she faced Drew again.

She wouldn't have turned back the clock on last night. If she had it to live over again, she knew she would have done exactly the same thing...because there was no way she could have resisted Drew at that moment when he drew her into his arms in her darkened living room.

But now there was the future to think about. And despite the wonder of their lovemaking, the essential situation between them hadn't really changed. That was the problem. What last night had done was made her all the more aware of the depth of her love for Drew. True, she'd already admitted—to herself—that she still loved him, that she'd loved him all along. But it wasn't until last night that she realized how very deep that love went.

She walked to South Beach, bought a cup of coffee and wandered out onto the sand. In the shadows of some palms she sat down and sipped. A couple of windsurfers were sailing around offshore, their sails splashing bright primary colors against a pale tropical sky. Other early risers strolled barefoot at the water's edge. It was a peaceful Sunday morning, a good time to think.

How had she thought that a single month out of Drew's life could change things for them? Christy asked herself. She'd hurled a challenge, he'd accepted it, and thus far he'd not only met all the tests involved, he'd passed them magnificently. Still, the basic circumstances of his life were bound to force him back to his old familiar patterns once this month was over, weren't they?

She asked herself that question again and again, and wondered if there might be hope that somehow, somewhere, they could make their marriage work. For even if Drew genuinely wanted her to return to Westport with him, she didn't think she could. Being on her own this past year had convinced her to never risk losing herself again. How could things possibly change in Westport so that risk would vanish?

Christy pondered that question and many others there on South Beach. Then she walked the full length of Duval Street and treated herself to breakfast. She hoped Drew would sleep late. Certainly he needed it. But, primarily, she still wasn't ready to confront him. They both needed to answer a few questions alone, in the wake of the question they'd answered together last night.

By his second Friday at Conch Town Motors, Drew was convinced he'd never been cut out to sell cars. The two other salesmen who worked for Conch Town Motors had each made a sale, but the closest Drew got was a sale that fell through because the prospective customer failed to qualify for financing.

"You got to learn to weed 'em out," Peters told him after this incident, referring to customers. "You get so you can tell whether they can come up with the cash and credit just by looking at 'em."

Drew didn't agree with Peters. He'd learned several lessons in Key West, he thought wryly. And the most important one was not to even attempt to judge books by their covers. Still, maybe he *had* been a little naive to think that a giddy young girl could finance ten thousand dollars in future car payments!

At nine that evening when the dealership was closing, Drew—who'd been standing at the showroom window looking out at the street for the better part of the last hour—decided it was pointless to try another week of car selling. There must be something else he could do better at and make more money in the bargain.

Peters was at his desk going over his figures. He looked tired and grumpy and in no mood to hear a man resign point-blank. Drew was surprised when Peters heard him out calmly, then said, "Well, if business was busier, I'd say you ought to give me two weeks notice. As it is, you happened to walk in on a slack period, but then you probably figured that, right?"

"I hope so, for your sake," Drew murmured politely.

Peters actually smiled. "I've been in this business almost twenty years. There've been tougher times than this, let me tell you."

"I can imagine."

"Okay, then you got today's hours coming to you," Peters pointed out. "The bookkeeper'll have to tally up what we owe you, so suppose you stop by next Tuesday and we'll have your check ready."

"Thank you," Drew replied and added, "I'm sorry it didn't work out."

"They come and they go," Peters shrugged. "Got the keys to that car I loaned you?"

Drew placed them on the man's desk. "Thanks again, Mr. Peters," he said.

"Good luck, son," Peters said nodding.

The day hadn't been a total loss, Drew decided as he headed out to the street. It had been a payday and he'd received a full week's check. The sum was still paltry, though. It made him wonder how people got by on such meager salaries, as many millions obviously did.

The dealership was about an equal distance from both Fancy's and the house, and Drew knew that Christy was doing the Friday late shift again. Cal had called her early that morning and asked if she wanted the extra work now that the season was peaking and she'd said yes without hesitation.

Drew thought about going over to Fancy's, then decided against it. He and Christy hadn't seen much of each other this week. It seemed to him she'd been working even more than usual, almost as if to avoid him.

They hadn't really talked since last Sunday. Drew had awakened to find Christy gone, and after taking a shower had wandered out into the morning sun himself. When he finally caught up with Christy at a café on Duval Street, she was with two friends having breakfast. Later Christy had done a thorough cleaning of the apartment, spent an hour plus at the laundromat, then another hour ironing her clothes. Finally she'd curled up in her armchair, intending to read. Instead she'd fallen asleep.

As he decided to head home, it suddenly struck Drew that half of his month was over. Two weeks gone, two more weeks to go. This time in Key West, he felt, was like a sand castle. Every day the wind blew away a few more grains. He wondered what would be left when the castle was gone.

Christy had arranged a picnic with a group of friends for Sunday. Again there was no chance to be alone with her, or talk with her in any depth. That night she was tired and slightly sunburned. After taking a shower, she told Drew she was turning in. She bade him good-night from the door of her bedroom, then gently but firmly drew the door shut behind her.

She was taking no chances, Drew thought somewhat resentfully. He was tempted to pound on her door and insist there were things they needed to thrash out. But he resisted the temptation. He had the funny feeling that Christy was running scared where he was concerned. Exactly how, he wasn't sure. But a gut feeling told him she was.

He was willing to wait a little longer to discuss what had happened between them with her—because neither of them could negate that a lot had happened.

In the meantime he tried to concentrate on other things. Monday morning he tried a new approach to finding a job. he located an employment agency and discussed his situation with a sympathetic young woman who gave every indication that she'd love to continue their discussion over lunch or dinner, if he were so inclined.

Drew wasn't. He was, however, grateful to the young woman, whose name was Cindy, for carefully evaluating what she termed his "employment potential."

He had to fake a few answers when it came to matters like past employment. But when she asked him about his hobbies and other interests, Drew decided it wasn't necessary to be quite so careful. He mentioned that he was an expert tennis player, swimmer, sailor and golfer, among other things.

Cindy smiled. "You sound like a walking country club," she observed, clearly impressed.

How true, Drew reminded himself, obviously not as thrilled as Cindy.

After she'd recorded all of Drew "Payne's" statistics, Cindy mulled over her employment lists.

"Aha!" she suddenly exclaimed. "This could be it."

"What?" Drew asked anxiously.

"Tennis instructor needed at one of the big resorts. They hired someone a couple of weeks back, but evidently he didn't work out. I doubt if the job's even been advertised yet."

She was dialing her phone as she talked. A few minutes later, Drew walked out of the employment agency with a lead considerably better than the ones he'd found on his own in the paper. If he got the job, it would cost him a hefty commission once he got his first paycheck. Still, the position of tennis instructor promised a relatively decent weekly salary.

"And if you charm your lady students you'll probably get some handsome tips," Cindy had purred.

Drew thanked her, trying not to wince at the implication.

The resort, he learned, was next door to the big motor inn he'd checked into when he'd first arrived in Key West.

Therefore it wasn't within easy walking distance, and Drew decided it was time to find out about the city bus line. Christy's bicycle, as it happened, needed considerably more than a couple of screws or bolts to be made operable.

Luckily for Drew, there was a bus that followed a very convenient route. He discovered he would only need to walk a block or so at either end of his trip. He splurged on a late breakfast, then hopped the bus in plenty of time to make the early afternoon interview Cindy had set up for him.

On the ride out he wondered what to say about past experience and fabricated quite a story. Instead of drawing attention to himself by mentioning the prestigious clubs he belonged to in Westport, Manhattan and Palm Beach, he planned to say he'd been on the tennis team at Brown, then had moved to San Francisco where he'd been a tennis instructor at a Bay Area club that had since gone out of business.

The resort manager liked the story. "Ever think of turning pro?" he asked while he showed Drew around the courts.

"I've thought of it," Drew said, which happened to be true. One of his rare fantasies had been to be a tennis star. "I don't have that kind of discipline, though," he admitted. "Or that level of talent."

He thought that the manager might suggest he play a set with someone on the premises, if only to validate his expertise, but to his surprise he was told to report for work at seven-thirty the next morning.

"Some people prefer to take lessons early," the manager said, "before the heat of the day creeps in. There'll be some paperwork for you to fill out, but let's leave it till tomorrow. I've got a meeting I'm already late for."

They shook hands and that was that.

On the bus back to the Old Town, Drew decided that as much as he disliked fibbing, he could see why people sometimes resorted to white lies. If bending the truth a little might open a door of opportunity for someone who really needed a chance, what was the harm? Performance in a job was what counted the most, not a list of credentials that might sound more impressive than they actually were.

He wondered how Christy would react to his new job. It tied in considerably with his privileged background, something he'd decided to use to his advantage. That, he realized, might very well strike Christy negatively.

He was wrong. Late that afternoon when he told her the news, she said, "Look, you use the tools you have at your disposal. That's how people make it after all. People hire you because you can do something. If you're good at it, that's when you start getting along."

She added, "You, of all people, should know that."

Drew was opening a cold bottle of beer when Christy said that. He took a sip and surveyed her coolly. She was sitting in the armchair dressed in yellow slacks and a white blouse. Her slight sunburn had faded, leaving a rosy glow on her flawless skin. She looked lovely and lovable, and Drew had to force himself to fight down his desire.

But he'd made himself a promise. Last time, where lovemaking was concerned, he'd taken the initiative. Next time—and he felt in his bones that there had to be a next time—*she* was going to be the one to make the first move. Since that incredibly sensual night between them, the signals she'd been sending out had been clear. For now at least, Christy didn't want to repeat history. Drew was determined to let it go at that. If she wanted him again, she would have to come right out and say so.

He reached out for the subject they'd been discussing. "What should I know?" he asked.

"Well," Christy said, "I've read about you several times in the past year, usually in articles about the up and coming generation on Wall Street."

"So?"

"So you're an expert at what you do," Christy murmured.

"Let's see how I do as a tennis instructor before we come to any conclusions about that!"

"Seriously, Drew..."

"Seriously what?"

Christy faltered slightly under his steady gaze. Then she said, her voice unusually small, "I guess I never appreciated how important you are, that's all. I never *really* thought that you used business as an excuse not to be with me more, but it did seem that way sometimes."

Her voice trailed off as Drew stared at her with an intensity that made her flinch. "That was never my intention," he said softly.

For a long moment they were both silent. Then, abruptly Drew stated, "I've got an idea."

"What kind of idea?" Christy asked warily.

"Well, I've still got most of the money I made last week at Conch Town Motors. In fact," he added, reaching into his pocket, "here's fifty dollars for my room and board."

"Drew—"

"Don't protest, Christy. I'm getting another small check from them tomorrow, and I've got enough left over right now to eke out a fairly decent dinner for four."

"Dinner for four?" Christy asked, puzzled.

"It's still early," Drew told her, smiling. "If Terry and Ben haven't eaten yet, why don't we suggest taking them to that little French place you pointed out to me the other day. The menu looked good, the prices were very reasonable and it's only a couple of blocks away."

"That's a great idea," Christy applauded. "I'll run down right now and ask Terry."

Terry hadn't started dinner yet and frankly admitted that going to an air-conditioned restaurant sounded like absolute heaven.

Half an hour later Christy, Drew and the Descarteses walked the short distance to the French restaurant. Drew insisted on ordering a carafe of wine, then was touched at the way Terry and Ben minded his pocketbook by ordering relatively inexpensive "blackboard" specials.

The restaurant had a delightful ambience. They dined by candlelight to the strains of romantic French music. Drew only hoped the dim light wasn't making it too difficult for Ben to see what he was eating.

Terry tasted her coq au vin and, murmured ecstatically. "This is absolutely delicious. Only you, Christy, could make a chicken dish this good. Maybe we could try it sometime...."

In the next instant, before Christy answered her, Terry dropped her fork on her plate and bent forward, clutching her arms around her abdomen.

"What is it?" Ben demanded urgently.

"I don't know," Terry moaned. "A pain. I...I think I'm starting labor."

"But the baby's not due for three more weeks," Ben said, dazed.

Glancing at Terry's face Drew swore under his breath. They needed a car, damn it! They needed transportation to get Terry to the hospital.

For the first time since he'd struck his bargain with Christy, Drew was tempted to tell her to get his credit cards and his cash. Then he realized that she'd get them herself, if it came to that.

As unobtrusively as possible, Drew hurried through the crowded restaurant and asked the cashier to summon the manager. The manager, who was very French, was also very excitable. By the time he reached the table and saw Terry for himself, the man was literally wringing his hands.

Within minutes the rescue squad arrived. And then Terry was carried out on a stretcher and on her way to Florida Keys Memorial Hospital, leaving her shaken husband behind.

"It would be better for us if you'd follow in a car," a female Emergency Medical Technician said, as the siren started to blare.

"I've got to get out there," Ben muttered helplessly.

"So do we," Drew stated.

He went back inside and paid the bill while the maître d' called a cab. "I hope the madame is okay," the man said then apologetically. "Please come back when you can and we will make this up to you."

"Thank you," Drew told him, then hurried back outside.

The ride to the modern medical facility seemed eternal, though actually it was not that far away. At the eastern end of Key West, they crossed the causeway over a narrow stretch of water dividing the Atlantic Ocean and the Gulf of Mexico and arrived on Stock Island. Shortly thereafter they pulled up to the hospital's emergency entrance.

Drew paid the cab driver, automatically adding a liberal tip because the man hadn't wasted any time getting them there. But as he followed Christy and Ben through the hospital entrance, he ruefully thought that maybe he shouldn't have been so lavish. Between dinner and cab fare, his resources were dismally low. Unless Christy had some cash with her, they just might have to ride the bus home.

These thoughts evaporated as a solemn-faced staff doctor appeared and asked, "Mr. Descartes?"

"Right here," Ben said nervously.

"Your wife *is* having labor pains, Mr. Descartes. She's okay, but she's quite uncomfortable. I've called your obstetrician, and he's on his way out. Meanwhile we're going to move Terry up to the labor and delivery area."

"How long will it be before she gives birth?"

"Well, that's hard to say. Twelve hours is not a long time for a first delivery. Eight hours would be on the short side. Given your wife's history of miscarriages and the fact that she's a couple of weeks early. Let's just say that she's not in any serious danger, Mr. Descartes, or we wouldn't hesitate to do a cesarean. Of course your obstetrician may decide that's the best way to go, once he's examined her."

"I see," Ben said miserably. Getting a grip on himself, he insisted, "I have to see her, Doctor. Where is she?"

"Right in there," the doctor said nodding. "But please, make your visit short. She needs to conserve every ounce of strength she has. It's apt to be a long night."

Chapter Eleven

This has to be the longest night in history," Christy whispered wearily.

"Very true," Drew whispered back. "But Ben *did* tell us to go home, you know."

"And sleep? Are you kidding?"

They were sitting side by side on a couch in a waiting area down the hall from the delivery suite. Ben sat slumped nearby, his elbows propped on his knees, his face buried in his hands. Drew put his arm around Christy's shoulder and tugged her closer. Five hours had passed since Terry's obstetrician had arrived, and not much had been said in the interim.

Christy's voice wobbled as she said, "God, I wish there was something I could do. This waiting is excruciating." In a very low voice she added, "Maybe I should tell someone that I'd be glad to donate blood if Terry needs a transfusion."

"Dearest, dearest," Drew murmured. "If either Terry or the baby had been in any danger, they'd have done a cesarean. And if anyone donates blood, I will. But you . . ."

He closed his eyes and shook his head. He wanted to tell her he thought she was the most generous and wonderful individual in the whole world, but words failed him.

"What about me?" Christy demanded softly, turning to look into Drew's eyes. "I'm stronger than you think."

"I doubt that," he told her, his smile bittersweet. "Lately I've been thinking you're one of the strongest people I've ever known."

Funny, Christy mused. That's exactly what she'd been thinking about Drew. Anyway, she'd meant that she was *physically* stronger than he might think. Emotionally...just then she was so shaken by the whole episode with Terry, she wouldn't have placed very high odds on her emotional strength. Terry wanted this baby so badly. It would be so terrible if anything should go wrong.

Drew released Christy gently, then stood and stretched. "I don't know about you," he said, "but I could use a cup of coffee. There must be a vending machine around here somewhere."

"The cafeteria might still be open," Christy murmured. "It was just a little while ago, when I used the rest room." She stood and stretched, too. Then she walked over to Ben and touched him lightly on the shoulder.

He jumped, then stared up at her anxiously. He'd taken off his glasses, and his pale blue eyes were red rimmed and unfocused. Christy wondered how much he could see without his glasses and wasn't sure she wanted to hear the answer.

"Ben," she said. "How about a cup of coffee?"

He shook his head. "I couldn't, Christy."

"You need something," she urged. "Look, Drew and I are going to see if the cafeteria's still open. Why don't you come with us."

"I'd rather stay here," Ben said quietly. "You go ahead."

Christy didn't press the issue.

There were a couple of surgical residents in their operating room greens sitting at a table in the corner of the cafeteria. Aside from that the room was empty. The kitchen was shut down—it was midnight after all—but coffee was available, and it was strong and hot.

After taking a sip, Drew reached in his pocket, withdrew some change and stood up.

"Going somewhere?" Christy queried.

"I thought I'd get a pack of cigarettes."

"Drew . . ."

"Yes?"

"I honestly wish you wouldn't smoke. I know your nerves are jangling just as mine are, but smoking's a temporary crutch, nothing more. I'm not going to lecture you on the subject, but considering the high-pressure life you usually lead, if it ever became a habit . . ."

As she spoke, Christy was thinking of Drew's father and what had happened to *him*. She knew Rogers Delahunt had dropped dead of a heart attack while still in his forties, and once Drew had mentioned that his father had been a heavy smoker. Considering how closely Drew was following in his father's footsteps . . .

And Drew *did* usually lead a very intense, high-pressured business life. She'd never fully realized that until now, and it made her wonder where she'd *been* during those years of their marriage. Oddly it was seeing Drew *away* from Westport that was making her really appreciate the demands normally made on him as chief executive of a very powerful corporation—demands heightened, made all the more difficult by his young age. Why hadn't she realized how wrung out he'd been so many of those nights when he'd returned home from Wall Street? Why hadn't she shown more interest in the affairs of his day?

She saw Drew stuff the change back into his pocket and sit down. "I really didn't mean to preach, Drew," she said hastily.

He smiled at her, a tired but very tender smile. "If you're that concerned about my health," he said gently, "the least I can do is comply with your wishes."

Christy didn't know what to say to that. But when Drew reached across the table for her hand, she was more than willing to give it to him. She felt the strength of his fingers entwined with hers, felt the strength of *him*. She loved him so much.

She couldn't help but think about the events that led up to her leaving him. She should have stayed in Westport, she told herself. Instead of running away from their problems she should have had the courage to face up to them, to level with Drew about the way she felt about everything. Then maybe they would have had a chance....

For a few minutes they sat in silence. Finally Christy said restlessly, "Do you suppose you could ask someone about Terry? I know nothing might happen for hours, but I'm really starting to worry."

"So am I," Drew admitted. "Come on, let's go back and see how Ben's doing. I'll check on Terry at the nurses' station."

Ben was sitting where they'd left him. He looked up as they approached to say, "No word yet."

As Christy took the seat beside Ben, Drew walked the short distance to the nurses' station. He automatically injected a note of polite authority in his request that the nurse find out anything she could, then came back to Christy to report, "She says she'll see what she can do."

Fifteen minutes later, an intern wearing hospital whites came into the waiting area and asked for Ben Descartes. Christy saw Ben reach for his glasses and put them on, as he looked up apprehensively. Then she heard the young doctor say, "It won't be too much longer, Mr. Descartes. Your wife's really hanging in there. She seems determined to have the shortest delivery in the history of the hospital. I'll keep you posted."

With that, he left and Ben appeared to momentarily relax a little. "Now you see why when the subject of the husband witnessing the birth came up, I politely said no!" he said.

Christy and Drew smiled appreciatively, then all three lapsed into silence. If waiting this long was taking its toll on them, Christy thought, she couldn't begin to imagine how Terry must feel.

At two-fifteen in the morning, the intern suddenly appeared, a wide grin crossing his face. "You have a beautiful little daughter, Mr. Descartes, and she and your wife are both doing fine. I'll come back for you as soon as we get them all squared away, so stay put if you will."

"Thank you," Ben managed hoarsely.

As the intern left, tears filled Ben's eyes. Noting the tears, Drew leaned in front of Christy and said, "Congratulations on becoming a father, Ben. If I were in your place, I think I'd feel all the waiting and anxiety was well worth it!"

If Drew were in Ben's place. Christy heard the words, and felt a sudden heavy ache. Maybe if she'd never left Westport Drew *would* have been in Ben's place by now. And she would have been in Terry's place. She pictured herself holding Drew's baby in her arms and wanted to cry aloud.

More minutes inched by. Drew and Ben were talking quietly, Christy was deeply absorbed in her own agonizing thoughts and wonder. Then, Terry's obstetrician came out to personally assure Ben that both Terry and the baby were in good health.

"Terry's a bit weak, which is to be expected. But very happy," the doctor concluded. With a smile he added, "Why don't you come see for yourself, Mr. Descartes, and meet your little girl?"

As Ben was led off for a brief visit with his wife and his new daughter, Christy felt tears begin to trickle down her cheeks, and noticed Drew's steel gray eyes were moist as well. "Thank God everything's gone so well," she murmured brokenly.

Drew's voice was husky as he began, "Christy..."

"Yes?"

"There's so much I want to say to you." He paused, then added, "It'll have to wait. Frankly I'm too tired to make much sense right now."

A short while later, with the stars glittering in a pitch black sky, the exhausted trio emerged from the hospital. Drew had called a cab after first checking with Christy to see if she could loan him ten dollars.

"I can't believe you're borrowing money from me," she whispered in his ear. "In the old days—"

"Things change," Drew answered her cryptically.

At the house Christy turned to Ben. "Ben, you just have to come upstairs with us for a few minutes. This calls for a celebration and I have something special."

Christy's special something was a bottle of choice Spanish brandy she'd been given for her birthday by Cal Fancy. "I decided when Cal gave it to me I'd save it for a toast to Terry's baby," she said.

Despite being dead tired, Ben grinned. "How about a toast to *my* baby?" he proposed.

"So, we'll drink two toasts!"

Actually none of them were up to a second shot of brandy. "If I don't get to bed within the next few minutes,

I'm apt to crash right here,'' Ben said weakly. He shook Drew's hand warmly, gave Christy a bear hug, then went back downstairs.

Christy returned the brandy bottle to the cupboard, turned toward Drew and her face crumpled. Everything she'd been holding in all evening surfaced, and as Drew took her into his arms, tears streamed down her cheeks. Feeling the need to be especially gentle with her, Drew led her into her bedroom, lay down on the bed next to her and let her cry herself out against his shoulder. Then he got a cool, damp washcloth and gently wiped away the traces of her tears.

All night he'd been thinking about how Christy had wanted to have his child—and about how he'd denied her. He cringed now, remembering how he'd crassly assured her that, should she come back to Westport, he would "bother" her with his presence for only as long as it took for her to become pregnant. Because *he* was now ready to have children.

Who the hell did I think I was? Drew cursed silently.

He felt Christy stir at his side, felt her reach out and tenderly stroke his cheek. If there had been any reserves, any doubts left in Drew, they melted at that feather touch. God, how he loved her!

Christy edged even closer to him. With a quick, almost convulsive movement, she flung her arms around him, drawing her toward him as if she wanted the two of them to erase all boundaries between them. And that, Drew sensed, was exactly what she did want. For suddenly she was moving her body over his in a way that left no doubt about her intentions.

"Drew, we need each other right now," she whispered.

Drew couldn't have agreed more. Regardless of what the past had held or of what the future might hold, this was their moment, and their need for each other blotted out everything else.

Drew began to stroke Christy, began to rain kisses on the soft curve of her cheek, her skin, the lovely column of her neck. Their hands sought each other and found, both separately and in unison. There was no haste in their lovemaking. They were too tired for haste. They yielded slowly, blissfully, each to the other and discovered yet another new way of transcending passion.

At a quarter to seven, despite the traumatic evening just past, an automatic alarm inside his head woke Drew up. He gingerly got out of bed, careful not to wake Christy, showered quickly, then dressed in a white sports shirt, jeans and his sandals. He'd made up his mind to raid the pro shop at the resort for shorts, sneakers and a racket. They'd simply have to advance him the items. If not, he'd look pretty out of place on the courts, especially for an instructor!

Luck seemed to be going his way when a bus came along after only a couple of minutes of waiting. Soon after that he was explaining to the manager, Dave Martin, how he'd come to Key West without any of his tennis gear.

"I'm out of cash, too," he admitted frankly.

"I wouldn't think it was funny, Drew," Martin told him, "except I once had a very similar experience. I got a job in an expensive men's store, and I didn't own even a single jacket or a decent pair of slacks. I was wearing their clothes the whole time I worked there. Which turned out to be pretty good advertising, come to think of it."

After he filled out an employment form, Drew was given keys to the pro shop and to an equipment shed by the courts. Then he was presented with his lesson schedule for the day.

The first lesson was scheduled for nine o'clock. Drew's first student was a spoiled, overweight teenage girl from Chicago who took one look at her handsome instructor and decided she'd rather flirt than learn. Drew fielded both her supposedly clever remarks and her sorry attempts to put the ball in action, and retaliated by sending some wicked serves in her direction that had her chasing balls all over the court. He was thankful when the hour was up and hoped she wasn't planning on a long Key West vacation.

After that things got better. There was a lesson with a delightful young couple from Toronto, followed by an empty hour during which Drew thoroughly familiarized himself with the resort premises, the workings of the pro shop and his office—a small thatched hut complete with bathroom, phone and a large daily planner. He even taped a new message regarding the scheduling of lessons and court hours.

After a short break for lunch Drew had four afternoon lessons scheduled, all with beginners. By three o'clock, it took every last ounce of his willpower to stay on his feet.

When he finally got back home, it was wonderful to find Christy there. "I called Cal and told him if he could do without me I'd rather not go in," she confessed. "Where did you get those shorts and those shoes, may I ask?"

He grinned. "You may, I liberated them from the pro shop at the resort." Saying that, Drew collapsed into the armchair.

"Honestly?"

"Honestly. I owe the shop for them. I told the manager I didn't have any tennis clothes with me or a racket, and he said to take what I needed, make a record of it and pay them back later. Not bad, huh?"

"Not bad at all," Christy agreed. "Pretty resourceful in fact."

She sat down on the couch. "Terry and the baby are doing fine incidentally," she told him. "They've named the baby Lucy, after Terry's mother."

"I like that," Drew said.

"Ben's back at the hospital now," Christy went on. "I called around to some of the people we know who have cars and they're going to take turns chauffeuring him while Terry's there."

Christy would think of doing something like that, Drew reflected, as he took a long cool shower. Christy was always thinking of ways to help out other people.

Could she be persuaded, maybe, to help *him* out one of these days? Was there a chance he could ever persuade her to come home with him?

Thinking of how much she valued her freedom, her independence, made the question become unanswerable.

The sun was setting as the two of them sat down to a light supper. Then, as dusk brushed away the last of the daylight, Christy let the shadows gather, leaving the candle untouched, saying that it seemed cooler that way.

They were quiet for a while. Then Christy asked, "When I woke up and saw it was past eight I wondered if you'd made it on time."

"I got to work with five minutes to spare," Drew said. Then he began telling her about the different students he'd instructed, beginning with the overweight teenager.

Christy chuckled sympathetically when he told her about the girl's attempts to flirt. "Poor kid," she said, "I can't say I blame her."

"Come on, Christy!"

"I mean it," she persisted. "Don't you ever look in the mirror, Drew? I mean *really* look, past the perfect grooming and the perfect clothes? I often had the feeling back in Westport that you weren't really seeing yourself."

"Maybe not," he admitted uncomfortably.

"You're a very attractive man, Drew," Christy said levelly. "A *very* attractive man. And I'm talking about you. Just you."

"As opposed to Drew Cabot Delahunt III, you mean?"

"Yes."

"I think I get your message," he said. He hesitated, "And," he finally added, "I thank you."

"For what?"

"For making me aware of myself as *me*," he told her.

"You've never had much chance to be you, have you?"

"No, I suppose not." He added, without thinking. "If Dad hadn't died when he did, things might have been different."

"It must have been hard on your mother, losing your father so suddenly." As Christy posed the question, she wondered why she'd never really *thought* of that before. Because Millicent Payne Delahunt seemed so totally in control of herself, perhaps. She presented as cool and perfect a facade to the world as her son did—perhaps more so.

"It was extremely hard on my mother," Drew said tersely. Again he hesitated, then continued, "My parents really loved each other, Christy. Theirs was a true romance. It withstood all the flak from the media, all the nastiness of people I can only think were envious of them. Wealthy people learn to live with envy," he added quietly. "It's not easy and it's never pleasant, but it's a fact of life, so you live with it.

"So many people think that having money is what it's all about," he went on. "The ultimate end of the rainbow. In college, as an example, everyone knew I was a rich kid. With my name there was no way of camouflaging it. I wasn't the only rich kid of course, but I always felt that being a Delahunt was, in an odd way, a strike against me. People just assumed my life was problem free. That my whole family was problem free. God knows that was anything but the truth."

It was Christy's turn to hesitate. Then she said slowly, "I guess I've always thought of your life as being pretty problem free myself, Drew."

Drew laughed harshly. "You couldn't be more wrong," he told her. Then, to his own astonishment, he felt himself really beginning to open up with her. The words started to pour out as he told her about the kidnapping and murder of his sister. About his beloved but alcoholic uncle, whose disease finally led to his tragic death. About the other misfortunes his family had suffered, culminating with his father's fatal heart attack.

He talked freely, letting it all out, making it clear that he didn't want her sympathy—never had, never would. But what he *did* want was to share with her the things that had affected his life so deeply. He wanted her to know all there was to know.

Christy listened to him, both shocked and spellbound. As close as she and Drew had been during the early phase of their marriage, she'd had no idea of the traumas locked up inside him. No idea that there'd been events in his past that had literally wrenched him apart. Now as she listened to him, she became filled with the wish that this sharing would last.

If only Drew would cast away his masks and never wear them again.

Drew's face was a silhouette in the darkened kitchen when he finished his story. Then, after a moment of total silence he said with obvious difficulty, "It's never been part of my nature to talk about my own problems, Christy. And certainly not part of my upbringing. I never realized how destructive the stiff upper lip policy might be until you left me."

"What?" She was genuinely startled.

When he spoke, the tightness in his voice conveyed his tension. "That summer when I met you was without a doubt the happiest period of my life. For the first time I was truly free and uninhibited—because that's the way you were." His voice grew husky. "If only...we could have gone on that way. If that spirit we captured hadn't needed to end."

Christy leaned forward, peering at him through the velvety darkness. "Why did it need to end, Drew?"

"Isn't that obvious? Running away, eloping with you, was as far as I could go. I knew I had to return to Westport, knew I had to join the company and take over what Millicent had been saving for me. I had to climb back into my mold. I neglected to tell you what was going to happen, though. That was a terrible mistake."

"As far as I was concerned," Christy said softly, "you were still you...in the beginning. Westport was a shock, but you were still you. You were the same Drew I'd met and fallen in love with. That was what mattered the most to me. But then I began to lose you."

"You were never in danger of losing me...until you left."

Drew heard the sharp intake of Christy's breath and wished he could have rephrased that last comment. The fact was, after she left him he'd forced himself to put her out of his life. To *try* to put her out of his life, he amended. She'd wounded his pride to such an extent that he'd had to convince himself—to try to convince himself—that they'd never belonged together in the first place.

He looked across at her and asked, "Do you still have that bottle of Scotch hidden in the broom closet?"

"Why, yes," Christy said. "I forgot all about it," she added, speaking carefully, afraid her voice was going to get stuck deep down in her throat. "Actually I bought it for you," she managed.

"Do you suppose I could sample it now?"

"Sure."

As Christy switched on the lights, then fixed a Scotch for Drew and a glass of chilled white wine for herself, her thoughts were in chaos. Initially Drew's sharing had made her hopes soar. Made her think that with his masks cast aside, there might be a real chance for them.

Also his confidences had evoked in her a real sympathy for Millicent Delahunt. She'd never realized how much adversity her beautiful, cool mother-in-law had faced and conquered. Was it possible that, with a little more effort on her part, she and Millicent could achieve a valid rapport?

Then, she'd felt a wild surge of exultation when Drew said she'd never lost him. And because her hopes had soared so high at that point they plunged all the more deeply when he followed with the admission that he'd always been hers, that is to say, until she walked out on him.

She felt almost sickened by the whirl of her own emotions as she gave Drew his drink, then sat down on the couch again with hers. She watched him lean back, studying the glass of Scotch as if there were a lesson to be learned in it. And suddenly she couldn't stay in the room a second longer. She had to divert her own tumultuous thoughts, stem this rush of emotions that threatened to sweep her away in a current too strong for her to handle.

Abruptly she got to her feet and blurted, "I imagine Ben's home by now. I think I'll run downstairs with the rest of the tuna salad and get an update on Terry and the baby."

"Fine," Drew murmured without looking up at her.

Christy's heart was pounding as she hurried down the stairs. She hoped against hope that Ben was home. She needed a little space from Drew. A chance to regroup.

Fortunately Ben answered her knock almost immediately. Then, after accepting the salad, asked rather wistfully, "How about hanging around while I eat?"

"Love to," Christy answered.

Ben carefully poured two glasses of wine, and it disconcerted Christy to realize how much trouble he was having gauging when the glasses were full. As she watched him move about getting a plate, a fork and a napkin, she felt that he was fumbling more than ever, and the thought that his eyesight was getting worse frightened her.

She spent nearly an hour with Ben, then reluctantly headed back upstairs. Drew was slumped in the armchair, his feet outstretched, his eyes closed. He'd switched on the radio and was listening to mellow jazz.

He opened his eyes when he heard her, but she couldn't read anything in his expression. Uneasy about it, she sensed that he'd reached for a mask again after all. Was he regretting those earlier confidences?

"How are things with Terry and the baby?" he asked.

"Fine," she reported. "Ben says the doctor wants to keep them both in the hospital for two or three more days, but then they'll be coming home. That'll be cause for celebration, won't it?"

"Indeed it will," Drew murmured politely.

The politeness got to Christy. She was right, she thought dismally. Drew had done some heavy thinking of his own while she'd been downstairs with Ben. And the result of it was his mask, firmly in place. The closeness they'd achieved earlier tonight might never have happened.

Suddenly the living room seemed too small a space to share. "I think I'll turn in," Christy said lamely.

"Okay," Drew said lightly. Only when she was at the door of her bedroom did he add, "Christy, don't go leaping to conclusions. We're both tired. It isn't the time to discover ultimate solutions."

Christy had to admit he was right. Certainly she was too tired and confused to do much of anything. She slipped on a thin, yellow cotton nightgown, climbed into bed and pulled a sheet up over her. The space next to her seemed so vacant. She wanted Drew to be filling it so much she nearly got up and went back into the living room to ask him if he'd sleep in her room tonight. Just to be with her.

Why didn't she? She asked herself that question as she lay on her back, staring at the dark blur of the ceiling. Pride maybe? Was that what was preventing her from asking Drew to assuage her loneliness? Maybe the fear he might refuse her? As he might, despite everything that had happened earlier. Or maybe the fear that if he accepted her invitation they wouldn't be able to resist each other, even though they were both weary to the bone. And were they to make love again, it would only be all the harder when, at the end of this month he'd given her, Drew left to go back to his own world.

Chapter Twelve

You're being needlessly stubborn," Drew said tersely.

It was Sunday morning. He and Christy had wandered down to South Beach after having coffee and croissants on her deck. They'd gone for a lazy swim, and were lying out on the warm sand on oversized beach towels. Drew had just finished anointing Christy's skin with a maximum protection sunscreen, and she was still tingling from the touch of his hands on her legs, back and shoulders.

It was the first time he'd really touched her since their lovemaking the night Terry's baby was born. After the confidences he'd shared with her the following evening, he'd withdrawn. As the week passed, Christy had felt he was deliberately distancing himself from her. Maybe preparing for the final separation so close at hand.

Even the excitement of Terry and Lucy's homecoming hadn't brought them together again. They'd gone down to the apartment to welcome Lucy into the fold, as Ben put it, and there'd been one moment that had been especially hard for Christy to get through. That's when Drew had held Lucy for a little while. The expression on his face, his gentleness with the baby, had played havoc with Christy's heartstrings. The thought that, under other circumstances, that could have been *her* baby Drew was holding so tenderly was overwhelming. Just then he'd looked up, and their eyes had met. Christy had been so choked up she'd had to turn away.

True, this week they'd both been very busy. Drew's lesson schedule was rugged, she knew he must be bushed when he got home nights. But that was something she hadn't been home to verify herself. This week it seemed as if she'd been working all three of her jobs full-time. What actually happened was she'd gone from one to the next with few intermissions—a combination of vacations and sickness had required her employers to ask more hours of her than they usually did. Which was as well. She wasn't sure she could trust herself to be alone with Drew for very long.

"You really are being *ridiculously* stubborn, Christy," Drew repeated.

She knew exactly what he was talking about, and she sighed. "Drew," she explained patiently, "you just can't go giving money away like it was bubble gum."

"You have a blind spot when it comes to anything involving money," Drew accused, "no pun intended. The fact is Ben's eyesight is going down the tubes. Unless he gets competent help *soon*, I'm afraid that he might wake up blind one day. What do you think his future as an artist would be if that happened?"

Christy turned on her side and surveyed Drew levelly. "You don't think Ben has much future as an artist anyway, do you?" she asked.

"Why do you say that?"

"When we went downstairs to see Terry and the baby, I noticed you scanning the paintings Terry has hanging in their living room. You didn't seem overly enthused by what you saw."

"That's not so," Drew protested. "Ben's paintings are different. He has a unique style. The two behind the couch were a shade too abstract for me, but that's a personal opinion. It doesn't mean I don't appreciate the quality of what he's accomplished." He paused, then added, "I get the impression that Ben is quite versatile, Christy. The two seascapes in the bedroom were quite different from the abstracts. In any event I'd like to see more of his work. I'd *have* to see more in fact before I could make any sort of judgment."

"You're hedging, Drew," Christy snapped.

"I am *not* hedging."

"Fine."

For a second they were silent. Then Christy said, "Okay, do you really think that several thousand dollars could simply be *heaped* on the Descarteses? Do you expect them to believe that the cash just fell out of the sky? Or do you propose to pin large denomination bills on the palm fronds outside their windows?"

"Very funny," Drew said caustically.

"Well, that's the real issue, isn't it?"

"The issue, damn it, is that I want to help!" Drew exploded. "And the fact is I'm able to. Can't you understand that? Or would you rather hold back and witness Ben losing his eyesight?"

"Damn you, Drew! Why must you twist things around like that? Don't you *know* how worried I've been about Ben, how concerned I am about his eyesight. Regardless I wouldn't think of just . . . just riding roughshod over him."

"And you think that's what I want to do?"

Christy's anger subsided. "Of course not," she said honestly. "What I *do* think is that you don't seem to realize Ben is a very proud person. No matter how you engineered your 'help,' he'd be crushed if he found out about it. And secrets like that have a way of leaking out."

She sighed again. "All right," she conceded, "I guess I can understand how you feel. I'd probably feel the same way if I were in your position. But can't *you* understand that the last thing Terry and Ben want is pity or charity, to say nothing of a combination of both?"

"Of course I understand that," Drew replied, his steel eyes cool. "I'm not as insensitive as you think I am."

"I've never said I thought you were insensitive," Christy muttered wearily. "Look, Drew...let's pass on this, shall we? You'll do what you want to do. So there's no point in our arguing over it."

There was a moment of ice-filled silence before Drew muttered, "I just want to say one thing."

"What?"

"Regardless of any conclusions you may have reached, I do like Ben's work."

"Please," Christy protested. "Don't try to mollify me."

"I wouldn't dream of it," he assured her. "But do you really think I'm so rigid in my tastes that I can't appreciate a talent that's different?"

"I can't imagine Ben's paintings gracing the walls in Westport," Christy told him bluntly. Those walls, she recalled all too well, exhibited original works by artists like Rembrandt and Gainsborough and Gilbert Stuart.

Drew said stiffly, "That's your opinion."

"Look," Christy sighed. "This isn't getting us anywhere."

"Don't blame me for that," Drew persisted. "You intimated that I'm hopelessly rigid. Have you ever stopped to think how rigid you are?" Without waiting for an answer, Drew turned over and stretched out flat, leaving Christy only an excellent view of his back.

She stared at his smooth dark hair and the well defined muscles of his neck and shoulders. Then her eyes followed the tapering contours to his slim waist where she encountered snug bright blue bathing trunks that ended where his muscular thighs began.

Drew had a beautiful perfectly toned body, Christy thought for the thousandth time. He kept himself in shape at the various clubs he belonged to and ate proper portions of only healthy foods. Here in Key West, especially since he'd been teaching tennis, he'd acquired an enormously becoming tan. He looked clean, strong, sexy and so insidiously desirable that Christy wanted to wail aloud.

She could allow herself only so much sun. Now she sat up, reached for a wide-brimmed straw hat and plopped it on her head, then slipped a beach robe over her shoulders and covered her legs with a towel.

She tried to stare out at the water, but the attempt was useless. She couldn't keep her eyes off Drew. It made her ache to think of the way they were wasting the little bit of time together they had left. After today there were six days left—unless Drew decided to stay through the last weekend. That would make it seven days. Seven days to last her for the rest of her life, she thought dismally. Unless, somehow, something happened to change things radically. She loved him. She had no doubts on that score. But, loving someone was one thing. Living in an alien world was another.

"Drew?" she said softly.

"Hmm," he mumbled, his voice muffled by the beach towel.

"Try to appreciate my reasoning, will you? It's really important to me to have you understand why I'm so wary of any attempt on your part to help Ben."

He turned his head and looked up at her. "I'm trying to," he murmured unconvincingly.

Christy expelled a deep breath, then began, "It's like Santa Claus, or more like *playing* Santa Claus.

"You think I want to play Santa Claus?"

"Not exactly, Drew. But the concept's pretty much the same," Christy stated. "What you have to realize is that people like Terry and Ben and me stopped believing in those kinds of fairy tales a long time ago. We learned there are seldom if ever any real miracles, and *never* to count on a miracle happening."

Drew rolled over, propped himself up on an elbow and reached for a pair of sunglasses at his side. "Do you think I believe in miracles?"

"I don't want to get personal about this. That's not the point."

"Well, you're getting personal when you express how you feel and how you think Terry and Ben feel, aren't you? So why shouldn't I get personal, too?"

Christy shook her head in frustration. "What I'm trying to point out to you," she began again, "is that it's no favor to people like Terry and Ben to have a benevolent Saint Nicholas wave a magic wand from the sidelines and temporarily smooth their way. They need to find permanent solutions to their problems. Real solutions."

"Real solutions?" Drew echoed sarcastically. "Are they any relation to the real world you've gotten me involved in these past few weeks?"

Christy ignored his prodding. "People," she stated firmly, "need to confront their problems by themselves. It's a basic law of survival, Drew."

"I see," he drawled. "So you're saying in essence that if a man is drowning no one should try to rescue him because he should have learned to swim in the first place."

"Don't be ridiculous!"

Drew didn't answer her.

"Look, try to see it this way," she tried again. "It's like winning a sweepstakes or a lottery. Most people aren't ready for anything like that. They're stunned by the quantity of money they suddenly have. More often than not, they'll either get swindled or fritter it all away."

"You've interviewed lottery winners, I suppose?"

Now it was Christy's turn not to answer.

After a moment, Drew ventured, "You know, Christy, when you shut off your mind it's like closing the door on a bank vault. I don't think anything I say would make you view this differently. So, I don't agree with you, and I'm not making any promises."

"That's your right," Christy muttered. "Anyway, in another week you'll be getting back your credit cards and your money and your . . . your identity," she stammered. "Then you can do whatever you damned well please!"

"Thank you."

"You're welcome. You're quite welcome."

Drew fell back onto the sand again, this time lying on his back and letting the sun caress his face and chest. With eyes closed, he said huskily, "Christy, we're behaving like a couple of kids. There's no law that says two people have to agree on everything. You have a right to your opinion and I respect that. I'd just like to think you respect my right to an opinion, too."

"I do," Christy managed, looking up at him. "I just don't agree with you, that's all."

Drew burst out laughing. "That," he said, "is a typically Christy remark!"

"What's that supposed to mean?" she asked suspiciously.

"You yield, yet at the same time you win your point." He paused briefly, then murmured, "God, Christy, I love you so much."

Time stood still. Christy became so unstrung she couldn't speak. For all the passion that had flowed between them since Drew had come to Key West, for all the endearing qualities she now knew he possessed, she never expected to hear him come out and say those words to her again. Stunned, she couldn't answer him, then was horrified when he obviously misinterpreted her silence.

"I think you've had enough sun," he said tight-lipped, "even with all that cover-up I suggest we go."

She wanted to tell him that it didn't matter whether or not she'd had enough sun, not right now. Right now they had far more important things to talk about. She wanted to explain that he'd just thrown her a curve—a beautiful curve. But she was hopelessly tongue-tied.

The silence between them was strained as they headed back toward the house. Christy felt as if she were walking on eggshells. As they passed the Descarteses door, they heard little Lucy crying, then the crying abruptly stopped. Christy suspected that the baby had been hungry and now Terry was assuaging that hunger.

If only her problems could be solved so simply!

Drew couldn't shake the feeling that Christy hadn't wanted to hear that declaration of love from him. Fortunately he had back-to-back tennis lessons all day Monday so there was little time for brooding. By the end of the day, though, he'd resolved not to make the same mistake again.

He tried to put Christy out of his mind—fruitless attempt that *that* was—and to concentrate on Ben Descartes's problem. His suggestion to Christy had been that she take the considerable cash he'd turned over to her at the beginning of their month, and somehow manage to bestow it on the Descarteses. Then Ben could make an appointment with an ophthalmologist and not worry about the cost.

In retrospect he realized it was a pretty inane idea. Christy was right. You couldn't give money away like bubble gum. You couldn't clip fifty dollar bills to palm fronds. Still, he had to do *something*. He couldn't simply stand by and let Ben go blind when it was in his power to help him save his eyesight.

He wouldn't have thought he would ever consider approaching the gallery owner who'd turned him away so rudely that day he'd first gone job hunting in Key West. But on his return from the resort Monday afternoon, he got off the bus farther up Duval Street and minutes later was walking through the door.

The man looked up from his desk and literally groaned. So Drew took personal delight in saying smoothly, "Some friends of mine up north contacted me to see if I can locate any work done by Ben Descartes. Do you handle his paintings by any chance?"

The gallery owner was tall, slim, gray-haired and fastidiously dressed in a pale beige leisure suit, with a yellow ascot knotted neatly at his throat. Business in the gallery was obviously slow. There wasn't even a single browser in evidence.

"I'm afraid not," the man said, his interest piqued.

"Then do you know who does handle Descartes's work?"

"As I understand it, he's pretty much of a loner. I believe McKenzie Studios has a few of his things, however."

That would follow, Drew reflected. Christy worked part-time at McKenzie Studios. Trust her to use her position to promote some of Ben's paintings for him!

She worked there in the afternoons, he knew. But whether or not she was working there now, he didn't know. The last thing he wanted was for Christy to become suspicious of what he was up to.

As he walked along Duval Street, Drew remembered the owner of the batik shop who'd been in the group that had gone out for pizza one night. He'd talked with Drew extensively about the artists and painters of Key West including Ben. Perhaps he would know if Ben's paintings were placed elsewhere around town. Other friends of the Descarteses, people who'd been at Christy's birthday party, might also know. The important thing would be to keep them from realizing why he was making his inquiries.

As it happened, Terry volunteered all the information he needed to know. On the way home, Drew passed a flower vendor and impulsively bought a little bouquet. When he reached the house, he knocked on the Descarteses' door before heading upstairs.

Terry was alone in the apartment. "Ben's gone to work at the salad bar," she explained as she let Drew in.

Drew held out the flowers. "These are for Lucy," he said.

Terry beamed, then led him into the bedroom on tiptoe so he could peep at Lucy, fast asleep in her crib. She was a cherub of a baby. Drew thought about how traumatic her entrance into the world had been for everyone involved and inwardly shuddered.

Back in the living room, Terry said, "I don't think Christy's home yet. Would you like a glass of iced coffee?"

"That sounds terrific."

While Terry stepped into the kitchen, Drew moved around the living room and examined Ben's paintings more closely. There were six altogether, including the two above the couch he'd studied the other night.

Ben's use of color reminded Drew of Gauguin's Tahitian scenes. Only Ben's treatment of tropical themes was more often than not abstract. He'd imparted his personal style to the setting sun, the swaying palms, the pelicans and the shrimp boats. He'd created evocative portraits of life in the Florida keys. All in all his paintings were excellent and quite unlike any others Drew had seen. Ben Descartes had a distinct and genuine talent.

He needs a break, Drew muttered to himself. Above all else he needs his eyesight!

He swiveled around as Terry emerged from the kitchen and accepted his iced coffee from her. Turning back to the painting he'd been studying, he said, "Ben's really good, Terry."

"Thank you. That's what I keep telling him. But Ben's so self-deprecating I get impatient with him sometimes."

Terry sat down on the couch as she spoke. She was wearing a long, loose-fitting cotton robe that only emphasized her frailness. She needed a chance to rest, a chance not to worry, Drew thought sadly.

He gritted his teeth. It was hell to think he could so easily give her that chance, if not for the fact his hands were tied. Or would be, if Christy had her way.

Terry was easy to talk to and interested in everything. She wanted to know all about his job at the resort and reacted with delight to the stories he told her about his more memorable pupils.

Finally Drew managed to say casually, "I can't help but think that if Ben were properly exhibited, he'd soon build up quite a following. Are his paintings displayed only at McKenzie Studios or do other galleries carry his work?"

Terry smiled. "Actually Ben has paintings hanging all around town. When we first came to Key West, Ben would set up his easel right on the street. He'd work all day at a painting, chatting with tourists and locals alike, and once or twice a week he'd make a sale."

"But he doesn't do that anymore, right?"

"Not since his headaches got worse, no." She paused, then went on, "Christy's really helped us. She got Ben's work into McKenzie's as you know. And at Violet's, as well. Another friend of ours has a whole wall of Ben's paintings in his gift shop."

"Are they all for sale?" Drew asked lightly.

"Yes," Terry said. "And it pains me that they're not selling better." She smiled ruefully, then admitted, "Painting for a living is hard for me to understand sometimes."

"You mean because Ben puts so much of himself into a work, only to trade it for dollars?"

"Strange, isn't?" Terry said nodding.

"Not necessarily," Drew decided. "I imagine Ben is so barraged by ideas that he doesn't see a finished work as something he owns."

"Ben has said those exact words, Drew," Terry exclaimed. "The only way he keeps a painting is by giving it to me! Still, if he'd only get out there and push a little. Push his name and talent, that is. . . ."

When Drew was silent, Terry continued, "Ben's problem, if you will, is that he's something of a loner. He's never been one to join anything, not even art associations. I've tried to get him to touch base with the Key West Art Center down on Front Street, for example. It's a non-profit artists cooperative, an excellent showcase for local artists. But Ben keeps stalling. To tell you the truth . . ."

"Yes?"

"Well," Terry said, "Ben hasn't done any paintings for quite a while now. He keeps insisting he doesn't have the time, but that obviously isn't true. I mean, he rarely puts in more than forty hours at the salad bar, and his mornings are free." She shook her head. "It's his eyes, Drew. I think painting's become too much of a strain."

"It sounds that way," Drew agreed softly.

Terry hesitated, then said, "I'm going to tell you something you must promise to keep to yourself."

"I promise," Drew assured her.

"I spoke to my obstetrician about Ben. He's arranging an appointment for Ben with a friend of his, an ophthalmologist. The problem will be getting Ben to keep the appointment."

"He has to," Drew stated soberly.

"Yes," Terry agreed. "I know."

A few minutes later Drew headed upstairs to an empty apartment. As he showered, he reflected that perhaps Christy wasn't entirely wrong. Maybe the Descartes would work things out by themselves after all, without help from him or anyone else. But that didn't mean they couldn't use a financial cushion, he told himself decisively.

Drew had no intention of going anywhere near Fancy's that night until it got dark. Then suddenly he couldn't stand the solitude of the apartment any longer.

As he walked along Duval Street, he once again told himself it was a free country and he had as much right to patronize Fancy's as anyone else did. If Christy didn't like it, too bad.

Christy in fact was more than glad to see him. When she glimpsed Drew standing near the bar, she went weak all over. He had to be the handsomest man in the world.

Why had she turned so tongue-tied yesterday when Drew had said he loved her? Christy had relived that scene a hundred times. And each time, in the privacy of her thoughts, she'd responded with the answer she hoped he wanted to hear.

Now, suddenly, she felt a rush of shyness toward him, a strange giddiness because he was only a few feet away. She watched him slide onto a bar stool and thought her heart would stop beating.

"Hi," he said easily.

"Hi, yourself," she said softly.

He was wearing a navy-blue knit shirt that emphasized his muscles and his tan, and he looked terrific. Christy's pulse bumped against the hollow in her neck as she tried not to stare at him.

"Something wrong?" he asked.

"Of course not," she murmured weakly. "How did your day go?"

"My day went fine. But my night's turned a little lonely." That was more than he'd intended to say, and Drew slammed on both his verbal and emotional brakes.

"What'll you have?" Christy asked.

"A beer will be fine."

"Draft?"

"Sure."

Drew watched Christy fill a frosted mug with icy beer and loved the way she moved. She worked swiftly, yet she never gave an impression of hurrying. When she placed the beer before him along with a dish of salted peanuts, he grinned.

"What's this? A bonus?"

"Peanuts have a lot of vitamins," Christy informed him.

She was surprised when Cal Fancy slid onto the stool next to Drew and ordered a beer for himself. He very seldom drank with customers. He knew Drew was her friend of course. Even so, he must have taken quite a liking to Drew to approach him like that.

The two men fell into an easy conversation. Christy cast surreptitious glances in their direction while she tended to the bar and decided they were getting along very well. She was astonished when Cal bought Drew a beer and ordered a second one for himself. She'd never seen him do anything like that before.

Then Luigi Amoroso stopped by for his usual Dos Equis and greeted Drew as if he were an old friend. Christy surveyed the two men, an odd and wondering expression in her eyes.

With business temporarily slack, she wandered down the bar and stood idly nearby. Luigi and Drew were having a deep discussion evidently about boats and the sea. She knew those were subjects in which Drew could very definitely hold his own. Though the beautiful yacht he owned was a pleasure craft, it took a high degree of seamanship to sail it. She'd observed Drew's expertise many times on those magical summer Sundays when they'd escaped together out on Long Island Sound.

"Hey Christy," Luigi said abruptly, motioning her to join them. "This fellow of yours knows his stuff."

It seemed strange even funny to hear Drew Cabot Delahunt III referred to as her "fellow." Christy nearly laughed aloud, then realized that her laughter could easily topple over the edge of hysteria. She was that upset—and that confused—about where she stood with Drew.

Drew studied her closely. "Is everything okay?" he asked.

"Everything's fine," she replied quickly. "Want another beer?"

"No, thanks." As Luigi looked on, he added, "Mind if I hang around till you get off, though? I guess it's foolish of me, but I still hate the idea of you walking home by yourself late at night."

"You're right," Luigi put in solemnly.

"Boys," Christy said with mock severity, "I can take care of myself. Besides it's not even ten o'clock."

"Listen to her," Luigi kidded. "Miss Tough Stuff!"

"Another comment like that," Christy kidded back, "and I'll shut you off!"

"It's me talking, not the beer, Miss DiMartino," Luigi countered. "A good Italian girl shouldn't be out on the street alone at all hours."

Christy saw Drew's mouth quirk, saw the hidden laughter in his eyes. But he contained himself. "He's right," he said solemnly.

Turning back to Luigi, Christy mumbled, "I'm no more Italian than you are."

"That makes you pretty Italian," Luigi chortled.

A few minutes later Luigi left. Then Cal Fancy came over and said, "Any time you want to take off, it's okay, sweetheart. You walking home with her, Drew?"

At Drew's nod Cal said, "Good."

"Hey, what is this?" Christy said. "Have I suddenly become incompetent?"

"She has no idea how young and beautiful she is," Cal informed Drew. "Or how vulnerable. When she looks in the mirror, I honestly think she sees a toughness that isn't really there."

"Maybe I should start taking lessons in self-defense," Christy muttered, scowling at both men.

"Good idea," Cal said easily. "Now get out of here."

As she and Drew started up Duval Street, Christy was still annoyed by the way the men had chided her. Yet it was wonderful having Drew by her side. It wasn't that she needed his protection. Rather she loved his company.

"This is your last week in Key West," she murmured absently.

"What made you think of that?" Drew asked.

"I don't know," she hedged. "Maybe it's because this month has gone by so fast. I mean, it seems like only yesterday that you showed up at Fancy's. There's so much you haven't seen here, Drew. So many things you haven't done."

"For instance?"

"Well, there's great scuba diving and snorkeling all along the keys. You'd love it."

"There's great scuba diving and snorkeling lots of places, Christy."

"Okay, then there's the aquarium."

"I've been to aquariums."

"Well, you haven't poked around Mallory Square, have you? Or Front Street? Or any of the other spots that are uniquely Key West."

"I've never been much for sightseeing," Drew confessed.

"You've done it all and seen it all, is that it?"

"I'm not saying that."

"Then tell me you've checked out the cemetery," Christy said defiantly.

"The *cemetery*?"

"The cemetery's something else," she stated. "Maybe kind of spooky on a moonlit night, but very special. A lot of people say it's the most *living* part of Key West."

"Why would anyone say something like that?"

"Because it *is* Key West. All the history and character of the town is there. It's kind of a permanent, visible time capsule, quite unlike any other cemetery I've ever seen—although I've heard the ones in New Orleans are similar. Key West has a coral rock base with only a thin layer of soil on top, so many of the graves are actually above ground vaults. James Merrill, a Key West poet, described them as 'whitewashed hope chests.' I think that's kind of a nice concept."

"Mmm," Drew murmured dubiously.

"Anyway," Christy continued, "many of the vaults are made of stucco and stacked one atop another because space is at a premium. Most are decorated with symbols that had special meaning to the deceased. My favorite memorial is the beautiful stone angel that commemorates a child's death."

"Sounds pretty gloomy to me," Drew mused.

"I don't know," Christy said reflectively. "After all, death is part of living."

Later, as he stretched out on the couch and gazed out the French windows at the dark southern night, Drew thought about that remark of Christy's. *Death is part of living.* It was a profound statement, indicative of an interesting philosophy. It occurred to him that Christy tended to be full of a lot of interesting philosophies. Most of the time he'd teased them away with comments about the night courses she'd taken. Comments she'd considered a put-down.

She hadn't been entirely wrong. Suddenly Drew was painfully conscious of how he'd underestimated his young wife. She'd never had even a fraction of his kind of opportunity, but she'd snatched every chance for learning she could get. In so many ways she was so much wiser than he was.

Drew thought again of her reaction yesterday to his having told her he loved her. He couldn't remember when anything had hurt quite so much.

Much as he wanted to make their marriage work, he was deeply afraid it was already too late. He just couldn't imagine Christy giving him another chance.

Chapter Thirteen

Drew was chagrined the next morning when, as he was leaving for the resort, Christy told him she'd be working at Fancy's again that night. He decided bitterly to leave her to her own devices. He'd wanted these last few evenings in Key West with her. Although they had a lot to talk about and a lot of decisions to make, he suspected Christy didn't want to face up to those decisions. Neither did he, when you got right down to it.

If only this interlude could last, if not forever, a lot longer. But he'd given her a month. He couldn't stretch it. It wouldn't be fair to his mother—a month was more than long enough for her to shoulder his responsibilities—or to the many others who depended on him.

So, like it or not, they were going to have to face the music...very soon. Probably, Drew thought cynically, the night before he was due to leave if Christy had her way.

He put in a long day on the tennis courts, had a lonely dinner in the apartment, then managed to dawdle until almost nine-thirty. At that point he couldn't stand it any longer. He had to see her!

He knew she would be off at ten. He decided to wander down to Fancy's acting as if it were an afterthought, have a beer at the bar and wait for her.

To his annoyance he discovered that Christy, as she'd done before, had made arrangements to go for pizza with some friends. Drew of course was invited to join them. He went along, convinced that she was definitely taking to some very delaying tactics. At least she didn't invite the others back to the house for a nightcap, he noted thankfully as they left the pizza place and headed home. But once they arrived home, Christy quickly murmured good-night and withdrew to her bedroom.

When Christy told him she was working till ten the next night, Drew was definitely suspicious. Christy rarely worked at Fancy's past eight in the evening on week nights. It seemed clear-cut that she was working long hours to diminish the time they would have alone. Especially the night time.

Was she so afraid he would want to make love to her if they were alone very much? Didn't she want to make love as much as he did?

It hurt to think that maybe, after all, she didn't.

Nevertheless, Drew again walked to Fancy's at nine-thirty and said nothing when Christy reported that they were meeting some friends for shrimp and stone crab at a waterfront café.

Shrimp and crab didn't exactly appeal to Drew's stomach at this hour. Nor did conch chowder, grouper or mako shark!

He tried to join in the spirit of things with Christy and her friends, but it was hard going. The girl who ran the bicycle shop finally asked, "What's with you tonight, Drew? You haven't said five words."

"Tired, I guess," Drew murmured.

"Don't you ever let this guy get any rest, Christy?" someone quipped.

Christy flushed and didn't attempt an answer. The moment passed but not before she'd wished she could sink through the floor.

She didn't dare glance at Drew. She'd already noticed how tired he looked. And though he hadn't retreated into the kind of cold shell she feared so much, he did seem unusually preoccupied. Was he thinking about the next step he'd be taking in just a couple more days? How could it be otherwise? she asked herself. Drew *had* to be thinking of this upcoming weekend, just as she was.

The whole thought of his leaving was tearing her to pieces. It was because she dreaded that soon-to-be separation that she'd been avoiding Drew these past few days. Avoided being alone with him, she amended. She supposed she was instinctively trying to cushion the blow to come. Her common sense told her that cushioning of any kind was useless. When Drew left, it was going to hurt. It was going to hurt like hell.

Since that declaration on South Beach, he'd been so distant. She read that as meaning that his love proclamation had merely been a casual remark and he didn't want her to attach a real significance to it. People sometimes said things like that without the words having the deep meaning they could have. True, she'd been so stunned she'd been unable to answer him. Even so if he'd really meant *love*, wouldn't he have said more by now?

Inwardly baffled, Christy forced herself to pretend a merriment she was far from feeling. She joked with her friends, laughed a shade too loudly, suggested they drink one last pitcher of beer even though the others probably wouldn't have ordinarily.

She was stalling. Stalling because she'd be walking home alone with Drew and it was a long walk. It would be incredibly difficult to keep a rein on her emotions during the course of it.

As it happened, she was temporarily reprieved. One member of the group said he had his car parked nearby and would be glad to run Drew and her back to Whitehead Street.

It had been a long day for Christy, working at the McKenzie Studios all morning and afternoon, then finishing up at Fancy's. She felt hot and sticky and in no state of mind to crawl under her covers once they were back in the apartment.

"I think I'll soak for a while in the tub," she told Drew, not looking at him. "Do you want to use the bathroom first?"

"No thanks," he said. "I'm going to read."

Christy was so conscious of Drew sitting right on the other side of the wall that she cut her bath short. She dried herself off, slipped on a clean nightgown and twisted her hair into a coil on top of her head. At her bedroom doorway she turned and said softly, "Good night, Drew."

He was sitting in the armchair. He glanced up and murmured, "Good night," then quickly looked back at the book he was reading.

She stood in the doorway a moment longer, wanting to say more to him, but the right words eluded her. She felt shy and confused. "Drew?" she managed tentatively.

"Yes?" he asked, not glancing up from the book.

Christy hesitated. She wasn't trying to entice him. In fact she knew she couldn't risk so much as the touch of his hand right now. She was so on edge that one kiss and she would dissolve.

Pride made her say, "It's nothing. I'll see you in the morning."

"Okay," Drew said nodding, still concentrating on the book as if he couldn't bear to give up a second of reading time. Only when the bedroom door had closed behind

Christy did he fling the novel to the floor, lean back in the chair and press his hands tightly over his eyes.

She'd looked like an innocent child, standing there in the doorway in her nightgown. At the same time she struck Drew as the most desirable woman he'd ever seen. She was such a paradox.

Which was the real Christy? Drew asked himself savagely. *Desirable young woman or guileless little girl?*

He knew the answer of course. She was both. An intriguing, fascinating mixture. Lovely and charismatic, stubborn and generous, giving, caring. Everything a man could possibly want in the woman he loved, Drew thought sadly, his heart torn.

Thursday morning, Christy said, "Terry wants us to come down for supper tonight."

"What did you tell her?" Drew asked.

"I told her I thought it was too much to tackle so soon, but she really wants us to come, Drew. I think she's a little stir crazy at this point. She's hardly been out of the house since Lucy was born."

"Lucy's not that old," Drew observed dryly.

"Even so, I said I'd make dinner. Maybe you could pick up some rolls at the bakery on the way home. Then all Terry will have to do is toss a salad."

"Okay," Drew said, "I'll get the rolls." He paused, then said, "You're not working at Fancy's tonight?"

"No, I'm not. Tomorrow night but not tonight."

Drew nearly swore aloud. Finally she was taking one night off—then managing to fill it up with other people when all he wanted was to be alone with her.

He was glad to get out of the apartment, glad to face a day booked solid with tennis lessons. He needed the diversion to keep his head on straight, but by the time five o'clock rolled around he didn't care if he never saw another tennis racket!

He stopped at a bakery for the rolls, then headed home. Christy was standing over the kitchen stove, stirring something that smelled marvelous.

"You didn't forget the rolls, did you?" she inquired, not pausing to look at the bakery bag he was carrying.

"No," he snapped. "Did you think I would?"

Christy shook her head and turned to ask, "Why are you so touchy?"

That, Drew decided, was the most direct and personal remark she'd made to him in days. The perverse thing was...he didn't know how to answer her.

"It was a long day," he mumbled and let it go at that.

"I imagine you'll want to take a shower?"

"Yes."

"Well, why don't I go ahead and take the food downstairs?" Christy suggested. "I put a bottle of Muscadet in the fridge to chill. Will you bring it along when you come?"

Drew nodded, not trusting himself to speak. Her one current aim in life seemed to be to keep them from being alone together as much as possible.

When Christy left the apartment, he rummaged in the cupboard, located the bottle of Scotch and poured himself a straight shot. He was restless and bothered by so many conflicting emotions, and he wasn't looking forward to this evening with the Desarteses. Much as he liked Terry and Ben, he just wasn't in the mood for being around other people.

Drew took a scalding hot, soapy shower, then turned the water cool for several minutes. Then he changed into his jeans and a sky-blue Key West T-shirt he'd splurged on when one of his female students—as the girl from the employment agency had predicted—gave him a generous tip for her week of lessons. Then, he still dragged his heels about heading downstairs, settling instead on pouring himself a second shot of Scotch.

Tomorrow was Friday. By Saturday night at the latest, assuming Christy was working her customary late shift at Fancy's, he and she were going to have to talk things out.

Drew closed his eyes wearily. After living in this conch house with her for almost a month, after seeing her both at work and at play, he couldn't imagine her ever coming back to Westport. He couldn't imagine her ever *wanting* to.

Here in Key West, she was a free spirit. The same free spirit he'd fallen in love with in Ogunquit six years ago. She made enough money to get by, kept her life simple and uncluttered. Very few things were lacking, he admitted fairly. He was sure she missed least of all the diamonds, furs and other accoutrements of wealth she'd never needed from him to begin with.

What she *had* needed was his time, his consideration, his companionship. The three things he'd pledge to give her in the future, if, somehow, he could persuade her to give him another chance. At least he would try his damndest to give them to her.

Drew had no illusions about radically changing his professional life. But his personal life was a different story, or should be. Certainly if he put the kind of effort into it he put into business, he could bring about results that would be satisfactory both to him and to Christy. But could he convince her of that?

Time passed while Drew sat lost in thought. Then he heard the doorknob turn and swung around to see Christy standing on the threshold.

She peered through the early evening shadows. "Drew?" she asked uncertainly.

"Yes."

Slowly she advanced toward him. "I thought maybe you'd fallen asleep," she said. "You looked exhausted when I left you." Spying the half-empty glass of Scotch he was holding, she added, "Oh."

"I was just relaxing," Drew told her.

"You don't have to explain to me."

"I wasn't. I only said..."

"I know what you said. Look, can you come down now? Terry has everything ready."

Drew nodded and tossed off the rest of his Scotch.

Christy preceded him down the stairs. She was wearing a lavender shift that floated around her knees as she moved, and she'd tied her hair back with a matching satin ribbon. Her hair, a pale gold mantle, swayed against her shoulders as she took each step. Drew, knowing how soft it would feel, could barely refrain from reaching out and touching it.

Terry had fed Lucy and was rocking her to sleep when they arrived. Ben was already seated at the kitchen table. Terry joined them, and they feasted on Christy's delicious meal. But the conversation, usually so stimulating, lagged. Ben was very quiet. Even Terry didn't have much to say. Christy tried to pick up the tempo, but her attempts fell flat.

Supper over, Ben said, "I could do with some ice cream. How about you guys?" Before anyone had a chance to answer, he suggested to Drew, "How about taking a walk with me to that ice-cream parlor a couple of blocks over?"

The two men set out. It was a cool cloudy night and the street was quiet. Drew had scarcely closed the gate behind them when Ben said tersely, "I had to get out of there, if only for a few minutes."

"Cabin fever?" Drew queried sympathetically. "Christy mentioned that you and Terry have hardly been out at all since the arrival of Lucy."

"No, it's not that," Ben said, carefully ducking under a tree branch that hung out over the sidewalk. "If I tell you something, Drew, will you keep it to yourself? I don't want even Christy to know about this. She might, maybe inadvertently, spill it to Terry."

"Of course I'll keep it to myself, Ben," Drew said quickly. "What is it?"

"I saw an ophthalmologist yesterday," Ben stated.

They'd reached a corner and Ben paused. After a rather long moment he said, "Let me take your arm, Drew. In this kind of light, I can barely see the curb."

Drew quickly proffered his arm and had a sudden, awful premonition of what Ben was going to tell him.

When they'd crossed the street, Ben said, trying to sound casual, "That's the problem of course. My vision is pretty well shot, has been for some time. The way things are going, I'll probably qualify for a white cane in eight or nine months."

Drew caught his breath, then managed, "That's what the ophthalmologist told you?"

"Essentially, yes."

"What do you mean 'essentially'? Did he say what the problem is?"

"Quite simple really," Ben answered flatly. "What I have is progressive glaucoma, Drew, stemming from an infection I got a couple of years back. I should have seen an ophthalmologist then, but I didn't. The infection, called iritis, left scar tissue on both my irises. Those are the tinted diaphragms that regulate the amount of light entering the eyes."

"Yes, I know," Drew said patiently. "But what does that have to do with glaucoma?"

"Glaucoma is a consequence of the untreated infection. Certain channels within my eyes are no longer capable of draining fluid, hence the fluid buildup, hence the headaches and steadily decreasing vision."

"Did the doctor offer any hope?"

"Oh, yes," Ben said shakily. "He said I could take a trip to New York where he can get me a consultation with a topnotch eye surgeon. A procedure called a bilateral iridectomy would basically set me straight."

"That's terrific, Ben," Drew exclaimed.

"Sure," Ben scoffed. "And after that I'll take Terry and Lucy on a trip around the world."

"Ben, it's not the same thing and you know it."

"It's exactly the same thing, Drew, as far as I'm concerned. We don't have any medical insurance. We haven't been able to afford it. So, we have bills for Terry and Lucy that have to be paid. I never would have thought of lining up an appointment with an eye doctor right now, and I wish to hell Terry hadn't."

"Are you saying you'd rather you hadn't gone."

"You're damned right that's what I'm saying!" Ben exploded. "Sometimes ignorance is bliss."

"But you've known, haven't you, that . . ."

"That my eyes were getting worse?" Ben cut in. "Of course I knew, but I had no idea how bad it really was. Now . . ." He paused, then added gloomily, "If I had life insurance, I'd get Luigi Amoroso to take me out shrimping and I'd conveniently manage to fall overboard in deep water where they'd never find me."

Even as he finished saying that, Ben laughed. "Strike that," he said. "I'm just letting off a lot of steam."

Drew didn't know what to say.

At the ice-cream shop, Ben insisted on paying and Drew didn't argue the point. He knew that, just now, even paying for a quart of ice cream was a pride-validating exercise for Ben.

On the way back to Whitehead Street, Ben said, "I'm sorry I laid all that on you, Drew."

"Don't be," Drew said quickly. "It's good to feel you trusted me enough to tell me about it. I only wish there was something I could do," he finished. Even as he said that, Drew's mind was buzzing with ideas.

"Who knows?" Ben speculated. "Maybe you can find someone who'll sell me a winning ticket to the Irish Sweepstakes."

"In the meantime I'll start collecting four-leaf clovers," Drew said, knowing that was the kind of quip Ben wanted to hear.

* * *

Drew woke up in the middle of the night, gazed out into a darkness unrelieved by moonlight and had a sudden vivid idea of what Ben's world might be like one day. By the time he got up in the morning, he'd determined his course of action. If Christy ever found out, she'd probably never speak to him again. But there were no guarantees on that as things stood now anyway.

His first tennis lesson wasn't until nine o'clock. He deliberately got to the resort half an hour early, went directly to his open-air thatched-roof "office" and picked up the phone.

In Westport a maid answered on the second ring and accepted Drew's collect call. A moment later Millicent came on the line. "I thought I'd probably be hearing from you soon," she said when they'd exchanged greetings.

"How have you weathered the month?" Drew asked her.

"Quite easily," she said, obviously pleased to be able to report that. "Everyone has been genuinely cooperative." She chuckled and added, "This time around they know you're here to stay, so no one's trying any executive takeovers. Now tell me about *your* month."

"It's been . . . an experience," Drew understated.

Millicent came directly to the point. "Will Christy be coming home with you?" she asked.

There was no point in dissembling with Millicent, Drew realized. She knew him too well. "I doubt it," he said honestly, his voice suddenly sounding as ragged as he felt.

"Oh," Millicent said. He heard the hurt in her voice. "I'd so hoped it would work out between the two of you," she added after a brief pause.

"So had I, Millie," Drew admitted.

"Drew?"

"Yes?"

"I need to ask this. Do you still love her?"

Drew felt his throat thicken. He said heavily, "I love her more than ever, Millie. She's a rare and wonderful person. One of these days after I've been back for a while, I'll tell you about her. I don't think you ever really knew her. For that matter neither did I."

"If you feel like that, Drew, are you sure you should leave Key West?"

"The month is almost up," he reminded her.

"Regardless, maybe you should stay a little longer."

"I doubt it would do any good," Drew said. He heard his words, and knew that, unfortunately, he believed them. Swiftly he changed the subject. "This isn't why I called you, Millie," he told his mother. "Actually I need a favor."

"What kind of favor?"

"I've met an artist in Key West I want very much to help," Drew said. "But this has to be a behind-the-scenes operation or it won't work out.

"This man is highly talented, I'd say he has a great future. But right now he desperately needs money for eye surgery." Drew continued. "The one acceptable way that money can be raised is for his paintings to be sold . . . in volume."

"And you want to arrange for the sales?" Millicent asked.

"No, I want *you* to arrange for the sales," Drew informed her. "The paintings in question are in several galleries, shops, restaurants and other places as well, all in Key West. They won't be difficult to locate. What's essential is for someone to come down here as soon as possible—tomorrow at the latest—and start buying them up. Ideally every outlet in Key West should be checked. Come to think of it, you'd better send down two or three people."

"That can be arranged," Millicent said serenely.

"The point is," Drew continued, "the people you send will need an extremely tight cover story. I don't want a single soul getting the idea they're connected with us in any way, or with Delahunt, Marcy and Bainbridge. Now does it sound easy?''

''Has this artist of yours ever sold anything?''

''Many times but not recently,'' Drew conceded. ''He's not very good at promoting himself. That's a major part of his career problem.''

''What kinds of paintings does he do?''

''Oil abstracts, mostly, with colorful tropical themes.''

''I see,'' Millicent mused. ''Are they good enough to be placed with a name gallery, do you think?''

''Definitely. Why?''

''Because I have an old friend in Manhattan, a gallery owner as it happens, who I think would be receptive. Maybe, just maybe...''

A minute later Drew hung up knowing that Millicent would waste no time in contacting her friend. And he was sure he wasn't being overconfident to assume that within a few days, every Descartes painting in Key West—except for the seven or eight in Ben and Terry's apartment—would be acquired for cash. Premium cash.

Drew hung up the telephone, satisfied with his own actions for the first time in quite a while. What he'd just done meant that Ben would have his surgery, with no ''charity'' involved, because Ben's paintings merited big prices. Ben's vision would be restored, and he would be able to continue to paint. If Christy wanted to call that playing Santa Claus, so be it.

Chapter Fourteen

Dave Martin, the resort manager, fixed Drew with a cold eye and said, "Are you aware this is Friday?"

"Yes," Drew said nodding.

"So, you're giving me two days notice. Is that it?"

"Yes," Drew admitted.

"Big of you."

"Look," Drew said, "I've told you I'm sorry about this. Some urgent personal business requires my presence up north."

"Then be my guest," Martin said. "You can walk out right now as far as I'm concerned."

"I've lined up a full schedule of lessons for both today and tomorrow," Drew pointed out.

The manager looked totally disgruntled, and Drew couldn't blame him. But after a moment he shrugged and said, "Oh, what the hell. Go ahead and give your lessons. You can collect your regular weekly paycheck tonight, and we'll mail the balance due to your *northern* address," Martin finished, snidely emphasizing the word.

"Thank you," Drew rejoined politely. Actually he was relieved. He'd expected more of a hassle from Martin than this and wondered what he would do, if he were in the man's place. It was the height of the season, and he was losing the most recently acquired tennis pro who'd been doing more than satisfactorily. He supposed there was always another tennis pro somewhere on the horizon.

Drew put special effort into his teaching that day, as it might compensate for his lack of giving adequate notice. But his efforts backfired because, as a result, the guests staying at the resort through the next week all wanted more lessons. Drew was forced to tell one, then another, that he was "leaving." It got so he hated to speak his piece, yet it was heartening to know that—despite the manager's understandable attitude over his quitting on such short notice—he'd scored this one definite success in Key West.

He collected his paycheck and left the resort late that afternoon. He'd made enough money to buy that special dress for Christy and wondered if the boutique still had it in stock. Then he reminded himself, as he climbed aboard the bus, that he'd better turn over room and board money to Christy before he went on a spending spree.

A spending spree! In two days, Drew suddenly realized, he'd be getting back the six hundred eighty-nine dollars plus five thousand in traveler's checks he'd handed over to her four weeks ago. Add credit cards to that, he thought, and the sky was virtually the limit. If he wanted, he could buy her every dress in the store!

Somehow there wasn't even a grain of satisfaction in that knowledge.

Drew was hoping to find Christy at home, hoping she would stay around long enough to have supper with him. This was probably their last chance to do that. If she followed her normal Saturday routine, she would be going straight to Fancy's after she finished work at McKenzie Studios. And she would tend bar at Fancy's till midnight at least.

He opened the apartment door and knew instantly she was gone. There was a note on the table saying there was plenty of food in the fridge for his dinner. Drew swore softly. He didn't want food. He wanted her!

Feeling utterly frustrated, he headed downstairs to see the Descartes. He thought of suggesting going out to get some pizzas or maybe fish and chips. Something, anyway, that they could all share back at their apartment. The thought of being alone tonight was too much to contemplate.

He rapped on their door. But when it opened a few seconds later, it wasn't Terry or Ben who stood before him, it was Christy.

"Drew!" she exclaimed instinctively stepping backward.

He noticed the retreating movement and didn't like it. "Oh, are you dining with Terry and Ben?" he asked coldly.

"No."

"Then what *are* you doing down here?" he demanded.

"Keep your voice down, Drew," Christy admonished. "You'll wake up Lucy."

"Sorry," he grumbled, lowering his voice. "I just came down to see if Ben and Terry wanted me to go out and get some food we could share. Are they home?"

Christy shook her head. "They really needed to get out for a while," she said. "I don't have to be at Fancy's until eight, so I volunteered to baby-sit."

"I see," Drew managed, none to graciously. "How late are you working at Fancy's?"

"Midnight."

He nodded, wishing he hadn't asked. He should have known.

Christy was waiting for him to say something. He groaned inwardly and asked, "Do you suppose I could come in for a minute? I'll be quiet."

Christy stood aside to let Drew enter and was well aware she'd annoyed him. His mouth was set in a tight line as he brushed past her, his eyes were glaring straight ahead. Then again, her own mood was anything but ecstatic. Tomorrow was technically the last day of the month he'd promised her. Sunday, she would have to live up to her part of the bargain, give him back his money, give him back his freedom. Unless...

Drew's valuables were locked away in a safe-deposit box down at her bank. The bank was closed from Saturday afternoon until Monday morning. If she conveniently forgot to stop by to retrieve his things before noon tomorrow, and if Drew forgot to ask her to...

Christy's spirits briefly soared. She didn't know why one extra day—and night—should seem so important when they'd had four weeks to work things out. Yet it was. Because she had been gearing herself to talk to him after she got through work tonight and all day tomorrow if necessary. Somehow they both had to keep their cool and talk things out together before he left. She was painfully aware that the rest of their lives depended on that.

Of course if he really wanted to, Drew could walk into the bank and identify himself, she reminded herself. His name alone would have any respectable bank manager bending over backward to accommodate him and retrieve his money without her help.

Except he didn't know which bank was hers!

Christy would have grinned if Drew hadn't been standing practically on top of her, staring at her with those steel gray eyes of his.

"What's with you?" he asked impatiently. "I wish I could read those expressions that have been playing across your face."

"What expressions?"

Drew looked away for a second, gritting his teeth. Turning back to face Christy again, he said, "Never mind about that. Look...tomorrow's my last official day here, you know. I'll be leaving Sunday."

"Please," she said unsteadily, "let's not get into that. Not yet."

"I suppose you've made up your mind about everything?"

"I've done a lot of thinking," Christy hedged.

"That's not what I asked you."

"Drew, please. I honestly don't want to go into this right now. I worked most of the day and I'm tired. I only have about an hour in which to relax, assuming Lucy stays asleep. Then I'm due at Fancy's."

She stared at Drew helplessly, not knowing what to say next. She had no idea what he saw or didn't see. She didn't know where he really stood on all the important issues that involved both of them, and there were so many.

She reached for something practical and mundane to suggest. "Look," she managed, "would you like a beer or something?"

"Not now," Drew said. "I guess I'll go upstairs and finish that book I've been reading." He paused in the open doorway and looked back into Christy's eyes. "I'll stop by Fancy's later," he informed her.

It was nearly eleven-thirty when Drew walked into Fancy's. Christy had been getting edgier and edgier, knowing that he would appear sooner or later. She hadn't planned any after-work excursions tonight. That meant the long walk home with Drew was going to be rough. She at least was laboring under so many heavy emotions she felt like she had a steamroller on her back.

Luckily Fancy's was incredibly busy. Christy didn't think she'd ever seen the place as mobbed as it was tonight. Every chair at every table was taken, as was every bar stool. The customers even seemed to be staying longer than usual. Most of the evening it was standing room only with people lined up at the back of the bar to get a drink. All in all there wasn't a dull moment.

Even with Cal helping out behind the bar, Christy was so busy she had long periods when she couldn't even think of Drew. When he finally did saunter in, all she could do was catch his eyes and call out, "Hi!"

For a moment she thought he might try to edge in close enough so she could pour him a beer. He didn't, though. And with a sinking heart she watched him leave—knowing he would be back later.

On leaving Fancy's Drew wandered down to Mallory Square. He strolled across the parking lot and stood at the edge of a pier. This was the Gulf of Mexico side of Key West and the site of a nightly ritual. It was here that tourists and locals alike gathered each evening to applaud the sunset.

Why didn't Christy and I do that? Drew wondered sadly.

He'd learned enough of Key West history to know that Mallory Square had been, in another era, the focal point for Key West's economy. Back in the 1830s wrecking and salvaging brought the island town fame and fortune. The area around the square was dotted with warehouses, auction houses, chandleries, piers and wooden wharves. Today only a few of the original brick buildings remained.

For a while Drew stood at the edge of the pier, staring into the dark night at the shadows of boats moored out in the harbor. There was a strong tropical breeze and the pungent smell of saltwater. Both soon to be memories.

It was after midnight when he started back to Fancy's, past time for Christy to stop working—ordinarily. Tonight, though, Key West nightlife was in full swing. Even Fancy's, which normally would have quieted down to only a handful of patrons at this hour, was still busy. Drew waited as a group of people boisterously emerged from the smoky red-lighted interior, then made his way inside.

Christy was bent over behind the bar, washing glasses.

"Hey," Drew said. "Almost finished?"

"Drew!" she blurted, looking up. "You startled me."

"Sorry, Christy. Look, when are you getting out of here?"

"I need about fifteen minutes to finish what I'm doing. Why don't you let me buy you a beer?"

"No thanks," he told her, barely containing his impatience. At this point Drew was tired and edgy and wanted only to get home. "I'll be back in fifteen or twenty minutes. Don't leave without me."

Before Christy could respond, he was gone.

Drew wasn't sure where he walked this time. He just walked. Finally he returned to Fancy's, feeling totally disgruntled. To his surprise—and only adding to his irritation—Christy was nowhere to be seen.

Drew was fuming, wondering if she'd deliberately left without waiting for him.

It was ten minutes to one in the morning, and Fancy's finally was nearly empty. Cal was standing behind the near end of the bar talking with his last two customers, and Drew tried his damndest to remain composed as he approached them.

"Drew," Cal said warmly, spotting him. "How goes it?"

"Fine, Cal. Just fine." He acknowledged the presence of the young couple Cal was talking with, then asked, "Did Christy leave?"

"No, no," Cal said quickly. "She's in the back room, cleaning up her act. We had a heck of a night tonight, Drew. I hope you don't mind that I asked her to stay late."

"It's Christy's choice, Cal, not mine."

"Yeah, sure," Cal smiled. "Hey Christy!" he called. When there was no answer, he said, "She probably didn't hear me. Go on and surprise her, Drew. She's been waiting for you. Around the corner down there and through the door."

"Thanks, Cal."

Drew walked the length of the bar, turned the corner, walked through the open door and froze in shock at the scenario confronting him. Two grimy looking men were in the small back room with Christy. One man held her firmly from behind with a hand clamped over her mouth. The other was on his knees before Cal's open safe, scooping cash into an open gym bag.

"What the hell?" Drew thundered. "Let her go!"

It was raw, primal emotion that sent Drew lunging into action. The man on the floor whirled around, his fists full of money, to be greeted by a stunning kick to the face. Even as he fell backward Drew wheeled on the other thief.

Shocked by the sudden, unexpected turn of events, this man momentarily panicked. Christy, however, did not. She wrestled herself free of his grip and bit down hard on the hand that had slipped off her mouth. The man would have screamed, if Drew hadn't connected with a right hook at the same instant.

"Cal!" Christy yelled, at the top of her lungs.

The next few seconds passed in a blur. The man on the floor struggled to his knees only to be plastered against the hard metal safe by a second punch from Drew. Then Drew was swinging around again....

And there was the knife, a glinting metal missile.

Drew felt a white hot thrust penetrate his chest, followed by a bolt of excruciating pain that sent him reeling to the floor. A moment later his assailant fell beside him, knocked out cold by a whiskey bottle that found its mark, courtesy of Cal.

"I'll call the police," Drew heard someone shout. Then he heard a woman scream, "Call an ambulance! Hurry!"

His eyes were closed, but he could feel Christy's presence at his side. Knew those were her hands cradling his head. Sensed those were her lips brushing his.

"Drew," she moaned, her voice starting to go far away from him. "My darling, darling Drew..."

Those were the last words Drew heard before the blackness took over.

Once again Christy sat in a waiting room at Florida Keys Memorial Hospital. She couldn't have imagined anything more emotionally wrenching than the other night, waiting for Terry to deliver Lucy.

This was.

Cal Fancy had driven her to the hospital shortly after the police had arrived, minutes after the ambulance had whisked Drew away.

"Christy?" Cal asked now. "Is there something I can get you?"

She shook her head.

"I keep feeling you're going to pass out on me at any second," Cal said.

She looked up and met Cal's worried gaze. "I'm all right, Cal. Really." She took a deep breath and made a decision. "Cal," she said. "Would you go to the desk, please, and ask them for some word. Tell them I have a right to know. Tell them I'm Drew's wife."

He stared at her, puzzled.

"I *am* Drew's wife, Cal," Christy said firmly.

And she was. She'd been Drew's wife ever since the day they'd eloped. She'd always be his wife. How could she have ever believed differently?

She knew Cal wanted to ask questions and was thankful when he didn't. He stood, then shuffled toward the desk. She saw him engage a nurse in conversation, saw the nurse glance toward her. Then the nurse reached for a telephone.

Christy shuddered. She closed her eyes, then quickly opened them again. Every time she closed her eyes, she could see that horrible man plunging a knife into Drew's chest. She could see Drew slumping, see the red stain gradually creeping through his shirt. She could hear herself screaming for an ambulance. She wanted to echo the soft moans she'd murmured as she knelt at Drew's side. She could see herself taking his head in her hands and whispering over and over again how much she loved him.

She heard an elevator door clang, looked up and saw a doctor in surgical greens walking toward her. He stood in front of her and asked softly, "Mrs. Payne?"

It took a moment for the name to register. "Yes," Christy said.

"I'm sorry, Mrs. Payne. We didn't realize you were Mr. Payne's wife. Even so, we couldn't have gotten to you any sooner. We did exploratory surgery to assess the extent of your husband's injuries. He came through okay and has been taken to intensive care."

"He's alive?" Christy managed hoarsely.

"Oh, yes, he's alive," the doctor assured her. "He's in critical condition, however."

"What . . . what are his injuries?"

"He's suffered from a punctured left lung and lacerated pulmonary vein. I know it sounds bad, Mrs. Payne, and it is. But it could have been worse. The knife came dangerously close to the heart. Just a fraction of an inch more and the consequences might have been fatal. As it is, he isn't out of the woods yet."

Christy couldn't speak.

"Did someone come out here with you?" the doctor asked.

"Cal did. Mr. Fancy, that is," Christy managed.

"I'd suggest he take you along home. Your husband's going to be pretty much out of it for a while."

"Please . . . can I see him?"

"There wouldn't be much point to that right now. He's being closely monitored, Mrs. Payne. I assure you, absolutely everything that can be done is being done."

"Please . . . if I could just *look* at him," Christy pleaded.

The doctor hesitated, then expelled a long breath. "Okay," he decided abruptly. "Who knows? He may even sense that you're there."

Intensive care was terrifying. Drew was unconscious, lying flat out on a narrow hospital bed, hooked up to an incredible assortment of medical machinery by more wires and tubes than were believable. As she approached him, Christy could barely breathe. There were tubes that connected him to a hissing, clicking machine the size of a dishwasher, dozens of IV bags were suspended all around him, and monitor wires were taped to strategic locations on his body. But worst of all there was an enormous surgical dressing covering his exposed chest and wrapping completely around his side.

Christy stared down at him helplessly, dying her own private death. Despite his tan, his underlying pallor was such that he looked as if every drop of blood had been drained out of his body.

They'd told her she could stand by his bed for only a couple of minutes. Her fingers trembling, Christy slowly reached out and touched Drew's hand. Then, gaining courage, she clasped her hand over his as the tears began to stream down her cheeks and again murmured broken words of love to him.

Was it her imagination playing tricks, she wondered a few seconds later? Or was she actually feeling the faintest return pressure from Drew's fingers?

A nurse came to tell her, gently, that time was up. Reluctantly Christy withdrew her hand. But she would have sworn she felt the slightest tug from his fingers, as if imploring her not to leave.

It was Cal who knocked on the Descarteses' door once he'd brought Christy home. Despite the hour—it was just past five in the morning—Christy wanted Terry and Ben to know what had happened but couldn't face them herself. Almost immediately Terry rushed upstairs.

Christy sat in the battered old armchair, feeling cold all over. She declined when Terry suggested brandy, accepted when Terry decided to make a pot of coffee.

She was frantic with worry over Drew, helpless and distraught. But something kept nagging at her, some idea that she couldn't quite pull out of her subconscious.

Terry handed her a steaming cup of coffee, then said, "Drew's strong, Christy. Physically strong. Mentally strong. Emotionally strong. He's going to make it. I know he's going to make it!"

"I know, Terry. I know," Christy murmured. "It's just...when I saw him, he looked so pale, so terribly weak. All those wires and tubes. God, Terry, I'm so scared. I've never been so scared."

"He's going to make it," Terry repeated. She sipped her coffee and stared across at her friend in silence. Finally she ventured, "Christy, there's something I have to ask you."

"Yes?"

"Cal said something about you and Drew being married."

Christy looked up and met Terry's eyes. "Yes," she said quietly, "Drew and I are married. I...I can't go into it right now, Terry. But as soon as Drew is out of danger, I'll tell you everything."

And she determined to do exactly that. There'd be no more camouflage where she and Drew were concerned. But for now, Christy couldn't begin to think straight. Thought of Drew filled her mind, her heart, her very soul.

Dawn was softly lighting the living room when Terry said, "Christy, you really need to get some sleep. I have some sleeping pills the doctor gave me. Would you take one? It won't hurt you."

"Thanks, but no," Christy said quickly. "I have to stay awake, Terry. The hospital has this number. They might call anytime."

Terry nodded understandingly. "Cal's downstairs, if you need him. He asked Ben if he could hang around in case you wanted to get back out to the hospital."

"Cal's been wonderful. And so have you, Terry. You should be in your bed asleep."

"Like Drew would say, friends are for listening."

"What do you mean, 'like Drew would say'?"

"When I was spilling all our problems on Drew a couple of weeks ago, I started apologizing, but he stopped me. He said friends are for listening, and he hoped Ben and I would consider him a friend."

Suddenly Terry's eyes filled with tears. "I'm sorry," she managed, turning away and sniffing.

"That's okay," Christy said softly. "I've already cried my bucket." She finished her coffee and sat up a little straighter. "Go on, Terry," she said. "Go back downstairs."

"I have no intention of leaving you here by yourself."

Christy managed a sad facsimile of a smile. "I'm a big girl, you know. Even if I weren't, you have a baby to take care of. It's not the time for you to wear yourself out anymore than you have to. I appreciate it, Terry. But please . . . go home."

It took a while to convince Terry that she should return to Ben and her baby. In the doorway, she asked, "Do you want Cal to come up and stay with you?"

"No," Christy answered quickly. "To tell you the truth . . ."

"Yes?"

"I don't want to hurt anyone's feelings, but I need to be alone for a little while."

Terry nodded. "I can understand that. Cal can use our bedroom to snatch some sleep. You come down whenever you want him to take you back to the hospital."

Alone, Christy wandered around the apartment picking things up, putting things down, feeling stunned and scared but restless. There was the book Drew had been reading. And, in the bathroom, his electric shaver and a comb. He kept his clothes in a closet just off the kitchen. She opened the door and stood sadly surveying his neatly arranged assortment of shirts and slacks.

She wandered into her bedroom. There was nothing of Drew in here, she thought, her heart sinking. Yes, they'd made love in her bed, but there was nothing *tangible* left of him in here. Only memories that just now were better suppressed.

She went over to her dresser and opened the top drawer, as if somehow he might have left something there. She saw the blue leather folder to one side of her lingerie, and suddenly her heart nearly stopped.

Christy opened the folder and stared at the photograph of herself and Drew in Ogunquit that long-ago summer. Then she spotted the little square of pink tissue, and a lump filled her throat. Opening it, her wedding ring fell into her palm. And the memories flooded back. She imagined she could actually feel Drew slipping the ring onto her finger as he promised his eternal love.

Her nerves tingling, she carefully slid the gold band onto the proper finger herself. And at that moment swore she would never again take it off.

Back in the living room, Christy sat in her armchair and stared out the French windows at the early morning pink sky. Now and then she rubbed the ring, with its lovely pattern of flowers and leaves, remembering how happy she and Drew had been in the beginning. Then Drew had taken her back to Westport...

Christy sat very still as her brain finally began to function clearly. And suddenly she realized what her subconscious had been nudging her about.

Westport. Millicent.

Drew was Millicent's only child. Her son. In so many ways, Christy knew now, her special link to the world.

Not hesitating for a second despite the early hour Christy picked up the phone and dialed.

Chapter Fifteen

Millicent Payne Delahunt arrived in Key West at one o'clock Saturday afternoon on a private Lear jet, courtesy of Delahunt, Marcy and Bainbridge. After Christy's call it had taken her precisely two hours and twenty minutes to make the necessary arrangements for jet and pilot, leave instructions with her staff at the estate, pack her bags and board the jet at Westchester County Airport, thirty-two miles from her front door.

Cal Fancy drove Christy out to the Key West airport and was standing at her side when the sleek jet came streaking in over the palms, touched down perfectly, then taxied back toward them, its engines making a deafening whine.

"Wow," Cal said simply.

Christy acknowledged his comment with a slight affirmative nod, but her pulse was pounding as the jet stopped not fifty feet from where they were standing.

"Come on," she told him, making her way through a gate onto the tarmac.

The door opened, and the pilot emerged first. Then Millicent stepped out. She was wearing a pale gray dress with matching accessories. A wide-brimmed hat shadowed her face, and she'd donned sunglasses. She looked as perfectly groomed as ever and presented the same cool facade Christy remembered so well. But when she grasped Christy's hand, her fingers were shaking.

"Christy," she murmured.

Christy never was sure what she murmured in reply. Something almost unintelligible, even to herself.

She was thankful that Cal didn't bat an eyelash when she made introductions. Of course it was possible that Cal didn't immediately recognize the name Millicent Delahunt. He wasn't exactly the type to keep up with "high society."

They went directly to the hospital. There, what Christy might have expected would happen, happened. Millicent walked in, and everyone she encountered seemed to snap to instant attention. She was charming and gracious, but a certain authority showed through. A definite call for respect.

She's so used to having her own way, Christy reminded herself. *She's so damned sure of herself.*

A few minutes later Christy began to revise that opinion. She was waiting in the hall when Millicent came out of the intensive care unit, having been allowed five minutes alone with Drew.

Millicent glanced at her daughter-in-law, her face ashen. "Could we go sit down somewhere?" she pleaded.

A passing nurse overheard and pointed them toward a small alcove at the end of the corridor where there was a couch and several chairs. Millicent sank down on one end of the couch and said, "Please, Christy...come sit beside me."

The request came as a shock, but Christy did as she was asked. Then she heard Millicent moan, "Oh God," and turned to meet a steel gray gaze so identical to Drew's it made her flinch.

Millicent asked, "Would you happen to have a tissue?"

Wordlessly, Christy fished in her handbag, brought forth a wad of pink Kleenex and handed them over to her mother-in-law. Then she watched in horror as tears spilled from eyes she was certain had never cried.

Finally Millicent murmured, "He looks so helpless. It's bad enough that he's still unconscious, but with all those wires and tubes, and all that noisy machinery..."

Christy hadn't seen Drew herself since ten o'clock that morning. After she'd talked with Millicent on the phone, she'd managed to doze for an hour. Then, wide awake again, she'd taken a quick shower and rushed back to the hospital.

"He isn't worse, is he?" she asked apprehensively.

"No," Millicent sniffed. "In fact the nurse in the ICU told me he's better." She looked up and smiled apologetically. "I guess the shock of seeing Drew like that set me off," she admitted. "He's always been...so strong."

Those disconcerting gray eyes met Christy's. "There is something I must tell you before any more time passes," Millicent said firmly. "The record needs to be set straight, and I'm not sure it has been. Drew loves you very much, Christy. I want to be sure you know that."

Christy was staggered. When she didn't speak, Millicent went on, "This isn't something I'm imagining. Rather it's something Drew told me himself just the other day."

"You talked to Drew just the other day?" Christy blurted.

"He called about something else entirely. It was a call he felt he had to make. Believe me, he wasn't violating the terms of your agreement."

So Drew had told his mother about the month he'd promised to give her! Christy tried not to let resentment take over.

"Please, Christy, listen to me," Millicent said quickly. "When Drew agreed to that month here, he *had* to call and tell me about it. He couldn't walk out on the company without making arrangements for things to be handled in his absence. He called me just before the month you asked for 'officially' started incidentally. I...I can't tell you how much I favored your suggestion."

Christy stared at Millicent Delahunt incredulously.

Millicent smiled faintly. "I'll elaborate on that sometime when we're both not so tense," she promised. "For now, well...unfortunately we seldom are given second chances in life. Given another chance, I would have behaved very differently when Drew brought you to Westport. Given another chance, I imagine you might have, too."

"Yes," Christy whispered. "Yes, I would have."

Millicent drew a deep breath. Then she said, "I need to hear you say you love him, Christy."

Christy's eyes pleaded for understanding. "Oh God," she cried brokenly, "I love him more than anything else in the world."

It was Millicent who made the first move. She reached out for Christy and embraced her tightly. Then the two women were clinging together, weeping without restraint.

At last Millicent said, "Now all we need to do is get him well."

It wasn't that simple. By sheer coincidence a columnist on a New York paper had gotten off a commercial flight only moments before Millicent's Lear jet touched down. His journalistic instinct prompted him to notice the sleek jet and wonder who it belonged to. Then, one glance at Millicent Delahunt had been enough to set his gears in motion.

Quickly grabbing a cab, he followed Cal's car to the hospital. A while later he discreetly intercepted Mrs. Delahunt and the young woman with her when they were having coffee in the cafeteria. Respectful of the strain they were under, he only asked a minimal number of questions. But that was enough.

By early evening the media knew that Millicent Payne Delahunt had made an emergency trip to Key West. And that her son, renowned young Wall Street financier Drew Cabot Delahunt III, was in Florida Keys Memorial Hospital fighting for his life.

Christy soon realized she'd never really known what being completely frazzled meant. Between trying to avoid eager newspaper and television reporters—who'd somehow swarmed to Key West like a proverbial plague of locusts—and spending five minutes each hour standing by Drew's bed in the ICU, she felt as if she'd run out of stamina and would crumble at any moment.

It was Millicent who sustained her. Millicent who counseled, "It's better to just go along with the press and be polite rather than shut them off. Doing that only antagonizes them, and when journalists become antagonized they become all the more persistent. Answer the questions you can answer, and tell them simply that you would rather not answer the ones you feel you must avoid."

Christy nodded, and thereafter went along with Millicent's advice, discovering it worked surprisingly well. Pretty soon the media definitely were on her side. And they were, all of them, rooting for Drew's recovery.

It was an eternity, though—or so it seemed—before Christy could begin to believe he would even gain consciousness again. Whenever she held his hand, she wondered if he was slipping beyond her grasp. Wondered if he'd be taken away her forever. Those thoughts paralyzed her with fear, and she prayed as she had never prayed before.

Then, at a few minutes past ten that night, twenty-one hours after he'd been in a fight that had nearly cost him his life, Drew opened his eyes.

He wasn't out of danger, the doctor warned. He was still alarmingly pale, alarmingly weak, and Christy still ached as she entered the ICU. She looked down into those clear gray eyes she loved so terribly much, and tears spilled down her cheeks.

Drew couldn't talk with the respirator tube in his mouth, but he managed to gesture very slowly with one hand. Christy quickly drew closer to his bed and leaned over him. He was making a writing motion, she realized.

"Oh, darling," she murmured. "Drew darling."

She quickly located a pencil and pad and helped him take them in his hand. Then, very, very slowly, he wrote, "Are you okay. How long?"

"You've been unconscious for twenty-one hours, Drew." Hearing that, he managed to roll his eyes. And trembling, Christy took his hand in both of hers. "I'm fine, Drew," she whispered. "And you're going to be fine, too."

Again he indicated the pad. And Christy watched him scrawl, even more slowly than before, "Never Leave Me."

"Oh, Drew," she moaned. She was on the verge of tears all over again, but seeing Millicent approaching, she managed softly, "Drew, look . . . look who's here."

He turned his head ever so slightly, and his eyes widened in surprise. On the pad, he wrote, "Hi Millie!"

"Thank God," Millicent whispered.

Drew looked from Christy to his mother and back to Christy again. Then, the shadow of a smile crossed his face. He closed his eyes and a second later fell into the kind of sleep that leads to recovery.

Christy had made Cal go home hours earlier. She'd pleaded with him to get some rest and reminded him that Saturday night was his busiest night. Cal couldn't have cared less about opening the bar. When Christy convinced him he had to, he groaned, "Without you there, the place is going to be a zoo!"

That just might be true. But the worst part of it was, any of her friends who'd watched the evening news on TV would know that Christy DiMartino was in reality Mrs. Drew Cabot Delahunt III. Terry and Ben and Luigi and all her other friends in Key West would soon learn—if they hadn't already—that she'd been a fraud all this time. How could she ever hope to make them understand?

Now, as she stood outside the hospital with her mother-in-law waiting for the cab they'd called, it suddenly occurred to Christy that Millicent had said nothing about where she was going to stay.

The question was settled very simply as soon as they were seated side by side in the rear seat of the cab.

"Where to?" the cabbie asked.

When Christy hesitated, Millicent said, "May I stay with you?"

"I . . . I just have a small place."

"Do you have room for me?" Millicent asked anxiously. "I don't want to crowd you, Christy, but . . . well, I'd just like to be with you right now, if that's all right."

"You're more than welcome to stay with me," Christy put in quickly. "It's just that I . . ."

Suddenly Millicent smiled. It was a smile so reminiscent of Drew, Christy gasped. "Why don't you stop worrying, dear?" Millicent advised gently. "Until Drew's well again, both of us have enough to worry about."

Christy took a deep breath and realized her mother-in-law was right. She leaned forward and gave the driver directions.

At the house Christy took the initiative and paid the cab driver. Taking her carry-on bag herself, the only piece of luggage she'd brought with her from the airport, Millicent explained, "I have more clothes on the plane if I need them. This is more than enough for tonight."

As they stepped onto the porch, Christy managed shakily, "My apartment's on the second floor."

"An authentic conch house," Millicent mused.

Christy was so surprised at her mother-in-law recognizing this basically Key West form of architecture that she almost dropped her keys before she got the front door open. Then, a few seconds later, they were standing inside her living room. "This is it," she said, her throat bone-dry.

Millicent set her bag down on the old armchair. "It's fascinating," she said, sounding one hundred percent sincere. "You and Drew must have had quite a month together."

"Yes, we did," Christy murmured, feeling her cheeks flame. "May I get you a glass of wine, Mrs. Delahunt? Or something else to drink?"

Millicent turned and took Christy's hand. "I'm not trying to rush you into anything, Christy," she said, "but, don't you think you could call me Millicent? Or even Millie? That's what Drew calls me."

"I didn't know, until he wrote it on the pad..."

"It's his secret name for me," Millicent admitted. "And, yes, I'd love a glass of wine."

Christy quickly poured the wine and handed a glass to Millicent. "I'm going to put you in my bedroom, and please don't say a thing. It'll only take a second to make the bed up fresh. Meanwhile, I have a wonderful old bathtub...."

A few minutes later the scent of pine bubble bath wafted through the apartment, and Christy felt unaccountably pleased.

She wouldn't have believed that the day would ever come when she and her mother-in-law could be on this kind of footing.

Christy awoke to sunlight streaming in through the French windows and the smell of freshly brewed coffee. Lifting her head to peer into the kitchen, she could hardly believe her eyes.

"Good morning," Millicent said, smiling across at her.

"Good morning."

"Ready for some coffee? Black with sugar, right?"

"Yes, but how did you know?"

Millicent actually laughed. "We lived under the same roof for five years, remember?"

"Yes," Christy murmured. She watched her mother-in-law move gracefully into the living room and settle herself comfortably in the old armchair.

"No one could have convinced me I'd be able to fall asleep last night," Millicent confessed. "But I did, and I feel worlds better. How about you?"

"I was exhausted," Christy admitted.

Millicent nodded sympathetically. "You know, Christy," she added, gazing directly into her eyes, "Today is not just another day, it's a special Sunday. I'd really like this to mark a new beginning for us."

Christy didn't know what to answer.

There was knock at the door, and Christy groaned. "I hope that isn't some reporter who's somehow tracked us down," she worried.

Millicent chuckled softly. "So do I. But if it is, tell them you just woke up and you'll get to them later."

It wasn't a reporter who stood at the door. It was Terry, holding a plate covered with a napkin.

"I thought you might like some homemade muffins," she said nervously. "I thought you'd need a bite of something." She glanced beyond Christy and saw Millicent. "Oh, I'm sorry," she said hastily. "I didn't know..."

"Come in, Terry, please," Christy urged.

Millicent stood and smiled easily, but Terry hesitated in the doorway. "Please do join us, Terry," Millicent encouraged. "I'm Christy's mother-in-law."

"Drew's mother," Christy added quickly.

"Terry Descartes, ma'am. Pleased to meet you." Turning to Christy, Terry demanded anxiously, "How is Drew? Ben and I have been worried sick."

"He's holding his own," Christy said. "Yesterday was a very bad day, but last night he finally opened his eyes." She paused, then added awkwardly, "Look, Terry..."

"Yes?"

"I can imagine what you've heard, and I don't know what to say to you except that whatever you're thinking..."

"Ben and I aren't 'thinking' anything," Terry said staunchly. "We know you must have had a good reason for doing anything you did. And we don't care whether Drew is Drew Payne or Drew Delahunt. He's a super, marvelous person." She turned toward Millicent, tears glistening in her eyes. "Your son's been a wonderful friend to us, Mrs. Delahunt," she said. "He's pretty terrific."

"Thank you," Millicent managed shakily.

The phone rang and Christy jumped. It took all her courage to pick up the receiver, not knowing what to expect. Bad news about Drew? Good news about Drew? A reporter?

"My car and I are ready when you and Mrs. Delahunt are," Luigi informed her. "Cal brought us up-to-date last night, Christy, and you don't need to worry about a thing. We're going to take turns driving you and your mother-in-law to the hospital, just like we did for Ben when Terry was there."

Christy immediately developed an enormous lump in her throat. Touched and grateful, she said, "Luigi, you don't need to do that."

"No," Luigi retorted cheerfully, "we don't need to, but we want to. What time do you want me to come around?"

Drew was kept in the ICU until late Monday night. During that time Christy and Millicent took turns maintaining an almost constant vigil, spending every moment they could by his side. It was especially heartening when the doctor in charge of his care removed the respirator tube from Drew's mouth. That allowed Drew to talk again—in a weak, hoarse voice—rather than scribble notes on his pad.

When Christy and Millicent stopped by Tuesday morning, Drew had been moved to a private room. There was a No Visitors sign posted on his door, but the special duty nurse assigned to Drew's care assured Christy that the notice didn't include her. Smiling at Millicent, she said, "Good morning, Mrs. Delahunt."

"Good morning, Celia. How's he doing?"

"He's doing very well, ma'am."

Christy was baffled until Millicent said, "I hired Celia yesterday to help out with Drew." She added to Christy in a low voice, "It wasn't with any intention of taking over, Christy. It just seemed the fair thing to do. The staff here has been absolutely wonderful, but it never hurts to have an extra hand. Now, shall we go in? I'll just say hello to Drew, then I'm going down to the cafeteria and Mr. Amoroso and I are going to have a late breakfast together."

Christy stared at her mother-in-law, astonished. That was a scene she could never have envisioned. Though it was true that on the drives to and from the hospital, Millicent and Luigi had quickly achieved an easy rapport, and Millicent seemed genuinely intrigued by his stories about Key West.

Millicent pushed the door to Drew's room open and went in. Christy followed, but just past the threshold she stopped. Once again, she felt that awful inner trembling creep over her—that dreadful reliving of the fight and what its consequences almost were.

She watched Millicent cross the room, bend down and kiss her son, then say lightly, "Well! You look considerably more human than you did yesterday."

Only at that point did Christy dare take a peek at Drew. The bed was angled in the middle so he was slightly propped up. Against the white pillows his thick hair looked raven black. His chest was still exposed with the enormous dressing that wrapped around his side, but the majority of wires and tubes had been removed. There was still an IV, but without the incredible machinery of the ICU the room was quiet.

Drew was watching her, she suddenly realized, his light gray eyes clearer than ever. "Aren't you going to say hello?" he asked, his voice surprisingly strong.

Christy moved toward the bed, her throat constricting. She felt shy, awkward, foolish. Christy tried to remind herself that this man was her *husband*, that she had every right to be here. But she still felt like an interloper.

Millicent said, "I must be off for a while. I have a breakfast date."

"Your mother and Luigi are having breakfast together in the cafeteria," Christy managed.

"Well, Millie!" Drew said with a grin. "Say hello to Luigi for me. Get him to tell you the story of our first night together in Fancy's."

"I can only imagine what that was like!" Millicent chuckled. And with that she left.

In the next second Christy literally collapsed into the chair next to Drew's bed, feeling like her legs had turned to rubber. She clasped her hands so they wouldn't shake and stared at her fingers. Suddenly she felt so absolutely *inadequate*. She would have given anything just then for even a little bit of Millicent's poise. There were a thousand things she wanted to say to Drew, but she couldn't manage to say even one.

Finally it was he who spoke. "Christy?" he asked softly.

She slowly raised her eyes. "Yes?"

"You don't have to stay here, you know. If you want to leave, it's all right."

Again, through no fault of his own, he was misunderstanding her. Christy stared at him helplessly, feeling that yet another impasse was about to develop between them. And that was the last thing she wanted!

She said huskily, "The other night you asked me never to leave you."

"I said that?" Drew asked lightly. "I must have been fantasizing."

Christy stared at him, bewildered and hurt. "Actually you wrote it," she told him. "But I'll leave now, if that's what you want."

"I didn't say that," he retorted.

"Then will you say what you mean?"

There was a stubborn thrust to Drew's chin. "I want you to do whatever you would have done if this hadn't happened," he told her. "My month has been up for a couple of days, you know."

"Yes, I know. And if I hadn't asked you for that month, you never would have gotten hurt. Oh, Drew..." The thought of how close he'd been to death was too much for her, and Christy's lovely face crumpled.

Drew looked at her and began to feel like he'd been in a dark tunnel for a long time and was just beginning to emerge back into the light. He knew he'd been near death, and he wondered if maybe that experience had given him a new kind of vision. He'd heard that people who came close to losing their lives sometimes became capable of seeing things all the more clearly.

Also even in the darkest moments when he'd been close to slipping away entirely, he'd felt Christy's presence by his bed. That, he *knew*, even though the time was pretty much a blank—a haze of pain, of semiconsciousness and of incredibly deep sleep. Yet somewhere beyond the normal reach of his senses, he'd known Christy was there. And his determined will to live had been inextricably linked with that knowledge.

Drew looked over at her now. He saw her uncertainty, her fear, but above all he saw her love for him.

Gently he said, "Come here, will you?"

Christy approached the bed gingerly and stood a foot or so away. Drew patted the mattress and said, "Come *here*," he repeated. "Sit next to me."

She shook her head. "I'm afraid I'll hurt you."

"Not by sitting on the side of my bed," he said rather cryptically. He reached for her hand and closed his fingers through hers. "Christy," he said then, "I have so many things to say to you."

"No," Christy told him, shaking her head firmly. "This is no time for you to talk about anything. You need to conserve your strength, Drew."

"I'll conserve my strength," he assured her. "A lot of what I have to say to you will of necessity be postponed a little longer. But even then it's apt to be pretty repetitive."

"What?"

"Mostly," Drew said, "I want to tell you that I love you...I love you...I love you. And I finally see and believe that you also love me. Am I right about that?"

Christy closed her eyes and nodded weakly.

"Could you possibly say it?" Drew urged.

She opened her eyes and stared into his. "I love you," she said brokenly. "Oh God, Drew, I love you so much."

Her eyes were swimming with tears as were Drew's. "I'd like to pull you close to me, put your head down on my chest and hold you tight," he said huskily. "But the doctors might raise a little hell if I tried that. Christy..."

"Yes?"

"Christy, when I said a few minutes ago it was all right if you wanted to go, that was my pride talking, not me. It definitely *isn't* all right if you want to go," Drew murmured, still holding her hand. "If I told you never to leave me the other night, I meant it—no matter what condition I was in. Do I dare say it again, darling?"

"Please..." Christy began, her emotions churning. "Please wait until you're feeling better."

Drew smiled. "I'm already feeling much better. And I'm not going to pressure you into doing anything you don't want to do. That's rule number one from now on. All I ask is that you give me another chance. Will you think about coming back to Westport with me after a while, Christy? I promise you that if you do it will be very different this time."

Christy couldn't speak, and Drew held her hand tighter, searching for an answer. Then suddenly as his fingers meshed with hers, a strange expression crossed Drew's face. He lifted her hand and stared down at the lovely gold band he'd given her so long ago.

"I thought I felt something," he said, his voice low. "Could this possibly mean what I think it means?"

Christy shut her eyes, squeezing her lids together so tight it hurt.

"Christy?" Drew persisted. "*Does* it mean what I think it means? Do you consider yourself married to me, Christy?"

Without opening her eyes, she shook her head in a violent affirmative.

"Christy!" Drew sighed. "Will you kindly look at me? Without a doubt, you can be the most exasperating person in the entire world. I need to *hear* something from you, Christy. When did you put the ring back on?"

At last she opened her eyes, still filled with tears. "I put the ring on early Saturday morning," she managed. "Not too long after Cal brought me home from here. I...I thought you were going to die, Drew, and I wanted to die, too. The ring made me feel like I still belonged to you. I...I always want to belong to you, Drew."

"And I to you," Drew promised her, his voice thick with emotion.

"But..." Christy began after a moment.

"But what, dearest?"

"Well," she said, her voice small and shaky, "about going back to Westport with you... I *want* to, Drew. But I... I'm still not sure I can live up to you, live your kind of life."

"Could you possibly just take things a step at a time?" Drew urged.

"That's what Millie said," Christy answered. Then added quickly, "Your mother asked me to call her Millie."

"I don't think you really know what that means," Drew murmured softly. "I'm the only person in the world she's ever let call her Millie."

"The two of us have been through a lot together, these last couple of days," Christy told him. "I... I feel so close to her, Drew. She's so different than I thought she was."

"Yes. I could have told you that."

"I think you tried to tell me. But I didn't do much listening, did I?"

"Christy..."

Christy frowned. "Your mother says that once you're well enough she wants to do some traveling," she said. "But I think what she really intends is to edge her way out of the Westport house if I come back with you and the thought of that kind of scares me. I don't think I could ever deal with being the lady of that house, Drew. I think it would be better if Millie stayed."

"You'd make a lovely lady of the house anywhere," Drew murmured huskily. "Anyway, I'm sure Millie will always come around when you need her."

Suddenly tired, he leaned his head back against the pillows and closed his eyes. "Do you want me to call the nurse?" Christy asked anxiously.

"No," he said. With his eyes still closed, he clasped her hand a little tighter. "I have exactly what I need right here."

For a minute they were quiet. Then Drew asked softly, "How are Ben and Terry doing?"

"You won't believe this," Christy said, "but an art dealer from New York saw some of Ben's work and became so interested that he's sending representatives down here to buy everything Ben's placed around Key West. Do you know what that will mean to Ben and Terry?"

As she posed the question, Christy glanced at Drew suspiciously. "You *do* know, don't you?" she accused. "You had something to do with the whole thing."

Drew hesitated. "Maybe a little," he acknowledged. "I couldn't just stand by and watch Ben go blind. But I promise you nothing was done that could in any way affront Ben's pride. The sales were honest sales. The art dealers involved have the highest praise for his work." He paused, then added uncertainly, "Christy, does my trying to help out make you very angry?"

She shook her head. "You did a wonderful thing, Drew. Tell me the details later if you want, but Ben and Terry don't ever need to know."

"Finally we agree on something."

Christy looked up and saw the glint of humor in Drew's silvery eyes. "Speaking of Ben and Terry," she said, "not to mention all our other friends in Key West...they've been terrific, Drew. I was so afraid they'd back off when they found out who you really are and who I really am."

"They already knew who both of us *really* are, Christy," Drew pointed out gently.

"Yes," she admitted shyly. "I couldn't have been more mistaken about that. All they care about is that you get well. And that we get back together. They treat our whole story as if it were some very special kind of romance...."

"It *is* a very special kind of romance," Drew murmured sleepily.

Christy's heart swelled with love. She leaned over and gently kissed Drew's lips. Then she sat quietly on the side of his bed, holding his hand while he slept. She was more than willing to hold his hand forever. To stay with him forever, no matter how difficult being Mrs. Drew Payne Delahunt III might be for her at moments.

Forever and ever and ever.

* * * * *

Silhouette Special Edition

COMING NEXT MONTH

#463 DANCE TO THE PIPER—Nora Roberts
When cheery Maddy O'Hurley (triplet number two of THE O'HURLEYS!)
scattered sunshine and color at cynic Reed Valentine, both were dizzied by the
kaleidoscope of emotions that began to swirl around them.

#464 AMARILLO BY MORNING—Bay Matthews
Chasing shiny city dreams, Amarillo Corbett tried to forget gritty Russ
Wheeler. But rodeo Russ kept bucking Amy's objections, refused to be thrown,
and vowed to hold on—forever.

#465 SILENCE THE SHADOWS—Christine Flynn
Pregnant, widowed and nearly bankrupt, Megan Reese had problems. Financial
wizard David Elliott offered assistance, but could he rightfully offer his heart to
his late best friend's wife?

#466 BORROWED TIME—Janice Kaiser
On the eve of Stephanie Burnham's wedding, tragedy struck, and the medical
profession abandoned hope for her fiancée. She found solace in compassionate
neurosurgeon Peter Canfield—until compassion evolved into something
more....

#467 HURRICANE FORCE—Lisa Jackson
Amid a hurricane and a storm of accusations, Cord Donahue had sailed away.
Heartbroken, Alison banning believed him dead. But now prodigal Cord was
back, accusing *her* of *his* crimes...and demanding sweet vengeance.

#468 WHERE ANGELS FEAR—Ginna Gray
When her twin tied the knot, Elise knew marriage was in *her* cards, too. But
could she accept intimidating Sam Lawford's chilly proposal? Find out in this
companion edition to *Fools Rush In* (#416).

AVAILABLE THIS MONTH:

#457 BEGUILING WAYS
Lynda Trent

#458 SUMMER SHADOWS
Pat Warren

#459 A DIFFERENT DRUMMER
Maggi Charles

#460 MOON AND SUN
Allyson Ryan

#461 INTENSIVE CARE
Carole Halston

#462 PROMISES
Mary Alice Kirk